X-Mas 2

☑ S0-AUV-732

Duets™

**Two brand-new stories in every volume...
twice a month!**

BRYAN'S WE BUY & SELL
BOOK STORE

Duets Vol. #97

Popular Nancy Warren returns with a quirky
DOUBLE DUETS about a couple of friends who
make the headlines—and more!—when they
each find Mr. Right. Nancy's previous Duets novel,
Shotgun Nanny, was "a fun, provocative, not-soon-
forgotten tale with a wonderfully offbeat heroine,"
says *Romantic Times.* This multitalented author is
also published in Blaze and Temptation.

Duets Vol. #98

Matchmaking is the theme of both stories this month.
Two-time Golden Heart winner Barbara Dunlop's
The Wish-List Wife is a fun story about a hero with a
detailed list of qualities he wants in a woman. Trouble
is, none of them fit the cute next-door neighbor
he's wildly attracted to! Toni Blake continues the
merriment with *Mad About Mindy...and Mandy,* a
story about a professional matchmaker heroine who
dons a disguise in order to date a hottie client herself.

Be sure to pick up both Duets volumes today!

A Hickey for Harriet

"Suck me."

"Are you sure?" Her words were like a blast from a cold hose. He wasn't on a date with a sexy babe, he was administering a charity hickey to a woman named Harriet.

"Yes, Steve." The sound came breathlessly.

Sighing, he rounded his lips and sucked her warm flesh, giving enough suction to guarantee a one-hundred-percent-genuine, no-turkey-baster-need-apply hickey.

"Ah." She gasped softly.

He stepped back, satisfied that no one would be in any doubt as to what this mark was on her neck. Unable to stop himself, he leaned forward once more and kissed the red spot gently to soothe it. She tasted like oatmeal cookies just out of the oven. Warm and fragrant.

"There you go. One hickey." Steve grinned. "Reapply as needed."

A soft, if slightly unsteady chuckle answered him. "Thanks."

"Anytime," he said. And the weird thing was, he meant it.

For more, turn to page 9

A Cradle for Caroline

"I miss you."

Caroline glanced down and fiddled with the edge of her manicured nails. "I don't know, Jon. I think some time apart is good for us."

"Well, I hate it. Come home with me."

"I can't." She shook her head. "Our troubles won't go away that easily. I don't even know if I want... I have to go."

"What about your article?" He shoved his hands in his pockets and rocked back on his heels.

"I'll make it up."

"Make it up?" Jon's jaw dropped, he was so stunned. "But you're a journalist."

"It doesn't matter."

He snorted. "Quote this."

Before Caroline could protest or run away, which she did best of all, he pulled her into his arms and kissed her.

For more, turn to page 197

If you purchased this book without a cover you should be aware that this book is stolen property. It was reported as "unsold and destroyed" to the publisher, and neither the author nor the publisher has received any payment for this "stripped book."

HARLEQUIN DUETS

ISBN 0-373-44163-0

Copyright in the collection:
Copyright © 2003 by Harlequin Books S.A.

The publisher acknowledges the copyright holder
of the individual works as follows:

A HICKEY FOR HARRIET
Copyright © 2003 by Nancy Warren

A CRADLE FOR CAROLINE
Copyright © 2003 by Nancy Warren

All rights reserved. Except for use in any review, the reproduction or utilization of this work in whole or in part in any form by any electronic, mechanical or other means, now known or hereafter invented, including xerography, photocopying and recording, or in any information storage or retrieval system, is forbidden without the written permission of the publisher, Harlequin Enterprises Limited, 225 Duncan Mill Road, Don Mills, Ontario, Canada M3B 3K9.

All characters in this book have no existence outside the imagination of the author and have no relation whatsoever to anyone bearing the same name or names. They are not even distantly inspired by any individual known or unknown to the author, and all incidents are pure invention.

This edition published by arrangement with Harlequin Books S.A.

® and TM are trademarks of the publisher. Trademarks indicated with ® are registered in the United States Patent and Trademark Office, the Canadian Trade Marks Office and in other countries.

Visit us at www.eHarlequin.com

Printed in U.S.A.

Nancy Warren

A Hickey for Harriet

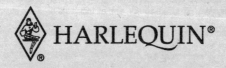

HARLEQUIN®

TORONTO • NEW YORK • LONDON
AMSTERDAM • PARIS • SYDNEY • HAMBURG
STOCKHOLM • ATHENS • TOKYO • MILAN • MADRID
PRAGUE • WARSAW • BUDAPEST • AUCKLAND

Dear Reader,

Did you have a dream when you were younger? Maybe something a little wacky that meant the world at the time? I would have loved to be a Broadway singing and dancing star. Since I can't sing and never took a single dance lesson, it was never going to happen, but I absolutely love musicals, and whenever I watch a show a little part of me is up on stage—invisible, luckily for the rest of the audience. In *A Hickey for Harriet*, Harriet MacPherson gets her chance to fulfill a high school dream, and her life will never be the same. Thank goodness.

In Harriet's story you'll meet some familiar friends from *Hot Off the Press*, my February 2003 Temptation novel. I hope you enjoy your time in Pasqualie, Washington, as much as I did.

Hearing from readers always makes my day. Visit me on the Web at www.nancywarren.net or drop me a line at Nancy Warren, P.O. Box 37035, North Vancouver, B.C., V7N 4M0, Canada. If you include a stamped, self-addressed envelope I'll send you a bookmark and an autographed bookplate.

Happy reading,

Nancy

Books by Nancy Warren

HARLEQUIN DUETS
78—SHOTGUN NANNY

HARLEQUIN TEMPTATION
838—FLASHBACK
915—HOT OFF THE PRESS

HARLEQUIN BLAZE
19—LIVE A LITTLE!
47—WHISPER
57—BREATHLESS

This book is for Emma,
who was born dancing, with love.
May all your dreams come true.

1

HARRIET! You can't call a beautiful baby Harriet, she'll grow up wearing twinsets and kilts. Call her Ashley, Crystal, Jennifer, Britney, Macy...

"Macy." The name passed softly between gently curving lips as Harriet slowly woke and the last wisps of her dream faded. Fully awake, she cursed her name as she did most mornings she wasn't running late for her job as copy editor at the *Pasqualie Standard,* Pasqualie, Washington's broadsheet newspaper.

A name like Harriet took the stuffing out of a person, robbed her of dreams. It was a name you couldn't help but grow into as surely as you turned out to have a red tint to your hair, freckles and one front tooth that overlapped the other. Harriet Adelaide Mac-Pherson. It was hopeless.

With a name like Harriet, it was fate that she'd been raised by maiden aunts. *That's right—aunts.* One wasn't enough. She got stuck with two. Great-aunts in fact.

Her mother had died giving birth to her, just as though it were still Victorian times. Death in childbirth had conjured Dickensian images and frankly encouraged the pair of maiden aunts to come up with a name like Harriet. Of course she was sorry her mother had died, but she'd never known her, after all, so

Harriet couldn't help being just a little resentful her mother hadn't hung on long enough to name her only daughter.

Still, Harriet was an optimist at heart. She pushed back the covers and rose, stretched in her flannel nightie and crept across her high-ceilinged bedroom to the ballet barre her aunts had installed for her years ago. Automatically, she put her feet in position one, held one hand gracefully outstretched, grasped the barre with the other and began her stretching routine.

Twenty minutes later she felt alive and ready to face the day. She showered, dressed, made her bed, carefully smoothing all the wrinkles from the bedcover patterned in tiny pink rosebuds, and then descended the stairs and made her way to the old-fashioned kitchen.

"Good morning, dear," Aunt Lavinia said, glancing up from today's copy of the *Standard*. Though she'd retired a decade earlier, Lavinia still dressed every morning in a crisply ironed blouse and one of her endless tweed skirts. She abhorred trousers for women and, even though the only makeup she wore was lipstick, she wouldn't be seen at the breakfast table without it.

The newspaper crackled as she turned a page and continued reading. She tsked and then turned to Harriet, tucking her chin so she could regard her niece over her reading glasses. "I can see you didn't edit this piece." She pointed to a long-winded editorial, which, thankfully, Harriet hadn't in fact seen. "Three comma splices, two misplaced modifiers and a dangling participle."

"Whoever wrote it was certainly never a student

of yours, Lavinia,'' Aunt Elspeth said, dishing oatmeal into three bowls. She wore one of her flowered cotton housedresses, support hose to ease her varicose veins, and the sheepskin slippers Harriet had bought her last Christmas.

A blue-and-white striped pitcher of real cream sat in the middle of the table; the aunts considered a brisk daily walk a certain antidote to cholesterol. A matching bowl contained brown sugar. A brown Betty full of strong English tea and three small glasses of fresh-squeezed orange juice completed the breakfast.

Harriet took her usual seat, the one she'd sat in since she was old enough to sit, shook out her crisply ironed napkin and laid it on her lap.

She should move out, Harriet thought, as she thought at least once each day. Then she scooped into her porridge, made exactly the way she liked it, and sipped the tea Aunt Elspeth passed her—already milked and sugared to her preference.

Guilt smote her. She was the center of their lives. How could she leave them?

''What are you going to do today, dear?'' Aunt Elspeth asked, her kindly wrinkled face turned to her.

''Never mind, Elspeth. Harriet's twenty-three. She's entitled to her secrets,'' Aunt Lavinia said firmly.

In a pig's eye. Harriet swallowed her porridge. Twenty-three or not, it would never do to speak with her mouth full. ''I've got field-hockey practice after work. I probably won't be home until about seven. But don't worry, I can get dinner out.''

''Nonsense, dear. Don't waste your money. I'll put on something you can reheat when you get in.''

"Don't you have a date tonight?" Aunt Lavinia asked.

The elder and bossier of the aunts, Lavinia was a retired history teacher whose formidable reputation was legendary in Pasqualie. She rarely asked a question if she didn't already have the answer.

The porridge hit Harriet's stomach like a rockslide and she glanced up in horror. "Is that tonight?"

"I would have thought you could keep up with your own social calendar, not rely on a seventy-seven-year-old woman to do it for you."

"I forgot," she groaned.

"It would be very poor manners to forget a social engagement to such a promising young man."

Harriet sighed grumpily. "He's a mortician. How promising is that?"

Aunt Lavinia stared at her as though she'd flunked a pop quiz. "The fastest growing segment of the population is seniors. I'd say his career choice was extremely intelligent."

Harvey Wallenbrau had lived in Pasqualie all his life. He was only a couple of years older than she so he wasn't exactly a stranger. If his career choice was intelligent, it was the only thing about him that was. "He smells of formaldehyde," she said, wishing she'd said no to a date arranged by her aunts, just once. She knew they loved her and wanted to see her happily married, but this matchmaking mania was getting to be too much. Aunt Lavinia needed a new hobby.

"Oh, my stars, that's right," said Aunt Elspeth. She turned to the gardening club calendar hanging beside the stove. ''He's coming for you at eight o'clock.''

She could get angry. She could tell them they had no right to interfere in her life. She could move out and get her own place. But all their dreams centered around her, and for some reason, Harriet tried to fulfill their youthful hopes for them. Maybe it was because of Aunt Elspeth's well-known but never-referred-to disappointment in her youth, and the fact that Lavinia's fiancé had been killed in World War II.

But they loved her, and she loved them, and she'd get through an evening with a greasy-haired mortician somehow. So Harriet smiled brightly at them as though she'd spend all day looking forward to her date, already planning how she'd get out of having to agree to a second one.

STEVE ACKERMAN was jogging past the bathrooms outside the *Pasqualie Standard* newsroom when he heard the cry of someone in pain. He glanced up, a hitch in his stride. None of his business, he told himself even as he paused.

The cry was followed by a loud moan.

It was coming from behind the door of the women's washroom. Another moan followed by a whimper kept him rooted to the spot. Somebody could be sick or dying in there. What should he do?

He glanced back into the newsroom, but at 7:00 p.m. on a Wednesday, it was quiet. The night news reporter was out on assignment and the night news editor was on the phone. There were no females on staff tonight.

Pushing up his glasses, he knocked softly on the door. He knew he'd have to at least check on whoever was in the bathroom.

"Is everything all right in there?"

"Fine." The single word should have reassured him, but it was delivered in a voice that even a dyed-in-the-wool jock like Steve recognized as tearful. He took a step away then cursed himself for a coward.

One peek, to ease his conscience, and he'd be out of here.

He eased open the door, hoping to hell he wasn't about to encounter "woman trouble" in there.

He couldn't have said what was going on, but it was the strangest thing he'd ever seen. The red-haired copy editor whose name he could never remember held a humongous syringe and was stabbing her own throat.

For a second he feared she had the biggest drug problem he'd ever seen. Then he saw the big red rubber bulb and recognized the apparatus as a turkey baster.

In the mirror he saw the girl's eyes, big and blue-green and focused so intently on trying to see beneath her chin to the turkey baster that she was going cross-eyed. He saw her take her bottom lip between her teeth and bear down, then she let go of the plastic squeezie part. She moaned as the plastic pinched the tender skin of her neck.

"That's gotta hurt," he said before he had time to stop himself.

With a startled gasp, the girl's eyes flew to the mirror and she stared at him in horror. The kitchen gadget clattered to the tile floor and rolled under a sink.

"What are you doing here?" the girl cried, her hand slapping over the red mark on her throat, a blush suffusing her freckled face.

"I heard moaning. I thought someone was hurt."

"Oh. That was very gentlemanly of you," she said in a clipped, formal tone, as though she'd walked off the set of *Masterpiece Theatre*. "But, as you can see, I'm fine."

"You were basting yourself," he reminded her, his curiosity engaged. "How fine is that?"

She buttoned the top button of her sweater, though he didn't see why she bothered. She was wearing another sweater beneath it, exactly the same but without buttons. She was one odd bird, that was for sure.

She bent to retrieve her utensil and he noticed that she was wearing the ugliest green plaid skirt he'd ever seen. She leaned farther under the sink and the skirt rode up, revealing surprisingly sexy legs. An amateur athlete himself, he loved muscular legs on a woman and hers were toned and firm like those of a serious jogger. The sight gave him a jolt of surprise.

She straightened and stuffed the baster in a big carry-all she'd placed on the counter beneath the mirrors. "I'm sorry I bothered you," she said pointedly, which seemed to him to mean, *There's the door, pal. Use it.*

But he was a *journalist,* even if he was the only one in Editorial who didn't consider sports journalism an oxymoron.

Because he was trained to get at the truth, and because she seemed like a nice girl—under the drab outfit—he leaned a shoulder against the wall and asked, "Do you want to talk about it?"

Her color was fading, but not her discomfort; he could see it in her eyes. They were big and aqua, innocent and dreamy. She didn't look nuts, but given his history of girlfriends—each one more psychotic than the last—he knew he wasn't one to judge.

"Well..." She seemed to hesitate, then with a determined nod, moved closer to him and lifted her chin, tossing her hair over her shoulder. "What do you see?"

White, creamy skin, an elegant curve, a pulse beating. A smell that reminded him of his grandmother's linen closet, flowery but comforting. "I see your throat."

"What about here?" she asked impatiently, jabbing her finger at the red spot on her neck.

"There's a red mark."

"What does it look like?" Her head tilted back and she pulled her double sweaters down—to reveal more of the flesh she'd been mauling.

He considered. "Like somebody attacked you with a vacuum hose."

"It doesn't look like a hickey?" she asked in a small, sad voice.

"Not a bit like a hickey." He couldn't keep the amusement out of his voice. "Is that what this is about? You trying to make your boyfriend jealous?"

She laughed at that, bringing her head to the upright position and patting her sweaters back into place.

"No. I'm trying to keep myself from getting one."

Privately he thought her wardrobe should do the

trick. She looked like the girls who'd joined the chess club in high school and spent all their lunch hours in the library.

Scary.

"You're giving yourself a hickey to keep from getting a boyfriend?"

She sighed, a deep, tragic sound, and stepped back to lean against the white porcelain sink, her shoulders slumping. "There's this man I don't want to go out with."

Of course she was nuts; he found her attractive, so she couldn't possibly be sane. His life wouldn't be normal if he'd felt something for a regular woman. He'd seen this one plenty of times at work, and he vaguely remembered her from high school, but he'd never looked at her closely before to see the killer body tucked inside the dowdy package.

He gave her the obvious advice in a hearty, no-nonsense tone. "Just say no."

"It's not that easy. My two aunts set me up with him. They think he'd be perfect for me even though he's a mortician and he smells of formaldehyde. I didn't want to hurt their feelings so I said I'd go out with him. That's why I need the hickey."

"I'm not sure I follow." He had to admit this was the most amazing story he'd ever heard.

"I'll show them the hickey after my date and they'll understand perfectly that I never want to see him again. No gentleman kisses on the first date," she informed him.

He couldn't keep the amusement out of his voice. "Isn't that kind of old-fashioned?"

She smiled grimly. "Welcome to my nightmare."

He should simply say goodbye and leave this woman to her turkey baster and her mortician, but somehow he couldn't make his feet walk out of the women's bathroom. Even though he'd seen her here and there throughout his life, he could never recall her name, and here he was feeling as if he ought to help her out of a jam.

He couldn't stand to see this woman with the sexy legs and quirky attitude stuck with a guy who smelled of formaldehyde. Not to mention that he couldn't imagine the perversions that might hide within the mind of a person who spent his working life with the deceased.

"Tell you what," he said. "I'll be at Ted's Sports Bar later. If you can drag the stiff over there, I'll help you get rid of him."

She gazed at him, her big blue-green eyes full of doubt. "How will you get rid of the stiff? I mean, Harvey."

His head jerked up and he pushed his glasses higher against the bridge of his nose. "Harvey? Not Harvey Wallenbrau?"

"Yes. Do you know him?"

He snorted. "I went to high school with him. Had a hairstyle right out of the fifties. I swear he used Brylcreem."

She wrinkled her nose, and under the fluorescent lights he watched her freckles dance across the surface of her skin. "He still does."

"You can't go out with him."

"Apart from being a mortician, is there something wrong with him?"

There was a guy's code Steve followed religiously.

It prohibited the spilling of the beans on certain un-savory activities perpetrated by men on women and it had an eternal statute of limitations. So he couldn't tell her about the peephole, a small hole drilled be-tween the boys' shower room and the girls' shower room during his days at Pasqualie High.

It had been the source of much snickering and jock-eying for position after phys ed class, but in truth there wasn't much to see apart from a lot of steam and the odd flash of skin that could have been any-thing. Of course, the guys all claimed they saw boobs, but he doubted any of them actually had.

But The Reptile, as Harvey Wallenbrau had been nicknamed because of his lizardlike habit of con-stantly licking his lips, had had his eye glued to that peephole so much that for Steve the prank had stopped being funny. One day, Steve and his friends had come into the locker room to find the hole in the wall had been refilled and the boys' gym teacher read-ing them all the riot act. No one had ever learned how the peephole had been discovered—which was fine by Steve. Once more he felt the urge to protect a nice girl from The Reptile.

"He's weird," was as far as he'd go to explain why she shouldn't go on this date.

"Well, my aunts are friends with his grandmother and she forgot to tell them he's weird. I can't get out of the first date. I already said yes. However, I'm determined to stop at that."

Even one date with Wallenbrau was one too many in Steve's opinion. "Well, get him to the sports bar. I'll think of something."

"How do I get him there? We're supposed to see a movie."

"Tell him there are strippers at Ted's."

She perked up. "Are there?"

"No. If you want to see strippers you go to— Oh, never mind."

"I see." She smiled at him, and an imp of mischief danced in her eyes. "I'll do my best. Thanks."

"You're welcome." He backed out of the ladies' room. As a last thought struck him, he stuck his foot against the door to stop it from closing and said to her, "Hey, if you go to the movies, sit up front where there are lots of other people. Don't let him get you in the back row."

She turned to the mirror and studied the red mark on her neck.

He narrowed his eyes so she'd know he meant business. "Hey!"

Their gazes met in the mirror. "No more turkey baster. If you need a hickey, I'll give you one."

2

STEVE SIPPED HIS BEER slowly and half watched the hockey game on the big-screen TV while keeping an eye on the entrance to Ted's. He was trying to figure out a smooth way to get the redheaded gal out of The Reptile's clutches without bloodshed. Not that he'd mind shedding some of Wallenbrau's blood—if he had any—but Ted, the bar owner, frowned on such things.

In an odd way, he felt responsible for her. He didn't like to think of an old-fashioned girl like that stuck with The Reptile. She arrived a little after nine. To his surprise, she was alone.

And she didn't look happy.

He rose from the bar stool and went to her. "Where's the stiff?"

This time she didn't correct him. "There was a problem at the funeral home. He had to leave early."

"That's great, then. You're home free."

She gazed at him as though tragedy had struck. "He wants to reschedule. But I can't go out with him again. He's so…" She shuddered delicately.

"Yeah. I know. Come on." He patted her shoulder. "I'll buy you a beer." He wondered why she'd bothered coming if she'd already ditched Harvey, but he imagined, knowing women, that she'd tell him soon enough.

They sat at a quiet table and Steve ordered a couple of pints of draft. He raised his eyebrows at the redhead to be certain she was okay with beer, but she was someplace all her own.

The buxom barmaid stared at his companion, then at him, as though she wanted to take his temperature or something. This gal was not the kind of woman Steve usually spent time with.

She was more of a charity case.

He sipped his beer and watched frustration build on her face until she said, "I hope you don't mind that I came here anyway. But I need to come up with a reason not to reschedule that date."

"Explain to me why you can't turn the creep down."

"It's my name," she said tragically.

Steve wasn't sure if she was answering his question in some oblique fashion or if she hadn't heard him at all and just blurted out this odd statement.

"What's wrong with your name?" He meant, What is it? He didn't have a clue.

"Harriet?" She stared at him in stunned disbelief. "What's right about it? It's ruined my existence."

"Well, I concede it's a superdorky name, but can't you change it?"

"My great-aunts named me. Harriet was my *mother*'s name.

It struck him that passing on that name was akin to passing on a curse, but even he could see that wouldn't be a very sensitive remark. He wondered what was wrong with her father to let a poor little baby get stuck with a handle like Harriet.

"Your father…" he said delicately. You never knew about fathers.

She blinked a few times, and he sensed he'd stumbled into the insensitive zone without meaning to. "My aunts told me my father was distraught over my mother's death. He thought Harriet was a wonderful name."

Of course he did. He probably bought her those kilts in bulk from Highlanders R Us.

But it turned out he was wrong about the father. Harriet sighed into her beer. "He's gone, too. I could never change my name."

"Gone? As in…"

She nodded, seemingly accustomed to her tragic history. "He was a photojournalist. Killed while filming a marathon." She shook her head. "He was trampled. Killed instantly."

"I'm sorry," he said.

"I was four at the time. I barely remember him. I'd always lived with my aunts because he traveled a lot so it wasn't as traumatic as it might have been." She sipped her beer, then licked the foam off her upper lip. "That's why I went into journalism. I want to follow in his footsteps."

Watching her, he hoped she didn't follow too closely in her father's footsteps. She was so different from most of the women he knew, she intrigued him. He was dying to ask why she hid her athletic body under all those prissy clothes, but before he could work out a tactful way to ask—if there was one—she was speaking again.

"Anyway, my aunts would be heartbroken if I tried to change my name."

He recalled their odd conversation earlier in the bathroom. "Right, right. The aunts." He drank his own beer, thinking there had to be something she could do about her name. "Don't you have a nick-name?"

"Harry."

"Hmm. I see your point." He tossed a couple of pretzels in his mouth and chewed thoughtfully. "What about your middle name?"

"Adelaide. It shortens to Addy. I've tried every-thing I can think of. H. A. MacPherson sounds like ha, ha. My initials spell 'ham.' It's hopeless. I'm hopeless."

"Look, I'm not exactly up on female psychology, but having a dorky name is not enough reason to go out with a guy like Wallenbrau. I mean, why stick yourself with a second handicap?"

She slumped forward, forehead in hand, strands of fiery red hair spilling over to trail into her pint. She didn't seem to notice, and he didn't want to embarrass her by pointing it out. He heard a couple of guys cheer and figured somebody must have scored in the hockey game. He'd tune into the late sports report on TV when he got home to find out.

"It's my aunts. They try so hard to get me married and settled down with a good man. And they love me so much I hate to hurt their feelings."

In his opinion, nobody could confuse The Reptile with a good man. The very idea was an insult to his sex. "Are they senile or something?"

"Of course not." She picked her head up off her hand and stared at him in surprise.

"No offense, but Harvey Wallenbrau is hardly Pasqualie's catch of the season."

"Well, neither am I." She'd said it so simply— and since she was absolutely right—he was rendered speechless, so he drank some more beer.

Over the rim of his glass he studied her. She wasn't a woman who'd stand out in a crowd, but he noticed her skin was creamy-fair with a bronze dusting of freckles across her nose and cheekbones. Her hair was red-gold and hung straight. Her eyes were kind of big and blue-green with a disconcerting way of staring at a person. Her lips were shaped nicely but sported neither color nor shine. In fact, in his admittedly inexpert opinion, he'd say she wasn't wearing a scrap of makeup. Maybe she wasn't a knockout, but she wasn't a troll either.

Wallenbrau was a troll.

"You can't go out with him again. That's all there is to it."

"You're right." She nodded with deliberation, as though she'd come to a decision, picked up her bag and started to rise.

"Where are you going?"

She blushed. "The ladies' room."

What was embarrassing about that? Then he eyed her bag and caught on, shaking his head. "Oh, no. Not the turkey baster."

"It's the best I can think of."

"It's barbaric. Besides, it doesn't look a bit like a hickey. If your aunts aren't senile, they'll figure it out right away. You need a man's mouth to make a decent hickey. Just the right suction and angle. It's not a job that can be turned over to a kitchen utensil.''

He was feeling a little huffy on behalf of his entire gender. Far too many of men's functions had been replaced by battery-operated devices and medical technology. Some things should be left to real flesh-and-blood men.

The hickey was one of those things.

Knowing he was standing up for all men, he rose from his seat with dignity. ''Miss MacPherson, if you need a hickey, I will provide you with one.''

She giggled, and again his attention was caught by the overlapping front tooth. It made him wonder what it would feel like if he kissed her. That slightly crooked tooth was sexy and when she giggled, her face warmed and he noticed an outrageous pair of dimples he hadn't seen before.

''Are you sure it's no trouble?''

He grinned back. ''It will be my pleasure.''

She blushed even more rosily and glanced around the crowded bar nervously. He thought she might bolt for the bathroom if he didn't plant a good one on her ASAP.

''Come on,'' he said, taking hold of her arm. ''I'll walk you to your car.''

''You mean...''

He nodded. ''Outside.''

Her breath seemed to shudder and she shot him a nervous glance.

''I promise it won't hurt as much as that turkey baster.''

That seemed to help her make up her mind. ''All right.'' She nodded and headed for the door.

He fell into step beside her, walking out into the quiet and relative cool of the night.

"Where should we... I mean..."

Her nervousness was kind of sweet. It wasn't even a real kiss he was proposing, merely a tug of his lips against her neck, a small price for either of them to pay to keep The Reptile out of her life.

A horse chestnut stood beside the parking lot, its spread branches offering a semblance of privacy. "How about here?" He motioned to the tree and with a nod she preceded him.

She put her back against the tree, took a deep breath that huffed her chest in and out like a bellows, then lifted her chin.

This had to be one of the strangest things he'd ever done. He shook his head then stepped closer. She was a few inches shorter than he, so he bent down, lifting the soft weight of hair off her neck. He moved closer and smelled again that old-fashioned scent of lavender and home baking. In the pale light cast by a streetlight and filtered by the chestnut, her neck was long and white. A pulse beat just in the crook where chin melted into throat.

Intoxicated by the warm flesh, the rich silk of her hair still in his hands and the scent of her, he pressed his lips to her throat. His eyes drifted shut as more sensory perceptions pelted him. *Soft*. Her skin was softer than down, but warm and exciting. A kind of buzz vibrated through her skin and set his body humming to her frequency.

"Suck me," he heard her say. He opened his lips against her throat and tasted her with his tongue. Oh, yeah. He wanted to suck and lick every inch of this delectable skin. He put both hands behind her neck and brought her forward so he could take his time, move from her throat, down to the curve of her shoulder and…

"Suck." She hissed the word and, like a blast from a cold hose, sanity returned. He wasn't on a date with a sexy babe, he was administering a charity hickey to a woman named Harriet. Get on with it.

Still, he hesitated. It seemed a shame to mar such gorgeous skin. "Are you sure?" he mumbled against her throat.

"Yes." The sound came breathlessly and it seemed the proximity was affecting her as well as him.

He hated to mark her, but she'd think he was a worse perv than The Reptile if he didn't finish the job. So rounding his lips and sucking her warm flesh into his mouth, he gave enough suction to guarantee a one-hundred-percent genuine, no-turkey-basters-need-apply hickey.

"Ah," she gasped softly, and he let her go, easing his mouth away.

He stepped back, satisfied that no one would be in any doubt as to what this mark was on her neck. Unable to stop himself, he leaned forward once more and kissed the red spot softly to soothe it.

As he straightened he noticed the light gleam on the wet patch he'd made against her throat. He licked his lips and tasted her. She tasted like oatmeal cookies just out of the oven. Warm and fragrant.

Slowly she lowered her chin and stared at him, her eyes wide and glassy, her skin flushed with the easy blush of a redhead.

He stared back, his breathing not quite steady. Even

for him, finding a girl like Harriet attractive was way out there. He forced himself to grin at her. "There you go. One genuine hickey. Guaranteed to prevent dates with reptiles." He stepped closer. "Reapply as needed."

A soft, if slightly unsteady, chuckle answered him. "This should do the trick. Thanks."

"Anytime," he said. And the weird thing was, he meant it.

3

HARRIET touched the spot under her sage-green turtleneck, where the hickey hid like a delightful secret. Who would have thought that last night's dismal date would have such a surprising conclusion?

She had to agree with Steve, his way was a lot more fun than using a plastic suction hose with a red rubber ball on the end. In fact, the feel of his lips against her throat had downright shocked her. True, he was a co-worker helping out the weird girl with the problem, yet when he'd touched her, she'd felt...well, sexy.

She sighed, and held her hand against that spot for a long dreamy moment. Steve Ackerman was a hunk. Athletic, good-looking, charming: everything a girl like Harriet could only worship from a distance.

Which she'd been successfully doing for the eight months she'd worked at the *Standard*. Long before that, if she were honest with herself. Steve Ackerman had been a dream at Pasqualie High. She'd first noticed him when she'd initially tried out to be a cheerleader, when she was a sophomore and he was a senior.

He'd been jogging the field—the quarterback who really worked at staying in shape—and she'd been captivated by his easy grace and his strong, even features. If he'd ever noticed *her,* either during their time together in high school or in the months they'd worked together at the *Standard,* he'd done a spectacular job of hiding the fact.

She couldn't believe he'd turned out to be a nice guy. *Don't work yourself up to a fatuous crush,* she warned herself, firmly removing her hand from her turtleneck and refocusing on the riveting report from Monday's city council meeting. The question of whether Pasqualie had enough money in its budget to update its street lighting was gripping stuff all right, she thought, changing an *it's* to an *its* and correcting the spelling of the mayor's name.

An exciting career in journalism she'd promised herself, even as she'd promised her aunts to stay out of war zones and marathons and to stick to safe stories. This job had seemed such a golden opportunity for a woman with a degree in English literature—specializing in the nineteenth-century novel—and a journalism minor. Her copy editing job was the first step toward her goal of becoming a reporter. The only trouble was she was excellent at what she did, which made it hard for her to snag a reporting assignment.

She felt eyes studying her and raised her head to find Steve Ackerman staring at her turtleneck. She could have sworn the hickey throbbed under his intent scrutiny and she felt the cursed easy blush of a redhead fire her cheeks.

He raised his gaze and looked at her. He was probably feeling mortified at what he'd had to do and hoping she didn't get any silly ideas.

As if.

She forced a bright smile to her face and tried to

pretend it was the future of Pasqualie's street lighting that had her heartbeat kicking up a notch. "Hi."

Now he seemed to be looking at her mouth. She closed her lips, certain she had spinach or something stuck between her teeth.

He pushed his glasses more firmly onto the bridge of his nose. "I just wondered how, uh…how it went."

She stared blankly, her tongue feeling around for stray greenery.

"You know, with the—" he touched his own neck significantly "—your aunts."

"Oh," she said. "It went fine. I showed them and they were shocked. I won't get any questions when I refuse to go out with the mortician again." Not wanting to appear too conceited, she added, "If he calls."

"Good. He's a creep. You shouldn't go out with him."

"Yes. I know." *We've had this conversation. Why does he keep bringing it up?*

"Okay, then." He hung around for another few seconds, picked up a pencil off her desk, put it down again, then said, "Well, see you."

She couldn't stop herself from watching him walk away. What a beautiful sight. She didn't even notice that her hand had crept up to touch her turtleneck again.

"Whoo-ee. Come to Mama, baby," murmured Cherise Talon, the crime beat reporter, unabashedly watching Steve as he strolled away from them. "Mmm-mmm, what that man does to a pair of Levi's! Too bad the brain doesn't match the bod."

"What do you mean?"

"Honey, he's your basic definition of all brawn and no brain."

She thought about the spark of intelligence and understanding he'd shown her. He hadn't seemed like a dummy. Not that she'd been that concerned about his IQ when he had his lips on her neck. "I didn't know he was...you know. Not very bright."

"Read his stuff sometime, hon. Besides, he's a sports reporter. I mean, come on. How hard can it be?"

But Harriet had spent her whole life being underestimated because of the way she looked, dressed, spoke and acted. She'd long ago learned not to judge people for superficial reasons. Still, she kept her mouth shut. She didn't know he was a mental midget, but she had no reason to believe he was an intellectual giant, either.

One thing she and Cherise definitely agreed on, however: the man was a gift to blue jeans. The crime reporter went back to her desk and Harriet was left to worship his back view all by herself.

He halted, as though he'd forgotten something, then turned and walked back to where Harriet was suddenly busy at work, eyes on her computer screen.

"Harriet," he said when he was beside her. "I knew there was something I wanted to ask you. Do you want to come out for the staff softball team?"

"Softball team?" She raised her gaze to his face, hoping her shock didn't show.

"Yeah. We're starting up again for the season. Last year the *Star* creamed us in the media tournament. Frankly, I still think Mike Grundel bribed the umpire.'' But he said it with a grin, to let her know he was joking. ''This year, that isn't going to happen.''

''What makes you think I can play softball?''

He wrinkled his forehead, ''I don't know that you can. I noticed you have, um…'' He petered out and suddenly looked at his feet.

Maybe Cherise was right and he was a bit thick in the brain department.

''I have…um…?'' She tried to help him out.

''I noticed you have runner's legs. It's not like I was looking up your skirt or anything, but you leaned over and…''

Steve Ackerman had noticed her legs? Harriet didn't think she'd ever felt so flattered in all twenty-three of her years on earth.

''Thank you,'' she said with real gratitude. Oh, Lord. She didn't want him thinking she was thanking him for looking up her skirt when she bent over. ''Thank you for inviting me. In point of fact, I haven't played softball since high school, but I'd love to try out for the team.''

He chuckled. ''We don't exactly have tryouts. It's more like we bully and threaten until we have enough people for a team.''

''Oh, of course,'' she said, flustered.

''Not that you wouldn't get picked for a team…''

''No. I understand. When's the practice?''

''Tomorrow night at six. Can you make it?''

''I'll check my calendar and let you know tomorrow,'' she said. Unless there was a dentist appointment she'd forgotten, she pretty much could guarantee she was free. But she'd swallow her own tongue before she'd tell a sports hunk that.

STEVE KNEW the first time he watched Harriet run the bases that his gut had been right about those athletic legs of hers. Although the plaid Bermuda shorts and yellow golf shirt had certainly caught his attention first.

Not that he was a *GQ* kind of guy, but some of the outfits Harriet put together were…well, out there.

Then her bat had connected with the ball, a nice respectable crack. She'd taken off like a scud missile, her long, muscular legs eating up the ground, her red hair flowing behind her like the mane of a Thorough-bred, silky and glowing in the evening light. He forgot all about her wardrobe as a huge grin cracked his face. Look out *Pasqualie Star,* the *Standard* had a new and lethal weapon. And her name was Harriet MacPherson.

His "team" had never played so well during a practice—or during an actual game. He had to think Harriet had something to do with that. He'd seen the jaws drop—as soon as he could snap his own jaw shut and look at something other than Harriet speed-ing around the bases, that is. That quirky redhead had hidden talents.

As the team captain, if they had such a thing, he felt it was his duty to congratulate her after practice. Which he did with a friendly pat on the back. "You were amazing, Harriet," he said. "You blew every-body away."

She flushed with pleasure. "I like sports."

He nodded. "You have talent."

"Thanks," she said again.

Her face glowed with health and a bead of sweat stood out on her upper lip, making him want to stroke it off with his thumb. "Coming to Ted's?" he asked her.

She blushed, looking as thrilled as though Prince Charming had just fallen at her feet to propose. "I'd love to."

They all piled into various vehicles and met for the weekly post-game conference at Ted's, where the beer was cheap, the nachos hot and the big-screen TVs blasted out all sports, all the time. To Steve, it was as near as heaven as he could imagine.

There were angels in his heaven, too. The Bravehearts—Pasqualie Braves' football team cheerleaders—also held their practices on Thursday nights and often found their way to Ted's afterward. Some people might think it was a coincidence that the *Standard*'s softball team practiced the same nights. If they wanted to think that, it was fine by Steve.

Sometimes the Braves players themselves showed up, as well. For them Steve had a darker reaction. Pure, plain envy. They were warriors with their bulky bodies, war paint and their perfect vision. Men who'd been blessed with extraordinary physical talent, twenty-twenty eyesight and thicker heads than he had.

He had other assets, of course, but Steve was an athlete at heart. He'd been given strength, agility, competitiveness, speed and an enduring love of sports. In fact, he played sports—particularly football—so eagerly and with such competitive zeal that he'd got himself one concussion too many, putting his brain—his whole life—at risk if he continued. His pro sports career had ended not long after he'd discovered it was what he most wanted.

Still, he couldn't complain. He was a pretty serious

recreational athlete and he made the best of things. If you couldn't play sports professionally, the next best thing had to be to write about professional sports.

And the next best thing after that was spending time with the Bravehearts. He perked himself out of his temporary gloom as the women invaded the bar en masse.

Steve might not see all that well long distance, but up close he did just fine. And he'd been up close and personal with his fair share of cheerleaders. There was something about them he found hard to resist.

All that perkiness, energy and their own brand of athleticism. They were gymnasts and dancers— women who could do amazing contortions with their bodies—on and off the field. His kind of woman.

You could feel the men, young and old, sniff the air as the Bravehearts bounced in. If there'd been a big thermometer hanging on the wall he imagined the bulb would explode.

The cheerleaders exchanged greetings, hugs and high fives with a few of the regulars and Steve sat back and watched. Those women were sex appeal in motion. Damn, he was crazy about them. Linda Lou spotted him first.

"Hey, Steve," she cried in the Southern drawl that turned each syllable into poetry. She'd been a runner-up to Miss Georgia Peach; he figured the competition must have been something to beat out Linda Lou.

He returned the greeting and earned a big hug and kiss, as though she hadn't seen him just a week ago in this very spot. She sat on the arm of his chair and curled her body into him like an affectionate kitten.

"How was practice?" he asked her.

"It was incredible. We're trying out some moves that are top secret, but man, are they somethin'." She put a bright-pink manicured finger to her lips. "Remember, top secret."

"Can't wait." He snuggled her over a bit with one arm so he could reach his beer. She anticipated the move and picked up the glass for him, helping herself to a hefty swallow first. She passed it to him with a wink and he thought Ted's draft beer had never tasted better.

"How was the softball?"

"It was great."

She shook out her mane of blond hair and rolled her shoulders. "I used muscles I haven't used in years. Sheesh, I'm going to be sore tomorrow."

He couldn't imagine what muscles those might be. Every part of her seemed in excellent shape to him. He didn't bother voicing his thoughts, though. Linda Lou wasn't the insecure type. She knew she looked fine. She gazed around the table, nodding to those she knew, then leaned into him and whispered in his ear.

"What's up with the redhead? She's staring at me like she wants to have my babies."

Startled, he gazed at Harriet, sitting across the table from him, and immediately understood why Linda Lou had asked the question. Harriet seemed starstruck. She gazed at Linda Lou with rapture in her face, a smile playing over her lips.

She looked as though she was in love.

With horror, he remembered he'd kissed her neck and felt a momentary zing of attraction. He had nothing against women who preferred women, but he didn't want to think about kissing one. It would be sort of like kissing a boy, he figured. And the fact that he'd enjoyed his brief encounter with Harriet's neck made him twitchy.

"I don't think she swings that way," he whispered in Linda Lou's ear. "Don't really know."

"Well, if she does, tell her Kelly's her gal. Definitely not me."

"I'll tell her." Kelly was a…one of those? He glanced over at the petite woman with short blond hair and a pixie face. He'd considered hitting on her once or twice. "They should wear a sign," he complained to Linda Lou. "Make it easier on a guy."

"I hear you. Same goes for us." She sighed into his beer. "Gay men are always so good-looking."

He couldn't think of a single thing to say to that. He gazed over at the table the cheerleaders had settled into, trying to detect some subtle difference in Kelly he'd never noticed before. Nope. He had to be honest, he wouldn't have known. A slim, pretty hand flapped madly in his direction. "Beth's waving to you," he told Linda Lou.

"I guess I better go sit with the girls. We're planning a shower for Ellen."

"Ellen's getting married?" he asked with casual interest.

Linda Lou smacked his shoulder. "She got married last year." She sighed. "Now, she's having a baby."

"You have a pregnant cheerleader?"

"For about another month. We're holding tryouts to replace her. I hate it when the team changes. Breaking in the new girls is so hard."

He commiserated and then she gave him another

kiss and a hug, waved to the others at the table, and
sauntered off to join her co-cheerleaders.

Harriet was directly across from him and she gazed
at him with her eyebrows raised, clearly wondering
about all the kissing and hugging he'd just received.
He shrugged. "Very friendly state, Georgia."

She still wore a fatuous expression. "She's so
beautiful," Harriet said softly. "They all are."

Oh, well. He didn't figure one kiss would mark him
for life. If that was her bent, he should at least steer
her in the right direction. "You should meet Kelly,"
he told her heartily, man to man, passing on the hint
Linda Lou had given him.

She sighed, the way a fan sighs when a movie star
walks down the same street, sprinkling a little fairy
dust onto their humdrum existence. "My whole life
I've wanted to be a cheerleader."

He blinked. *Harriet wanted to be a cheerleader?*
"Is that what all the sighing and goo-goo eyes are
about? You're not..."

"Not what? One of those women who think cheerleaders are antifeminist, you mean? No. They're ath-
letes and dancers and...so...beautiful."

Feeling a whole lot better that the woman whose
neck he'd kissed hadn't turned out to be playing for
the other team after all, he asked, "Why weren't you
a cheerleader in high school?"

She stared at him as though he wasn't all that
bright. "I had red hair, braces, and weighed a few
pounds more than I do now." Her face wrinkled as
though her high school memories weren't the best. "I
tried out." She sighed. "I never had a chance."

He knew about those kinds of dreams. Something

you wanted so badly that was always out of your grasp. You were a superb athlete, but had taken one hit to the head too many, for instance. Still, people who didn't make teams—even cheerleading squads— usually lost out for a good reason. Harriet could blame her high school failure on her braces, but it was more likely she had two left feet.

"Not everybody's cut out to be a cheerleader," he said.

"Oh, I am," she told him with a bland confidence that had him smiling. "Twelve years of gymnastics, fourteen of ballet. I could outdance and outflip them all. But only the popular girls got to be cheerleaders. Only the pretty girls."

Had a truly talented athlete like Harriet been barred from being a cheerleader because she wasn't pretty enough?

"I'm sorry," he told her with real sincerity.

She shrugged. "I got over it. I still love to watch them and imagine that's me out on the field."

He knew how she felt. She could be describing him watching the Braves play. "You never get over it, do you?"

"If I could be a cheerleader, even for one day, I'd feel like I fulfilled a dream. Instead, I watch them at halftime and pretend I'm one of them."

"Really?" He set his elbows on the table and leaned closer to her. "I thought I was the only one who did that."

She blinked. "You dream of being a cheerleader?"

"No. No! I imagine I'm the quarterback on the team."

Sympathy flooded her face. "You mean…?"

He pointed to his head. "When the doctors warned my parents that one more concussion could leave me a vegetable for the rest of my life, they made me promise I'd give up football. Toughest thing I ever did."

"I guess some dreams aren't meant to become real," she said, and sipped her beer in a ladylike way that barely got her lips wet.

It was too bad she'd never had a chance. A few pounds and some braces shouldn't have stopped a girl with all that potential from having her moment in the sun.

He put down his beer mug with a thud as an idea—starting out as a niggle behind his belly button—hit him. Linda Lou said they were holding tryouts for a new cheerleader. Harriet no longer wore braces and those extra pounds seemed to have melted away just fine. Harriet would never qualify for Miss Georgia Peach, but... What if...

Trying to keep his voice casual, he said, "Did you keep up your ballet or gymnastics?"

"I still do a ballet stretching routine every morning, and I take classes to stay in shape. When I came home from college, I used to teach in the summers, but I gave that up when I started working at the *Standard*."

The niggle in his belly became a burn. "How about the gymnastics?"

She shrugged. "I can still do a back flip."

"Only one?"

An impish grin lit her face, bringing the dimples to life and making her look about twelve. "I can back flip from the edge of the street in front of our house all the way to the back fence. It's an acre lot. But don't tell my aunts. They'd be horrified.''

"My lips are sealed." Sealed maybe, but he couldn't keep them from curving into a grin. Damn if he couldn't just picture the tartan skirt flipping end over end as she covered an acre of lawn. Of course, when she was upside down the skirt probably rode up, exposing those sleek legs and muscular thighs. He was going to have to spend some time on Harriet's street in case the back-flipping urge took hold.

His idea was probably completely insane, but why not? He might never be a pro football player, but there was no reason Harriet couldn't live out her own dream. She obviously wanted to be a cheerleader and this was her chance. And if someone on the staff of the *Standard* became a contestant, he'd have the makings of a behind-the-scenes sports feature that could win him a coveted newspaper award. Talk about a win-win situation.

"Harriet, I just had a thought." He glanced up and grinned at her, feeling as excited as a kid on Christmas morning. "And it involves you."

Her eyebrows rose. "Me?"

He nodded. "One of the Bravehearts is leaving to have a baby, so they're going to have an opening. I think you should try out for the squad."

Harriet blinked, feeling as if she was underwater. Steve's lips were moving, but she couldn't seem to grasp the words. Excitement mixed with dread built in her chest so that all she could hear was the roar of her own blood pounding. Her throat felt so dry she reached for her beer and gulped.

"Well," he asked after a long silence had stretched between them, "what do you think?"

"I think," she said very slowly, "that you need to say that again."

He repeated it and the meaning appeared the same. Still, she felt wise to confirm she hadn't made some ghastly mistake of comprehension. "You are asking me, Harriet MacPherson, to try out for the Bravehearts?"

"Yes."

She said the first thing that came to mind. "But I'm not beautiful."

"So what? You don't have to be beautiful to be a cheerleader. I guess most of them are pretty cute, sure, but..." Steve gazed at her. "You could be pretty cute yourself, you know. Besides, you've always wanted to be a cheerleader."

It was easy to smile at him, for she was truly grateful. But she shook her head all the same. "Some dreams aren't meant to be, Steve. I'm happy to gaze at them from the sidelines and imagine I'm there."

"But what if you could be there? Really and truly?"

"I couldn't." Why didn't the man understand? "Trust me, they don't choose girls in—" she gazed down at herself "—twinsets and kilts. They don't choose girls who don't know how to put on makeup or how to look...well, sexy."

"I think you look very sexy," Steve said.

Her jaw dropped. It really did. Not all the scolding she'd received for twenty-three years from two very proper aunts could stop the lower jaw unhinging itself from the upper and dropping in a most unladylike fashion. "You must be making fun of me," she said when she could force her poor jaw to function again.

"No," Steve said, "I'm not making fun of you. I do think you're sexy. I'm not saying you'd notice it straight off, because you don't. But it's there. You've just buried it under all that—" he glanced up and eyed her twinset "—wool."

As hard as she looked, she couldn't see any sign he was mocking her. In all her days, no one but no one had called her sexy. Hardworking, yes. Reliable, yes. Intelligent, yes indeed. Athletic even. But never, ever had anyone suggested she, Harriet MacPherson, was sexy. But it was sweet of him to try to make her feel better. "Well, it's kind of you to say so. But I already have a job."

"I'll talked to Earl if you want. I don't see why he'd say no as long as it didn't interfere with your work at the *Standard*."

Her darn jaw must have come loose or something. Down it dropped again. "You would talk to the managing editor for me?" Her voice squeaked on the last word. Oh, Lord. It was like asking a little brown sparrow to audition to be a peacock.

"I bet he'll like the idea. You could write a feature about the tryouts as a trade for the time off."

"But I don't have a hope in…in Hades of making the squad. Look at those women," she said, waving her hand toward the cheerleaders' table, "they're magical, so pretty and…well, not like me at all."

"Harriet, you're looking at this all wrong. All you have to do is try out. Who cares if you don't make the squad? At least you can give it a shot. That way you'll never regret not trying."

"Why are you doing this?" she asked.

"Because everybody should get a shot at their dream."

Since she already knew she didn't have a real hope of becoming a cheerleader, there'd be none of the hot heartache she'd suffered as a teen when she hadn't made her high school team.

But, for one shining moment, she'd get her chance to dance with the squad.

She took a deep breath, let the excitement build within her. "All right," she said to Steve. "I'll do it."

4

HARRIET'S EYES WELLED as she gazed in the mirror of the women's bathroom—the same washroom where Steve had found her with the turkey baster, and where this craziness had begun. Raggedy Ann stared back at her. Harriet didn't have much of a temper, but she was a redhead after all, and when she got mad, she got mad.

Right now, she was steamed. She threw her cosmetics bag on the floor and let out a very un-genteel shriek...just as the door to the ladies' washroom swung open.

Mortification flooded her as she slapped a hand to her open mouth.

Tess Elliot strolled in, paused, and gazed first at Harriet, then at the open bag on the floor, and the lipsticks, powders and potions scattered far and wide on the dingy tile.

Tess was the *Standard*'s movie writer, a classy woman and a great reviewer. Harriet always agreed with her reviews, unlike Tess's fiancé, Mike Grundel, who wrote reviews for the *Star*. She couldn't figure out how those two had ended up together, when, in print, they couldn't agree about a single thing. Tess looked awfully happy, though, especially now that she was covering hard news stories as well as doing movie reviews.

Harriet felt more than ever like crying. She liked Tess, but of all people for Raggedy Ann to bump into right now, Tess, with her perfect blond beauty, wasn't the one she'd have chosen.

"Looks like the makeup counter at the Bon Marché just exploded," Tess said, bending to retrieve the bag.

"Please, leave it. I'll clean that up," Harriet muttered, her throat raw with unshed tears. Tess must have heard her screech.

Harriet tore off a piece of paper towel from the industrial dispenser and ran it under water then scrubbed at the circles of rouge on her cheeks.

Tess didn't reply, but kept gathering the makeup off the floor and replacing it in Harriet's bag.

She rose and put the bag on the counter under the mirror, close to where Harriet was still scrubbing her cheeks. She turned to the bathroom stall then turned back. "Is there anything I can do to help?"

Harriet laughed with a jerky hiccup that sounded like popcorn popping. "Make me look pretty enough to be a Pasqualie Braves' cheerleader."

Instead of joining in the laughter, Tess stared, excitement dancing in her eyes. "I saw the notice in our paper that they're holding auditions. Are you trying out?"

Harriet gazed at herself in the mirror. The fluorescent lighting was no flatterer; she appeared pale, freckly, carrot-haired and over made-up. Where she'd tried to rub the rouge off her cheeks she'd merely spread it around in an uneven, blotchy mass. Now she looked as though she had a bad rash.

She sighed. If she couldn't even manage to slap on makeup, what hope did she have? "No." She sighed heavily. "I changed my mind. It was a ridiculous idea."

"No. It's not." Tess patted her shoulder in a sisterly gesture that made Harriet's throat clog again. "I saw you playing softball, you're a natural athlete."

"It's not the athletic ability that bothers me. It's…it's…" She made a sweeping gesture from the top of her styleless red hair to her little-girls'-dress-up-party makeup to her frumpy clothing to her Mary Janes. "Everything else." She sniffed. "I look as though I just stepped out of an English boarding school."

"Well," Tess said, "at least you got a great education."

"But I didn't go to English boarding school," Tess wailed. "I went to Pasqualie High."

Tess pressed her lips together and cocked her head to one side, squinting at Harriet in the mirror. "When's the audition?"

"Today. After work. But I can't do it."

"I'm sure they'll teach you the moves."

"I can do the moves with my eyes shut," Harriet said, closer than ever to tears. "But I don't *look* like a cheerleader."

Tess smiled, a smug, woman-to-woman smile. "I don't know a thing about cheerleading moves, but I can help you look your best. You are as pretty as any of those cheerleaders. You just need to make the most of your natural beauty. Hang on for a minute, okay?"

Harriet nodded glumly while Tess went to the washroom then washed her hands. Tess glanced at her watch and the light caught her engagement ring, gleaming with newness. "It's three-thirty now, we'd better hurry."

"I don't get off shift until four-thirty," Harriet protested.

"Well, tell your editor you've got a headache or something. We haven't got a second to waste."

Before Harriet knew what had hit her, she was sitting beside Tess in her perky red BMW speeding through the streets of Pasqualie.

"Where are we going?" Harriet finally asked.

"My mother's. She's a genius."

"Your mother's?" Harriet asked in horror. No, no. She wanted to look hip and contemporary, not put together by someone's mother. The only thing that could possibly be worse would be if Aunts Lavinia and Elspeth were her makeup artists. She imagined herself going to the audition looking like a Betty Grable Second World War poster. She hadn't even told her aunts about the audition. They'd watched her break her heart over tryouts in high school, and now that she was older she didn't want to put them through the ordeal again.

Tess laughed. "Don't worry. My mother's brilliant. Trust me. I called her while you were getting your things together. She'll be ready for us when we get there."

For one wild moment Harriet considered opening the door of the BMW and throwing herself out. But they were going too fast and head-to-toe road rash seemed an extreme price to pay to avoid an audition. With a sigh, she resigned herself to showing up as a redheaded Betty Grable.

While Harriet was watching her last chance at her dream fizzle away, Tess pulled over to the side of the road and took a cell phone out of her purse. Although Harriet knew that now was her best chance to run, she remained in her seat. It would be rude to run away, and besides, on her own she was no better. On the cheerleader scale, Betty Grable still beat Raggedy Ann.

"Hey, Caro. It's Tess. I've got a bit of an emergency." Tess flashed Harriet a conspiratorial smile and winked at her.

Harriet was too stunned to wink back. *Caro.* Could Tess possibly be calling Caroline Kushner, *Standard* publisher Jonathon Kushner's wife? Now she thought of it, Tess and Caroline were both society types and moved in the same circles—or at least they had until Caro and Jonathon split up, which pushed Caro out of Pasqualie's power circle faster than you could spit the seed out of a grape.

But where Tess was approachable and someone Harriet actually knew, Caro was like a visiting cover girl when she showed up at the paper, always perfectly groomed and gorgeous, so it was really hard to see the person underneath the gloss.

"You have all that chichi exercise wear for Pilates and dance classes, right? I need a favor for a friend. Harriet MacPherson. She works at the *Standard* and she's trying out for the Bravehearts.… That's right, the cheerleaders, but she…" Tess glanced at Harriet and Harriet waited for her to explain that her wardrobe was beyond hopeless. "She forgot her workout gear and she lives clear across town. No time to pick it up. Could you be an angel and meet us at my mother's with some of your stuff?''

Tess nodded and mmm-hmmed, then glanced at Harriet again. ''She's about your size. Maybe a little bigger in the bust and a couple of inches shorter.'' She gave Harriet a thumbs-up. ''Thanks a lot, Caro. Right. We'll meet you there. I don't know. You can ask her when you see her.''

She hung up and then pulled back out onto the road. ''Was that who I think it was?'' Harriet asked, hoping against hope that she wasn't about to borrow clothes from a stranger who also happened to be her newspaper publisher's estranged wife.

''Haven't you met Caro? Jonathon's wife? Or, uh, you know. I guess they're separated. I'm not sure what the term is for that. They're not divorced, but not living together. His separated wife doesn't sound quite right. Makes her seem as if she split in two. Hmm. There should be a term, don't you think? If only to ease social conversation.''

Harriet couldn't help but laugh. ''Uncoupled?''

Tess's nose wrinkled. ''That sounds like his truck uncoupled from her trailer hitch.''

She shook her head, the short blond hair dancing. ''Hitched then ditched.'' She glanced at her ring. ''I hate seeing people break up before I've even got married. It makes me nervous.''

''I can imagine,'' said Harriet, wondering what it would be like to be as confidently in love as Tess and Mike. She had a sneaking feeling it would feel pretty wonderful and all of a sudden an image of Steve Ackerman popped into her head. She really needed to get over her adolescent crush before she embarrassed herself.

"You'll look great in Caro's workout gear," Tess said, interrupting her thoughts. "Everything she wears has a designer label, even the stuff she sweats in."

"I only hope it's big enough." She was going to look like an X-rated Betty Grable if her breasts burst out of a too-small dance suit and all the designer seams split open.

This whole nightmare just kept getting worse and worse.

Before she was ready, Tess's car pulled through imposing black wrought-iron gates, fortunately open, and buzzed around a crescent drive to pull up outside a gracious white-stone mansion.

Tess popped out of the car and ran up the three shallow curving steps while Harriet followed slowly, feeling certain she was going to wake up from this bizarre dream any second. Or throw up.

But the moment she met Tess's mother, Harriet started to feel a niggle of hope.

Rose Elliot was beautiful. She might be Tess's mother, but it didn't stop her from choosing modern clothes, hair and makeup. Not only was she modern, but, Harriet soon discovered, very determined. And opinionated. She had a musical British-accented voice and Harriet suddenly felt as though she were being made over by Julie Andrews. She fought the urge to break out in song.

Almost as soon as introductions were made, Rose cupped Harriet's chin and tipped her face to the light. "Hmm." She turned Harriet's face to the left and right, hmmed again, so that Harriet began to feel as though she were a show dog being judged. "Excellent possibilities. Wonderful bone structure, clear skin, lovely eyes." She patted Harriet's cheek then rubbed her hands together with glee. "How long do I have?"

"Less than an hour, Mother. Come on," Tess urged.

Rose Elliot tsked. "I don't know what you expect in an hour. I'll do my best, Harriet, but it won't be as much as I could do if I had more time. Never mind. You'll still be the prettiest cheerleader on the field."

It was such a motherly comment, and so much like what her aunt Elspeth would say, however patently untrue, that Harriet relaxed. What the heck. She was in this now, she'd have to see it through and simply remember she was doing this for a newspaper story. Nobody would care if she did poorly at the audition.

Except her.

Mrs. Elliot ushered Harriet up plush carpeted stairs, down an endless wide hallway and into the largest bathroom Harriet had ever seen, with acres of marble, huge mirrors and a full vanity. "I've got the hot rollers already warming. Now sit down here, dear." She all but pushed Harriet into a velvet-upholstered chair in front of the vanity mirror.

"I wish we had time for a facial," she said, shaking her head.

"We don't," her daughter reminded her.

"I know. I'll only cleanse Harriet's skin, then we'll get the rollers in and then do the makeup."

Harriet started to rise so she could wash her face with the bar of soap at the sink. But Tess's mother pushed her back into the chair and secured her hair back from her face with a hair band. Then she squeezed some goop onto a cotton pad and smoothed the cool, scented cream over Harriet's face and neck.

She removed that with another liquid from a different bottle, then came a third application.

"There we are," she said. "Nice and clean."

Harriet was amazed. No water? No soap?

Trust rich people to find a way to wash without having to get their hands wet. Still, her skin did feel nice.

"Now, I'll put a light moisturizer on you. It gives the foundation a smooth base."

Harriet nodded as if she had a clue what the woman was talking about. Foundation? Base? She felt more like a building under construction than a cheerleader.

Now her skin was left alone to *absorb* the moisturizer.

Mrs. Elliot removed the hair band and picked up a hairbrush. She brushed Harriet's hair until it shone and floated around her shoulders, snapping with electricity and sparkling with highlights. Then Tess's mother began winding chunks of hair onto wide rollers in some complicated arrangement.

Harriet was so fascinated to be part of this very female ritual that her nerves settled while she watched the other woman's deft fingers make fat red sausages of her hair. She'd come to the point where she felt fatalistic about the whole tryout. She'd purchased a videotape of the cheerleaders and practiced every move. She'd worked out at her old gymnastics club every day after work and hit as many dance classes as she could squeeze into her schedule for the past two weeks.

Physically, she was as ready as she'd ever be. And now, her looks were in the hands of Tess Elliot's mother. She eyed the rollers skeptically. Maybe she'd come out looking like a Raggedy Ann doll who had stuck her finger in an electric socket, but she couldn't look any worse than she would have if left to her own pathetic makeup bag and inept hands.

"Lean back and close your eyes, dear. I'll start with a nice neutral foundation."

Harriet did, and followed all Mrs. Elliot's instructions while she was painted with a bewildering number of substances applied with more brushes than Picasso could have used in a lifetime. Finally her hair was released from the rollers and combed out and sprayed.

She emerged, choking and coughing from a cloud of noxious hairspray, to the satisfied smile on Rose Elliot's face. "Well?" the older woman said, turning Harriet's chair to face the mirror, "What do you think?"

To say a stranger stared back would have been an exaggeration. Certainly that was Harriet's own reddish-brown hair, but it was styled so it fell in soft waves to her shoulders, with the front pieces gathered on top of her head. "To keep the hair out of your eyes when you perform," Rose explained.

Her eyes looked huge and somehow sultry. Her skin glowed and her cheekbones glinted with some kind of bronze sparkly stuff. Her mouth looked coppery and wet, though she knew it wasn't water but some multistep process that had involved two shades of lipstick and a lining pencil.

To top it off, her brows and lashes were darkened.

She looked… She was so amazed, she said the word out loud. "Pretty."

Cinderella's fairy godmother couldn't have looked more proud. "Oh, no. No. Not pretty, my dear. Beautiful."

Tess, who'd disappeared when the doorbell rang a quarter of an hour earlier, now came in with an armload of mostly black exercise clothing and grinned. "Now you look more like a cheerleader."

Harriet nodded, feeling a blush heat her cheeks.

"Mom." She gave the older woman a quick hug. "You are a genius. And look at all this stuff Caro brought over. Come in, Caro. You don't mind, do you Harriet?"

What could she say? She shook her head, even though her stomach was wobbly at having yet another fairy godmother, or sister or cousin or whatever fairy role the younger women were playing.

She'd only ever seen Caro at the office, and they'd never been introduced. A few weeks ago, Harriet had stopped seeing Caro at all and had heard through the gossip vine that the publisher and his wife had separated. Harriet was less shocked than some since she'd worked there less than a year, but even so they'd seemed like a perfect couple to her.

"I hope you don't mind me coming in. It sounds like you're having so much fun," said the woman herself, entering the bathroom.

Harriet's first thought was that marital separation didn't agree with Caro. A former model, she still looked as elegant, and as coolly beautiful as ever, but, where she'd always been model-slim, she was now hovering on the hostile border between svelte and skinny.

Then she smiled, and Harriet couldn't imagine any man, even handsome and successful publisher, Jonathon Kushner, ever letting her go. "You look wonderful, Harriet," she said. Harriet felt flattered to think Jon's wife had noticed her before today. Tactful and classy, she cast an experienced eye over Harriet's figure and bit her lower lip. "I hope something fits. You're more, um, voluptuous than I am."

"Everything will stretch," said Tess with the breezy determination that made her one of the *Standard*'s top reporters. "Come on, Harriet. Let's see what works."

She ended up in black dance tights courtesy of Caro and a black top from Tess's mother, who also took Pilates but was bigger in the bust than Caroline. It was really just a fancy sports bra as far as Harriet could tell and it left little to the imagination.

"I can't wear this in public," she cried, gazing down at the firm mounds of her breasts rising from the bra like overrisen bread.

"Wow," Tess said. "I never knew you had so much, um, cleavage."

Instinctively, Harriet crossed her hands over her chest and dived for her pale blue Shetland sweater.

"Stop!" said Rose.

She stopped.

"You've got to learn to make the most of your assets, Harriet," she said. Picking up the big soft brush she'd used to put the bronze sparkle on her cheeks, Rose dashed some of the sparkly powder across Harriet's exposed, blushing chest.

''There, that's better. Now stand up straight. You look lovely.''

Harriet caught Caro's eye and of all places to see sympathy, she read it in the woman's cool blue gaze. ''I remember feeling exposed a few times when I was modeling. You look fine, but if you really think you're half naked...''

Harriet nodded frantically.

Caro nodded in understanding and hunted through the pile of stuff to pull out yet another black stretchy item. ''Here, put this over top. But remember, attitude is half the battle.''

Harriet thankfully donned the garment, careful not to muss her hair, and found herself in a sleeveless dance wrap that covered a bit more of her breasts but left her belly bare. Somehow she didn't think she was going to get any more cover-ups so she did her best to straighten her shoulders and summon some ''attitude.''

The three makeover mavens glanced at her, then at each other, smiled and nodded. ''Perfect,'' they said in unison.

Harriet wasn't at all certain she was anywhere near perfect, but they'd been nice to help her and, besides, she'd run out of time.

''Can you drive me back to the newspaper and I'll pick up my car?'' she asked Tess.

''No way. I'm not missing out on all the fun. I'm going with you to watch the audition.''

''Well, you're certainly not leaving me behind,'' exclaimed her mother.

''Or me,'' said Caro.

The quartet spilled down the stairs giggling like schoolgirls, and ran for Tess's car.

Harriet had been so wrapped up in her transformation she'd forgotten to be nervous. But now, as the car neared the Pasqualie auditorium, her stomach cramped with nerves. She started to pant like an overheated dog.

"Breathe, dear,"

"Yes, Mrs. Elliot," she panted.

"Please, you're wearing my bra. Call me Rose."

Harriet choked on a laugh. "Thanks for everything…Rose." She turned to glance at both of the younger women. "And you guys, too. I can't believe you did this for me."

Her happy bubble just about popped when they pulled into the stadium parking lot. There were an awful lot of cars there, and seven or eight young women heading toward the auditorium reminded her so strongly of the cheerleaders in high school that she wanted to turn around and bolt.

"I think I'm going to be sick."

"Nonsense," said Rose. "You'll muss your hair."

"I should go home and put on something else," she said desperately to Caro. "I don't want to sweat on your stuff."

"It's sweat. It'll launder."

From thinking of the three women as fairy godmothers, she now saw them as a trio of Mafia heavies frog-marching her to certain doom. They didn't leave her until she'd given her name at the registration table and received a number. Harriet tried to pin it so it covered her cleavage, but Rose grabbed it and pinned it to her waistband.

"Good luck," said Rose.

"Break a leg," said Tess, giving her a quick hug.

"I admire you for this," said Caro, surprising her most of all.

Then she was alone. But it was too late to run.

5

THE AUDITION HALL was Harriet's worst nightmare. She'd never seen so much lip gloss in one place.

She was sent to the "dressing room," which was a fairly large meeting room that had been converted for the tryouts. There were mirrors, outlets for curling irons, even an ironing board and a small table with hairpins and safety pins.

Harriet inhaled deeply and nearly choked on the sweet sticky pall of hairspray hanging in the air.

Young women were chatting in groups, giggling nervously, fluttering, adding last-minute touches to their makeup, switching hair clips.

Blue exercise mats were scattered across the wooden floor and some of the other contestants stretched and bounced on those. It seemed like a good idea to limber up; besides, it might stretch out the huge knot in her stomach.

She ought to act reporterly and chat to the other hopefuls, but she was too darn nervous. To Harriet, this wasn't a lark. She wasn't a reporter going "undercover" for an insider's look at cheerleading. This was her last chance to fulfill a lifelong ambition.

Steve had told her to listen to chitchat and to get a sense of the atmosphere before telling anyone she was a reporter, so by standing here mute and bashful she was actually following instructions.

Not that she could take in a word, or describe the atmosphere in any terms other than terrifying.

"All right, girls!" A woman who glowed with perkiness bounced in. "Is everybody ready?"

"Yes!" shouted everyone but Harriet it seemed. She would have shouted, too, but her tongue had just become paralyzed. She hoped like heck it was a localized paralysis or she was in big trouble.

Move, she told her feet. She glanced down in panic. Had someone nailed them to the floor?

Nobody else seemed to have that problem. They all bounced, giggled, danced and tumbled out the door.

She'd have called for help but her tongue was still numb.

Dreadful moments passed when she saw her dream vaporize, her closest-held wishes smash like crystal under a hammer.

She looked at her hand, welded to the barre and thought of all the countless hours she'd pirouetted, stretched, leaped and practiced, practiced, practiced. It had led her here, all the ballet and the gymnastics, the summer jazz and trampoline camps. Here to this moment and her chance.

Her last chance.

It was hopeless. Even though she could feel the sweat building under her palm, she couldn't get her fingers to uncurl from the smooth wood rail. A quiver broke out on her upper lip and humiliation washed over her in a tidal wave.

"What's going on?"

She jumped at the sound of Steve's voice as familiar as it was dreaded. ''What are you still doing back here?'' he asked.

''How did you get in?'' she asked in a ghost of her normal voice.

He flashed his press card. ''Came to check on my undercover agent.''

Harriet gave a final desperate tug on her hand, but it might as well have belonged to someone else for all the notice it took of any messages her brain sent.

''I can't do it.'' She moaned. ''I can't go out there.''

He was behind her in an instant. In the mirror above the barre she watched him watching her face. Instead of derision, she saw understanding, even sympathy. Or was that pity? She could stand anything but pity.

She narrowed her eyes at him just as she felt his hands drop, warm and solid, onto her shoulders.

''I know,'' he said, squeezing the boulders of tension in her shoulders, and sending her an enigmatic look. ''It's no big deal. If you can't do it, you can't.''

''I'm sorry.''

''Forget about it,'' he said heartily. ''I never thought you could do it. Cheerleading takes a lot of physical strength and talent. It's not just tossing pompoms around and saying 'Go team' anymore.''

''I know, but I'm—''

He slapped her on the back. ''Don't sweat it. Stand at the side and watch them and you can interview the candidates as they're disqualified.''

Stand on the side and watch. Hadn't she been doing that most of her life?

Watching while other girls got all the attention.

Watching from the sidelines while guys like Steve chased after women with perky breasts and limp brains. Maybe it was her turn to shine for once.

Her spine straightened and she raised her chin. Wasn't it better to fall on her face at least knowing she'd tried than to give up before she got started? *Attitude,* Caro had said. How hard could that be?

"I'm going out there." She took a deep breath and suddenly everything was moving at once. Attitude, huh? She'd show Steve so much attitude his eyes would bug out.

She yanked the dance sweater thing off and tossed it at him, pulled herself up straight, fluffed her hair and pasted on a smile that only wobbled at the corners.

"*You* can watch from the sidelines," she told Steve with false confidence.

Then she noted that his jaw had dropped and he sported a peculiar expression.

The false confidence fled in an instant and she stared down at herself in apprehension. "What? Is something wrong?"

He just stared at her, his gaze scanning her from top to toe with the oddest expression on his face, as though she'd just turned into an alien in front of his eyes. "No," he said at last, his voice sounding oddly strained. "There's nothing wrong." He cleared his throat. "Nothing at all."

"Well..." She glanced down again, turned her back to the mirror and craned her neck over her shoulder for a rear view. Everything looked tucked in and neat. "If you're sure."

"You look terrific." He pulled himself together

and gave her a grin. "Gorgeous, **in** fact. I never knew..." He shook his head. "**Knock** 'em dead, babe."

She nodded, oddly reassured that he was there then skipped out to the rock-concert size wooden stage where the other women were being placed in order. Another perky woman with a big smile checked Harriet's number and took her to a spot about two-thirds of the way back.

Nerves jiggled in her stomach and she looked toward the stage entrance to see Steve lounging in the doorway, his gaze on her. He gave her a thumbs-up, and somehow it gave her courage. The overhead lights glinted on Steve's glasses and she reminded herself that her dream was in reach while he'd never had a chance at his. She had to do this—for both of them.

A scary-looking woman in a Braves' tracksuit appeared at the front of the stage with a megaphone.

"I'm Betty Lederhammer and I'm the choreographer and cheerleader director of the Bravehearts. I want you all to welcome our girls."

There was general hooting and clapping as the squad bounded out in their spangly blue-and-silver uniforms. Envy smote Harriet's heart. She wanted one of those uniforms more than she'd ever wanted anything in her life.

"All right, girls. Watch closely. The cheerleaders are going to do a routine. Then we'll teach you and see how well you can do it. Don't worry about those people roving around with clipboards, they're helping us judge the talent out there. So put on your best smile and your best foot forward!"

Harriet held her breath as the high-energy music boomed out with a beat that made you want to dance and cheer, and she watched carefully as the cheerleaders went through a simple routine, one she'd seen on their video and practiced dozens of times as, she was certain, had all the other contestants. It wasn't a long routine, and it wasn't difficult. They went through it a second time then each cheerleader took her place in one of the lines.

The woman in Harriet's line was the former Miss Georgia Peach. Merely looking at her in all her blue and sparkly glory brought all Harriet's insecurities rushing back, until the woman glanced down the line, giving them all her beauty contestant smile. Her eyes widened slightly when she saw Harriet. "Good luck, y'all," she said, and Harriet was so thrilled to be recognized, she fully believed Miss Georgia Peach meant it.

But it wasn't luck that was going to help her tonight, she reminded herself, it was all the years of work. Whether she'd consciously realized it or not, she'd never stopped training for this moment.

She was as ready as she was ever going to be.

The music started up. "And, five, six, seven, eight!" The coach boomed and they were off. She strutted up and down, giving it her all, going through the routine in her head.

Remember to smile, Harriet told herself.

As she tried to put a smile on her face she discovered it was already there. She was having fun!

Suddenly it didn't matter that she'd probably be knocked out after the first round; here she was, for this one moment in time, dancing with the Brave-hearts.

She had maybe two minutes and she gave it all she had, seeing in her mind's eye not a hundred other women in exercise gear, but the roaring crowds in the stands. She could practically feel the swirl of her blue-and-silver skirt.

The music wound down and she found herself jumping with a whoop, clapping and waving to the imaginary crowd of fans.

She caught herself with a blush, only to find the woman with the megaphone staring at her, a "You betcha!" grin on her face. "That's the way to show the team spirit. Yeah! Woo!"

Woo-oo! shouted her inner cheerleader, a grin on her own face. "That was so much fun," she said to the young woman beside her, who gave her an anxious smile.

"I guess."

The real cheerleaders jogged forward, along with the other six women and two men who'd been wandering around with their clipboards, observing and making notes. They all huddled with the coach while the contestants chatted nervously, paced, ran for their water bottles. After what seemed like an eternity, the megaphone squealed. "All right. Listen for your number, girls," the woman bellowed. She called out a list of numbers.

Harriet waited, feeling the euphoria settle to a contented glow. She'd done it. For two minutes she'd felt like a real cheerleader. She hadn't fallen on her face, or embarrassed herself, Steve or the *Standard*.

As the numbers were called, some jumped up and

down and clapped. Some hooted, most merely stood silent.

Her number wasn't called, but that was okay, she'd never expected to get further than the first round. She'd shown up and she'd given it her best. For that she'd always be proud.

She turned toward where Steve was still standing, and shrugged, letting him see by her huge smile that she was just happy to have had the chance. He grinned and gave her a wink.

Then a remarkable thing happened.

"Thank you very much, ladies. Those whose numbers I called are free to go."

Harriet's jaw dropped.

Steve's didn't. He nodded to her as though he'd expected her to do well.

The megaphone woman had called out the numbers of those who *hadn't* made it to the semifinals. So, if Harriet's number hadn't been called, then it meant…

She'd made the first cut.

The field was now down to fifty and this time they were taught a cheer that was a little more challenging.

Harriet forgot to feel nervous, instead adrenaline and excitement coursed through her body as she watched carefully, still riding the high of knowing she'd made it to the second round.

Whatever happened, she'd always remember this day.

6

STEVE COULDN'T TAKE his eyes off Harriet. He removed his glasses, polished them on the bottom of his shirt and put them back on, but she still looked amazing.

He was no expert on female stuff, but he couldn't get over the changes. Her hair, which normally hung straight, swirled around her shoulders like hot silk, catching the light and gleaming crimson, gold and bronze. He wouldn't have known hair could go from boring to sexy, but today he'd discovered it could.

Her face looked different, too. He knew it must be makeup, but he didn't see the makeup, he saw Harriet's eyes, big and aqua and dancing with excitement as though the sun had hit the Mediterranean. He saw Harriet's lips, curving in a smile, looking full and wet and oh, so kissable.

But when his gaze had first dropped from her face to her figure he'd experienced the biggest shock of all.

Those kilts and sweater things should be outlawed. It was criminal to hide a chest like that under layers of wool and plaid.

Whew, it certainly wasn't hiding anymore.

The Harriet he knew wasn't willowy. She had a womanly shape and muscles. Strong, defined legs and arms. A belly that was as close to washboard as he'd ever seen on a female, a round, athletic butt, high-perched. And, more amazing still, breasts that were the stuff of fantasies.

It seemed to him she'd tossed her shyness along with the sweaters. This woman sparkled, bounced and danced with life.

He couldn't keep the grin off his face. She was a natural cheerleader. Just watching her made him want to cheer. It made him want to do a lot of other things, too, that wouldn't be appropriate in a sports stadium.

He let the discouraged first-cut gals stream past him, ignoring Harriet's pantomimed request that he interview them. No way he was going to miss a single minute of her time in the sun, however brief it might be.

He wanted to enjoy every minute. And after this was over, he planned to spend some time up close and personal with the most surprising cheerleading contestant he'd ever been privileged to watch.

Of course he knew the routines would increase in challenge as they weeded out more and more candidates. Today they'd choose two, three at the most. A full-fledged cheerleader and a couple of on-call alternates. Out of almost a hundred hopefuls.

He settled back to enjoy every minute of the try-outs, moving slightly as the lines of contestants shifted so his view of Harriet was unimpeded.

"Hiya, Steve," said Rock Richards, appearing at his side.

"Hey, Rock." He tried to sound friendly, but in truth he couldn't stand the guy. Sure, part of it was that he had the job Steve would like most in all the world—quarterback of a pro football team—even if it was in Pasqualie. The other part of his dislike stemmed from the fact that they shared similar tastes in women.

Apart from Steve, the guy who showed up most reliably to cheerleader practices was Rock.

The quarterback wore a sleeveless vest and workout shorts. He'd obviously been pumping weights, and, just as obviously hadn't showered. Steve's nose twitched. Still, Rock's muscles bulged from the workout and shone with sweat. Or it could be baby oil. Steve wouldn't put it past him.

His delight in the day began to dim.

"Seen any good talent?" Rock gestured to the lines of bouncing beauties and winked.

Steve shrugged. "Most of the usual girls came out. A few new ones. Nothing special."

Rock nodded and leaned his shoulders back against the wall, jutting his chest out like a rooster.

Steve wasn't a small guy, but standing beside Rock he felt like a mortal next to a superhero. The possibility of steroids crossed his mind, but he knew it was spite that had him thinking that way.

The music blared and he forgot all about the sweat-sheened hulk next to him as the contestants began moving once more.

Neither man said anything during the full routine. Steve deliberately turned his gaze to the gal farthest from Harriet, even going so far as to nudge Rock and point her out. But the hulk's twenty-twenty vision reverted firmly to the one cheerleader Steve wanted him to ignore.

When it was over, Rock said, "I like the moves on that redhead. Don't think I've seen her before."

Steve grit his teeth. "I didn't notice a redhead. I was watching the blonde in the corner. Real hottie."

Rock spared her a glance. "Minister's daughter," he said. "I dated her a couple of times. Couldn't get past first base. But that redhead looks like a homerun kind of gal."

Steve tried to keep his hands from fisting, but it wasn't easy. If Rock had any inkling he was interested in Harriet he'd work harder than ever to muscle his way in and get his meaty paws on her first.

Shock speared him even as he had the thought. *He, Steve Ackerman, was interested in Harriet?*

As the truth sank in, he realized he'd been drawn to her from the moment she'd bent over in the women's washroom and he'd caught sight of those sexy legs. Not even her antics with the turkey baster had prevented the rush of attraction he'd felt. Then, later, when he'd talked to her in the sports bar, he'd enjoyed her company and found he'd admired her guts. She made the best of what she had, but life couldn't have been any picnic being brought up by two spinster aunts instead of parents.

He thought of his own noisy family—a mom and dad who'd been together thirty years, four kids who all still lived in the same town—and he realized how lucky he'd been. Sure, sometimes money'd been a little tight, and he'd hated wearing his older brother's hand-me-downs, but at least he'd had a regular family.

No wonder Harriet came across as a little eccentric. It wasn't her fault. She also had a quirky innocence that brought out his chivalrous impulses. Especially since she seemed like a creep-magnet. First, The Reptile, now The Boulder.

Harriet wasn't used to guys like Rock. She wasn't the sort of woman a professional athlete usually spared a second glance. Steve's grin faded in annoyance. Why hadn't she shown up to the audition in her kilt and sweaters? It was the best defense there was against a shallow womanizer like Rock.

While Steve steamed and Rock leered, Harriet danced and bounced and…jiggled. There was probably a better verb than *jiggled,* but it was the best he could do. Not jiggled in a centerfold way, but a kind of happy wriggling from top to toe.

It made his mouth dry.

Not wanting to drip drool—the last thing Rock needed was more shine on those biceps—he grunted a goodbye and left the stage.

Only to hit the bleachers to continue watching the tryouts.

Family members and friends of the contestants and quite a few of the gals who'd already been cut sat around watching the remaining contenders. He recognized Tess Elliot with an older woman he was willing to bet was her mother, and realized with a jolt of surprise that Jonathon's soon-to-be-ex-wife, Caro, was sitting with them. They were three of the classiest women in town, but no one would know it to see their anxious faces and the way they passed vending-machine popcorn back and forth, munching ferociously.

His stomach gurgled and he realized they'd all missed dinner. It wasn't much of a compliment to

Harriet, but he imagined they'd all assumed they'd be out of here after the first round.

"Hey, Tess," he said, plopping himself down beside her.

She turned to him, her eyes full of excitement. "Can you believe it?" she squealed. "She's doing a fantastic job up there. I never knew she had it in her."

He hadn't known Harriet had all those curves in her, either, but decided not to say so in front of the three most elegant women in Pasqualie. "She surprised me, too."

Tess introduced him to her mother, and he shook hands. He said a polite hello to Caro and then all four of them fell silent as the coach announced the next round of cuts. The three women clung together, muttering, "Please, please let Harriet make it."

He wouldn't do anything so lame as hold hands with women he barely knew and beg the gods for Harriet's success, but in his head a similar incantation played over and over. *Come on, Harriet. You can do this.* Over and over as number after number boomed out from the megaphone.

It took a few moments of stunned silence before they realized the cuts were done and Harriet was still a contender. They were down to six contestants for the finals and Steve discovered his palms were sweating.

Now came the ultimate test. Each finalist had been asked to come up with an individual routine. He'd offered to help Harriet with hers last week, but she'd told him she was fine. At the time he'd wondered if she didn't want him to see her mediocre talents, but now he puzzled over her refusal. She must have a coach somewhere who helped her. At least he sure hoped so.

Three other women did their routines. None of them fell even though inside his head he willed them to. Maybe it wasn't very chivalrous, but he didn't figure anybody deserved this chance more than Harriet. They were all great. His heart sank as they danced, leaped in the air, backflipped and smiled, smiled, smiled.

Then they called Harriet's name. Without meaning to do it, he jumped to his feet and yelled. "Come on, Harriet. You can do this."

Flushing, he sat with a bump, only to have Tess's mother pat his arm. "I'm sure she heard you."

And it seemed she had. As Harriet took up her position at the back of the stage she looked out over the stands and flashed him a big, happy, cheerleader's smile. *Come on, Harriet.* The words looped repeatedly in his head.

Then the music swelled. Not the boom-boom rock that the other three had chosen but more of a hip-hop beat. Was that okay? Or had she screwed up in some way with her choice of music. He wiped his palms on his sweater. This suspense was killing him.

And then she launched herself into the air and he forgot there was any kind of music anywhere. All there was was Harriet, sailing through the air, landing on her hands in a perfect handstand to back flip. She was up, doing some kind of complicated dance moves. Whew, that lady could move. She jiggled, she twirled, she high-kicked and then she back-flipped. One, two, three, four perfect flips, a gleam of red hair flapping on her black bodysuit.

She leaped and spun in the air and slipped down in perfect, graceful splits, her hands rising straight up in the air and her smile as bright as the sun in August.

Of course he'd applauded politely for the previous three contestants, but now he was on his feet along with Caro and Tess and her mother, yelling and hooting. Forming, he dimly realized, their own cheerleading section for a cheerleader.

The other two contenders showed up and did their best, but it was over. Steve knew it in his gut. Harriet had blown the lid off the competition.

When they called her name as the winner of the contest, Steve felt his eyes prick. He felt like a damn fool but he couldn't help himself. She'd just attained the dream she'd thought was unattainable. She'd grabbed it with both hands and made it hers.

Her smile lit the whole stadium and, as corny as it sounded, even in his head, he felt as if he was watching the ugly duckling find her new home in the swan pond.

"She did it. She did itshededitshedidit!" shouted Tess, grabbing Caro, who yelled, "Who-hoo!"

Mrs. Elliot didn't do any screaming, merely clapped with enthusiasm as befitted a respectable society matron. "I'm going to give Harriet that top. She'll be needing it more than I will, and—" she sighed "—she looks so much better in it."

"I'll give her the tights, too," agreed Caro.

Ah, so there was one mystery solved. Steve had been wondering where Harriet had come up with the figure-hugging duds that didn't jive with her usual fifties schoolgirl wardrobe.

Harriet's fan club rose together and made its way

to the stage area. He watched as the coach gave Harriet some papers and the other cheerleaders patted or hugged their newest recruit.

She glanced up and saw him and the smile broadened. She was just flying.

With a last nod, and mumbled thanks, she slipped away from the coach and jogged to Steve and the three women. He stepped forward with his arms out. Everybody on the damn team had given her a hug. It was his turn.

She hesitated for just a second, then walked straight into his arms. "I did it!"

"I knew you could," he said into her hair as he wrapped his arms around her.

Everything about her seemed unfamiliar to him— her looks, the bright verve, even the smell of her. The sticky-sweet scent of hairspray assailed him. But under it, he smelled the sweat of a healthy workout and a hint of fresh-baked oatmeal cookie.

She felt so good squeezed up against him that he never wanted to let her go. But, of course, he had to. Tess was waiting. After he eased back, Harriet tumbled into Tess's arms, then Rose's and even Caro's.

Then, most unwelcome of all, the hulking Rock Richards was suddenly muscling in. Now, nobody would ever accuse Rock's brain of being bigger than his biceps, but from the narrow-eyed glare he sent Steve, it was clear he'd figured out he'd been trying to keep him away from the hot redhead.

"Hey, babe," he said in his gravelly voice. "I'm Rock. Team quarterback. Want to welcome you to the team."

"Thanks," Harriet said, turning her sparkling gaze

his way. She put out her hand politely, but Rock had other ideas. He pulled her body flush against his and kissed her full on the mouth.

Harriet gave a little squeak and her hands went up to Rock's shoulders to push him away.

Steve's blood pounded behind his eyeballs and his hands fisted as he watched the big gorilla do his best to eat Harriet for lunch. He was about to break up the clinch when she managed to pull away with a flustered giggle.

"You need anything, anything at all. You call on Rock." He gave Harriet a smile, sent them all a general wave and lumbered off.

"Wow. What a hunk," Tess said.

Steve almost snarled.

"He was certainly…friendly," Harriet said breathlessly.

At that moment Steve vowed that Rock may have beat him in the gene pool lottery, but he wasn't going to beat him to Harriet.

"I don't know when I've been so excited," Rose said, then paused. "Not since you got engaged, I suppose," she said to Tess. She shook her head. "I never thought my daughter would marry a man with long hair and an earring."

Tess snorted. "You're not fooling anyone, Mother. You love Mike almost as much as I do."

"And I got rid of all my odd earrings, too. You know, when you've lost one and can't bear to throw the single away?" She beamed. "Now I can just give them to my almost son-in-law."

"No more rhinestones, Mom. I'm warning you.

He's threatening to wear the long dangly one to Christmas dinner.''

"Oh, dear. Whatever will your father say?"

"Exactly."

"Oh!" Rose put her hand to her cheek and glanced at the watch on the opposite wrist. "Speaking of your father, I never told him I was going out. He'll wonder what's happened to me."

Tess glanced at her watch, too. "Oh, shoot. I was supposed to pick Mike up at the boxing ring ten minutes ago. We'd better get going. Harriet, I'll drop you back at the office on the way."

"Oh, but that's out of your way."

"I'll drive her back," Steve said, only too happy for the chance to be alone with this intriguing new Harriet.

"Is that all right with you?" Tess asked her.

"Yes, of course. Thanks for everything."

"I'll hitch a ride back to your parents' home to pick up my car if that's all right," said Caro in her well-modulated voice. She didn't seem to be late for anything or have anyone waiting for her. Steve felt a twinge of sorrow. She and Jon had seemed like the perfect couple.

But, as Caro strode away with the two Elliot women, Steve was happy to put her problems out of his thoughts and to concentrate on the newest Braveheart—a cheerleader who looked as though she didn't have a problem in the world. She was absolutely glowing with a combination of recent exercise, excitement and sparkly makeup.

"Do you have to go straight home?" he asked her.

"No. Why?"

He grabbed her hand and started walking toward where he'd left his car.

Harriet's article for the sports section was going to be more than he'd originally envisioned. He could see the headline now: I Am A Braveheart. A Behind-The-Scenes Look.

Not Pulitzer-prize material, certainly, but something the good people of Pasqualie would all be fascinated to read. The women would want to know what it took to be a Braveheart. And the men, well, they just wanted to look at the pictures of all those delectable babes posing and prancing.

Steve had a bit of a rivalry going with the sports editor at the *Star*. Jim Cole had been trying to get a Braveheart to pose for the scantily clad *Star* Gal feature on page three for as long as Steve could remember.

None of the cheerleaders would pose for the *Star* Gal, but he imagined they'd love a decent feature story in the *Standard* about the squad. And who better to write the inside story of what it was like to be a cheerleader than a budding journalist and part-time Braveheart.

If everything fell into place her piece might have a real shot at a journalism award, something else he and the *Star* sports editor were in hot competition for.

"Steve!"

"Hmm?" He came out of his reverie to find Harriet calling his name in a way that made him think this wasn't the first time she'd done so.

"Why are you staring at me like that?"

"Was I staring? Sorry. I was thinking of something else."

He was thinking of more than one article. A whole series.

Along with his own reports of the Braves' games, he could sidebar stories from Harriet with her view from the cheerleaders' squad.

This was one of his greatest ideas. He, Steve Ackerman, was a journalistic genius.

"Harriet, I just thought of something." He looked at her with a gleam in his eye. "What do you think of this? Now that you're an official Braves' cheerleader, how do you feel about writing about your experiences in first person for the *Standard*?"

She just stared at him, shocked for a second time that day. "You want me to write an article about *myself*?"

"Well, sure. I'll help you. But yeah, that's the whole point of this. You'd have the inside scoop."

"Would it have my name on it?"

"Absolutely," Steve said with confidence.

Harriet bit her lip.

"Harriet," he said when he saw her reluctance. "This is a great story." Enthusiasm built as he thought about it. "You had a dream. You worked at it, made it come true. I want a first-person account of what it was like up there, how it felt, the moment you knew you had a real shot at it. Everything."

They walked hand in hand and it felt like the most natural thing in the world.

"It felt…" She blew out a breath. "It felt so incredible I don't know if I can even describe it to you."

"Well, we'll have to work on that otherwise your article isn't going to be too interesting," he joked.

She stopped dead and turned to stare at him. The day was just heading for dusk and lit up her still-bouncy curls with fire. With the unusually bold makeup, her eyes looked huge and mysterious, her lips glossy enough to lick. "Oh, my gosh. That's right."

He grinned. "We've got some time. I'm thinking about a big spread to celebrate your first game. We can tie it in with some kind of promotion. A contest to win game tickets or something." He was thinking not only of boosting the paper's circulation, but of upping his chances at the sports section award in the upcoming journalism awards.

"A spread about me?" She still sounded stunned.

His enthusiasm built as he dragged her along to his car.

"Sure. You're a Braveheart now." He gestured to her luscious curves lovingly outlined in black. "Look at you."

A huff of impatience was his only reply. No, there was also a muttering under the breath that sounded like *"Men!"*

"What?"

"This isn't about lip gloss and jiggling around in tight clothes."

"It's about dreams," he insisted.

"Exactly." She suddenly dropped her snarly attitude and smiled at him. "And I didn't thank you enough for getting my sorry butt out there today." She lifted up on tiptoe and kissed his cheek.

Her lips were butterfly-soft against his skin, and once again he caught her scent and had to restrain himself from dragging her against him and giving her a "you're welcome" kiss that would curl her toes.

"So, a woman who just fulfilled her dream deserves a night on the town to celebrate."

She blinked at him, and the Harriet of the plaid skirts was back. "A night on the town?"

"Sure. You, me, we'll paint this town red."

"But I have to work tomorrow."

Boy, she sure didn't get out much. "Don't worry. This is Pasqualie and it's Tuesday. Last call is eleven."

"Well…" She glanced down at herself. "I should change first."

No, he wanted to yell. *Don't change.* He nodded.

"And shower."

No, no! She'd shower the sexy do out of her hair and the makeup off her face. All the stardust would drain away with the water. "Sure," he made himself say. "I'll wait."

"I'd like to pick up my car."

"All right. I'll drive you to the office, do a bit of work, and pick you up at your place at—" he glanced at his watch "—eight."

Her brow puckered. "Are you sure?"

"Of course I'm sure. This is your day. We have to celebrate."

She beamed at him. "Okay."

So he drove her to the newspaper office, where she glanced around the empty parking lot nervously. It was seven o'clock. Was she expecting pre-dinner muggers or what?

"Do you want me to walk you to your car?"

"Hmm?" She glanced at him as though *he* was odd. "It's seven o'clock. I think I'm safe, thanks."

"You seem nervous."

"Oh, that. I just don't want anyone to see me like…" She glanced down at herself and he could have sworn she blushed. "Like this."

"You look great," he assured her, but she just gave him one of those looks that went with *men* muttered sotto voce and, with a final quick glance around the parking lot, scuttled out of his car and into her own so fast you'd never have known she was there. The lady would be tops in the spy business.

She drove carefully out of the parking lot in a sensible tan compact that had to be as old as she was and he let himself back into the *Standard* building.

Already he was planning the two-page spread showcasing not only Harriet's talent and the tryouts, but how she, a hometown girl, had made her dream come true.

He was also playing with layouts in his mind. Harriet, the high school geek. Maybe the art department could do something funky to make it appear the photo was torn out of a yearbook. Then, beside it, he'd get a picture of Harriet, the newest Braves' cheerleader in the uniform, full makeup, the hair, the whole bit. No one would believe it was the same person.

After checking his e-mail and phone messages, he settled down to play with some headline ideas.

"Cinderella Finally Gets Her Pom-Poms." No, that wasn't right. It sound as if she'd had a boob job or something. He deleted that and tried again.

He liked the Cinderella aspect, though. "Cinderella

Scores A Touchdown.'' Better. Not quite there, though.

He left that as the header and let his thoughts flow, jotting notes. First-person account. High school heartaches. Tryouts, failure. Other athletics? Boys? Had she had a date to the prom?

Soon he realized he was working more on a hybrid feature/sports story. There was her first-person article, and then an article that he would write about her. The combination might bring more readers into his section. It might finally win him that award and show Jim from the *Star* a thing or two. This was the kind of story the jury loved. Soft sports.

And he couldn't think of anything softer, or more uplifting to the reader than the story of an overlooked athlete finally achieving her dream.

But, for tonight, he was determined not to talk shop. Tonight was about Harriet and her new job for the Braves.

He gave her a few extra minutes more than the hour they'd agreed on, then picked up the neat little note she'd written with her address.

When he pulled up to her home, she emerged from the front door as soon as she saw him. It was just about the trimmest, best-kept house Steve had ever seen, in a neighborhood of well-maintained homes built in the forties.

Symmetrical flowerbeds, velvet lawn, swept path. Even in the dim light he could somehow tell the paint was fresh and the windows gleamed. It was that sort of house.

Harriet jumped into his car. Yep, as he'd feared, she'd done away with all traces of Harriet the cheerleader. This was everyday Harriet. The gal with the straight hair, cosmetic-free face and the Mary Janes.

"Tess's mother said she was going to give you that workout stuff," he said, thinking how great she'd looked in it.

"I don't know. It was kind of…skimpy."

"Harriet, I have to tell you. Skimpy is good when you're a cheerleader. Skimpy is great. See, mostly guys watch sports, and guys like eye candy."

Her eyes and mouth both widened, as he'd known they would. "Eye candy. I'll have you know, Mr. Sports Reporter, that cheerleading is a real sport. Lots of colleges are offering scholarships to top cheerleaders. It's not just pom-poms and…and wiggling butts anymore."

He let a beat pass. "We should take a poll of the Braves' fans to see whether they like the cheerleaders best for their athletic ability or their butts."

A sound that was an awful lot like a kitten's growl came from the passenger seat. "Are you implying…" They passed under a streetlight and she must have caught sight of his face. "Oh. I should have known you'd just be joking with me. You're never serious."

"I'm always serious about sports." He paused for a moment. "And butts."

She wouldn't be drawn in a second time, so he chuckled and let it go. So she thought he was joking. Fine by him. In truth, he was willing to bet that the good gentlemen of Pasqualie, while no doubt appreciating athletic ability, still watched the Bravehearts for the eye candy.

"Where are we going?" she asked after they'd driven a few minutes in silence.

"Hungry?"

"Starved. I was too nervous to eat for most of the day."

"Like Italian?"

"Love it."

7

HARRIET SIGHED, her whole body feeling relaxed and yet tingling with excitement. Her muscles were pleasantly tired, her nerves finally back to normal after being on high alert for weeks.

She sipped at the red wine Steve had ordered and felt further relaxation seep into her bones. She closed her eyes for a second and savored the moment, the smell of garlic and cream and the fact that she, Harriet MacPherson, was sitting having dinner with studly Steve Ackerman. Of course it wasn't a real date, it was more a work thing, but she could dream.

Today was, after all, about impossible dreams coming true.

When she opened her eyes, Steve was grinning at her. "I bet you feel like you just reached the summit of Everest," he said.

"I knew you'd understand."

"Better than anyone. At least you don't have thick glasses and a thin skull."

"Steve." She leaned forward, feeling her forehead wrinkle in earnestness. "I know there's nothing you can do about your head, but couldn't you have laser eye correction? I understand it's very successful these days."

He shook his head. "It doesn't work for everyone.

I'm not a good candidate. My eyeball's the wrong shape or something.''

She stared into his eyes, a beautiful clear gray with long, sweeping dark lashes. They were almond-shaped and gorgeous. "I think they're the perfect shape," she said. Then realizing what she'd said, blushed deeper than the Chianti. "I mean, they seem like they're normal eyes."

He let her embarrassing compliment pass without teasing her, for which she would be eternally grateful.

"I see fine with glasses. Sure, for a while I wanted perfect eyesight as much as…" he chuckled softly "…as much as you wanted pom-poms. But it wasn't meant to be." He shrugged. "I can still play sports, even with weak eyes and a weak head. I'll never play pro, but I've made my peace with it. Writing about sports is a pretty great consolation prize."

"But you miss it. I can tell." From the way he'd worked so hard to help her become a cheerleader she knew that he was in some small way making up for never being able to attain his own goal.

He didn't lie, as she'd known he wouldn't. "There's a smell in the dressing room sometimes after a game. It's pretty disgusting really, all that sweat and the smell of the champagne they've dumped over each other after a big win, the steam and soap from the showers. It all comes together and hits me that I'll always be on the outside looking in. I'll never be one of them."

She reached over impulsively to touch his hand and he turned it palm up, gripping hers so she couldn't take it back without tugging.

"But it doesn't happen often. And then I think

about five, ten years down the road when they're all washed up and wondering what to do with their lives, and I've still got the second greatest job in the world.''

Harriet could barely take in his words. She felt the warmth of his palm against hers, the tough leathery feel of it, the calluses that lined up with hers. It was difficult to explain, but their hands seemed to fit together.

After a long moment when they stared into each other's eyes not speaking, she said, ''I got my calluses from the uneven bars mostly. How about you?''

He turned her palm over and studied it in the light from the candle. Usually she was embarrassed at how battle-scarred her palms were, but Steve ran his index finger across her skin in a way that made her shiver.

''Impressive,'' he said, and she knew he meant it.

He let her see his palm, which sported a pretty impressive pattern of calluses all its own. ''Mine are from squash, tennis and baseball mostly.''

Their dinner came then, so she was able to get her hand back without making an issue of it. *Don't make a fool of yourself, Harriet.* Steve Ackerman was merely being kind to her; she mustn't embarrass them both by developing a raging crush. She wasn't the sort of person who could have a crush in secret. Her cursed blushes always gave her away.

As they tucked into their pasta, he asked her how she'd come up with her routine and who was her coach.

''I don't have a coach,'' she said, surprised at the question. ''I watched a video of the Bravehearts. No,'' she amended, always truthful, ''I memorized it.

Every routine, every move, every posture. Then, when I put together my own routine, I used some of their moves and added in some gymnastics and dance moves of my own. It wasn't that hard. I love choreography.''

"You know, Harriet, you have got to stop hiding your talents. You were absolutely amazing out there. I knew you'd be good, but you blew the doors off the place.''

"So, when you said I should forget it..."

He laughed. "It worked, didn't it? My saying you couldn't do it got you out there faster than any pep talk.''

She nodded. "When you came into the dressing room I was literally scared rigid. I couldn't move. And you told me it was okay and I could just stand at the sidelines and watch. That's the moment I knew I was going out there. I had to show you, show those other girls, but most of all show myself that I could do it.''

His eyes twinkled behind his glasses. "You showed us all.''

"I know." She couldn't keep the smug smile off her face. She forked more lasagna into her mouth, enjoying every bite now that she was relaxed enough to eat.

"You'll have to get started on the first article.''

The first article, she liked the sound of that. "Yes, of course. But without any interviews...''

"I got a list of a few names and phone numbers of women who are willing to talk to you. They were hanging around watching the rest of the practice so I asked them then.''

"Why didn't you do the interviews yourself? While the moment was still fresh in their minds?"

He leaned forward. "Because I couldn't take my eyes off you. You were amazing."

She blushed and couldn't think of a thing to say.

"It's mostly about you, now, anyway. How you felt, what it was like. You can call a couple of those women and add in some reactions from other contestants. The Braves know you're a reporter, right?"

"Copy editor," she corrected him. Though the fact that he'd referred to her as a reporter sent a thrill through her. "And, yes. I had to fill out an application and have a short interview before the tryouts. I told them about my job."

He raised his glass in a toast. "To your career as a cheerleader and your budding career as a journalist. May they both be full of success."

When they tapped glasses and sipped, she made a silent addition to the toast. *And may this be the first of many intimate dinners together.*

Before she realized it, her plate was empty.

"Want to try some of my linguini?" Steve asked her.

Her gaze dropped to his plate in horror. He still had about a third of his dinner left and she'd practically licked her plate clean.

"Oh, I was starving. I haven't eaten anything all day and I didn't realize…"

"Are you kidding? It's great to see a woman enjoy her food. I'm not a big fan of skinny women who pick at their food as if they're counting the calories in each grain of rice. Where's the fun in that?"

"Really?" Harriet raised her gaze to his to find him staring at her with an expression of approval.

"Harriet," he said, "you have a fabulous body. It's not heavy at all. It's muscular and...well it's beautiful," he finished in a rush and she had the feeling he was as embarrassed as she'd been when she'd told him she loved the shape of his eyes.

With a huge happy sigh, she said, "I'd love a bite of your pasta."

Even the way he wound linguini onto a fork with his big, capable hands had her stomach going squishy. He really was an extremely attractive man. How was she going to hide her embarrassing crush?

He reached toward her, the pasta creamy and glistening, a plump shrimp perched on top. She opened her mouth and he fed her in a distinctly intimate gesture.

Nothing had ever tasted as good as that pasta.

Between them, they finished his food, all the bread in the basket and then he looked at her with devilry in his eyes. "Dessert?"

She laughed. "Love it."

She ordered the tiramisu and he ordered a chocolate gelato, but they shared.

Afterward, when he'd waved away her offer to pay for half, she sat back thinking she'd never had a better day.

"Thank you," she said simply. "Not just for dinner, but for encouraging me to try out."

He leaned forward, and, for a crazy moment she thought he meant to kiss her. His face swam into her vision and he cupped her chin in his hand.

But he didn't kiss her. He dampened his fingertip with his tongue and ran it along her cheekbone.

She gasped at the feel of his rough skin sliding against her cheek.

Then he held out his finger and she saw sparkles from the makeup Tess's mother had applied.

"All the stardust didn't wash away," he said softly.

Now that dinner was over, he would probably take her straight home, which was fine. Good, really, as she had a big day tomorrow and would finally get a decent night's sleep now that she wasn't so nervous about the cheerleading tryouts. Still, she wasn't a bit sleepy.

"Would you like to walk by the river?"

"I'd love it." In fact, she couldn't think of anything she'd rather do.

They left the restaurant and walked to his car where he opened her door first and held it for her. Just like a real date.

It didn't take more than five minutes to drive to the public riverfront park. He parked the car and she was almost reluctant to leave the intimate space, where just the two of them sat in the dark, soft jazz playing on the car stereo.

But he opened his door and climbed out, so she followed suit. They made their way to the gravel path that meandered along the riverbank. It was peaceful and serene, with a clear indigo sky dotted with stars and a sliver of moon.

"Are your shoes okay for this?" he asked, looking down.

"Perfect." She stuck one of her sensible leather flat-soled shoes up in the air for his perusal.

"I thought you might be wearing heels or something," he said, a ghost of a laugh in his voice.

"No." She felt like laughing herself. "I'd only fall flat on my face. My aunts were always telling horror stories about their friends with crooked spines and sprained ankles from wearing high heels." She shrugged. "I tried them a few times but I felt like an idiot."

"I like flat shoes on women. It's nice to walk at a normal pace," he said.

In fact, they were striding along. Harriet hated dawdling walks and it was clear Steve did, too. If she was going to walk, she liked to walk, arms swinging, legs eating up the ground. The gravel crunched underfoot, the river lapped in quiet accompaniment and the evening air was fresh and cool in her nostrils.

Her hand accidentally bumped Steve's and, without saying a word or making any kind of fuss, he simply held on to it. It was nice walking along holding hands with him. Once more she felt the connection, the warmth flowing between them.

She wondered with a leaping hope whether he'd kiss her, then clucked her tongue in annoyance. Steve Ackerman was a hunk, a chick magnet, a ten out of ten on Harriet's scale of male attributes. Well, if it was true he was kind of thick upstairs, she might have to knock him down to a nine. She glanced at his profile, strong and perfect in the starlight. Call it nine and a half, she decided. And no one had proven to her satisfaction that he was a dummy, anyway.

She wondered how she could find out. Not that it

really mattered. The chances that he'd be interested in her romantically were about the same as him kissing her tonight. Still, out of academic interest she'd like to know something of his mental capacity.

She could ask her aunt Lavinia, who'd most likely taught him, but her aunt had a policy of not discussing her students' academic records at home. She felt they were entitled to their privacy. Harriet admired her integrity, but it was annoying never to be able to pump her for info.

She'd simply ask Steve herself, that's all. Since they'd been walking in silence for a few minutes, now seemed like the perfect time.

"Did you enjoy school?" she asked.

He glanced at her oddly, and she realized this wasn't exactly after-dinner date conversation. Except it hadn't been a real date, of course, so she ought to be able to talk about anything she wanted to.

He shrugged. "I guess."

That was a point in his favor. If he liked school, he was probably good at it.

"What was your favorite subject?" she asked.

"Phys ed."

Well, duh. "How about academically?"

He shuffled a bit on the gravel path almost as though he was in danger of falling into the river and her hand tightened automatically in his. "I was more interested in sports than anything else."

"Oh." She was disappointed, but it looked as if he was stuck with a 9.5. Close enough to perfect. So, they wouldn't discuss symbolism in the Brontës' novels and poetry, or discuss calculus. It didn't mean he was less attractive, or less fun to be around.

"How about you?" he was asking. "Did you like academics?"

"Oh, yes. Very much." She'd topped the honor roll two years in a row and won a few chess championships. Still, it hadn't made her popular, only more geeky.

"You don't sound all that happy about it."

"Well, the truth is, being smart just made me seem more of a freak, I guess. I was that geeky smart girl with carroty hair."

He turned to her, and, dropping her hand, cupped her chin. "You should be proud of yourself for getting good grades and not caring what the other kids thought," he said firmly. "That takes guts."

Something about the way his eyes stared down into hers so intensely made her stomach feel more nervous than she'd felt before her audition today. She swallowed, wishing she were glamorous and sophisticated and knew how to wear the right clothes and style her hair. Wishing she were the kind of girl...

Steve lowered his head slowly and kissed her.

Her eyes opened wide as she took in the amazing fact of his lips, warm and sure against hers. Then they drifted shut as she kissed him back.

The warm connection she'd felt when they'd held hands was nothing compared to this. His lips teased and soothed her at the same time, making her feel both desired and cherished. She sighed into the kiss and leaned into him, wondering which fairy godmother was responsible for this part of her fantasy coming true.

His arms wrapped around her and she found her own circling his waist. As he pulled her body against his, she felt the firm muscularity of his chest, his hands tracing patterns on her back.

She couldn't seem to get close enough to him. She moved deeper into the embrace, feeling that warm connection everywhere they touched.

He tasted of red wine and a hint of garlic, which only reminded her of how much fun they'd had at dinner and how much they had in common. To heck with his brain. His kissing ability alone shot him back up to ten out of ten on her personal scale.

Her own hands traveled up his back and she loved the sculpted feel of his muscles beneath his skin. He wasn't bulky; you'd look at him in his day-to-day clothes and see a normal-size man. But being this close, she felt his athleticism and loved it.

"Excuse me," mumbled a man's voice. She and Steve broke apart guiltily, letting an older gentleman and his ancient spaniel squeeze around them on the narrow path.

Steve took her hand and they walked a few more steps before he moaned. "Oh, no!"

"What?" she asked alarmed. Was it her kissing? Was she so hopeless he was moaning?

"That kiss," he said.

Oh, Lord. It *was* her kissing. She felt the blood rush to her face as embarrassment swamped her.

"I've ruined everything," he muttered, sounding annoyed.

"No, you haven't," she retorted swiftly, rigid with mortification. "We'll pretend it never happened."

"Really?" He sounded so relieved she wanted to kick him or to push him into the river. "I'd really appreciate it."

The jerk. She tried to tug her hand out of his, but he held on tight.

"I'd forgotten about your aunts," he said.

"My aunts?" After insulting her kissing technique, he'd moved on to a critique of her family? "What have my aunts got to do with it?"

"Well, you told me they wouldn't want you to go out a second time with a man who kissed you on the first date. Remember? That's why I had to give you the hickey. If they find out I kissed you on our first date, it will be all over for me."

Where embarrassment had barely receded, a new blush suffused her cheeks, this one caused by pleasure so acute she wanted to jump up and whoop for joy. All the time she'd been telling herself this was about work, he'd been on a date. With her. She couldn't imagine a day could get any better than this one. And if he was talking about a second date, it meant...

"I won't tell them about this," she promised happily.

"I'd really appreciate that, Harriet. I want to see you again."

"You mean, like a date?"

"Definitely 'like a date.'" He was laughing at her, she knew, but in a good way. It made her want to laugh along with him and at her old-fashioned lifestyle and her old-fashioned aunts.

He gazed at her in a way that had her licking her lips in anticipation. "And I'd better get you home right away, or there will be two things you can't tell your aunts."

8

HARRIET AWOKE the next day feeling as though she must still be dreaming. Had she really won the coveted cheerleading spot?

She hugged her pillow to her as she let it all sink in. Yes, she was fully awake and she'd not only won the cheerleading competition, but she'd had dinner with a man she'd worshiped from afar for almost a decade. She giggled to herself when she recalled his wonderful kiss and the promise that he wanted to do it again. That he wanted to see her again.

Aunts Lavinia and Elspeth's proud delight when she'd told them the news last night had capped off her perfect day.

In no hurry to jump out of bed, she reached for her bedside table and picked up the sheaf of papers she'd been given the day before. There was her contract, which required her to be present for all the Braves' home games. They sent a smaller squad on the road, and tried to work around the women's work schedules. No trouble with either of those provisions, Harriet thought with glee.

She'd also be asked to take part in certain local charity events. She liked the idea of that, too, and hoped she'd be an inspiration for other young girls like her who might not be Miss Americas, who loved athletics more than the latest fashions.

She had her first practice tomorrow and had made an appointment for costume fittings first thing in the morning.

Yes. She'd be custom-fitted for one of those sparkly blue costumes she'd dreamed of for so long.

She'd also be responsible for her own makeup and hair.

Her happy glow dimmed in an instant. Do her own hair and makeup? The rest of the squad would find out she was a fraud, a geek in cool girl's clothing. A nerd, a loser, a...

She jumped out of bed and started to pace. She'd never thought about the consequences when she'd let Tess and Caro and Rose make her over into a glamorous woman. She hadn't watched every move Rose made or memorized what was in the forty-seven products she'd used or the seemingly endless number of brushes and pencils it had taken to effect her transformation.

And that was just her face. The hair was a whole other matter. It had involved hot rollers that burned her fingers just by looking at them, more than one brush, a spray for this, a tube of that.

"Don't panic," she said out loud. The Braves didn't choose her for her hair and makeup, they were simply part of the package. She'd have to learn how to do herself up, that's all. Had she really expected makeup artists and her own hairdresser?

In truth, she hadn't thought that far ahead. She'd focused on giving the best audition she could, not on the specifics of being a cheerleader.

While she worked through her morning stretching and ballet routine, she continued to worry about hair and makeup, two subjects she'd barely thought about in her whole life. She had almost a week until her first practice so she'd have to learn how to beautify herself on her own by then.

She could phone Rose Elliot and ask for a lesson, but Harriet was too shy to approach a virtual stranger.

Tess wasn't exactly a close friend, but they had a good working relationship and she'd pulled Operation Rescue Harriet together yesterday, and done it brilliantly. She'd ask Tess for guidance when she saw her at work. Perfect.

ONCE IN THE OFFICE, she started right away on her article for Steve. She pulled out the wrinkled page he'd ripped from his notebook and given her the night before. It contained the names and phone numbers of half a dozen women. He'd scrawled little notes beside some of the numbers. *Made it to semis* beside one. *Terrible dancer, nice personality* beside another. *One pom-pom short of a pair* beside a third. Harriet chuckled and decided to leave that one for last.

She smoothed out the wrinkled page, taking a moment to gaze at Steve's handwriting. It was a cramped scrawl, not a bit elegant, but still she loved looking at the words he'd made, touching the paper he'd touched...

Gasping in annoyance at what Aunt Lavinia would term featherheaded pining, Harriet picked up the phone and started calling.

Amazingly, she was able to talk to all six of the young women who'd given Steve their phone numbers yesterday. After she got off the phone with the last finalist, she had to admit she agreed with his scrawled comment next to the girl's name. She was one pom-pom short. Still, Harriet had managed to get some gushing praise for cheerleaders in general after some careful prodding, so it wasn't a completely lost cause.

Harriet gathered her notes, turned to her computer and started typing. She kept an eye on the clock on her screen, knowing she had to get the story written in plenty of time for Steve to read and edit it before deadline. Plus, she still had some of her own copy-editing to do. She could pretty much write off lunch.

STEVE WONDERED how long it would take Harriet to finish her article.

He jumped up. Maybe he should help her. Poor kid was probably flustered and nervous working on her first byline piece. Would she blush in that adorable way she had when she saw him? Would her dimples peep out?

Get a grip! he snarled to himself. Harriet could manage the article fine without his help, and he could manage to get through another hour without seeing her.

He pulled up a story from a stringer about some high school baseball meet and forced himself to concentrate on giving it a read. But somehow he kept seeing Harriet as she'd been yesterday, so full of life and on top of the world and so amazingly responsive to his kiss.

She was obviously very traditional and in some ways he thought she was much younger than her years. Dating Harriet would be like entering a time warp, he felt sure. There were the aunts to worry about, the social niceties. Did Harriet have a curfew? He grinned. It had been years since he'd had to worry about getting a girl home on time.

Amazingly, he didn't think he'd mind at all. There was something about Harriet that brought out the old-fashioned values in a person. He knew already that he'd pretty much let her set the pace for their relationship. It would be a novel experience.

He was ashamed of how little work he'd accomplished when a tentative tapping on his open door had him glancing up to find Harriet standing there. Definitely everyday Harriet, not cheerleader Harriet.

And she was blushing as adorably as he'd imagined she would.

He couldn't keep the smile off his face. "Hi," he said.

"Hi," she replied, and there were her dimples peeping out from her flushed cheeks. "I've finished the article."

He watched her mouth form the words and remembered how soft her lips were to kiss and how they'd trembled when he took her in his arms. "Article?"

Her dimples deepened. "I wrote the article about the cheerleaders that you asked for."

"Oh." He pulled himself together with an effort. "Right. Come on in and let's take a look."

"Okay." She seemed jumpy and he remembered the first time he'd written an article that had ended up in print. He'd been nervous, too.

She passed over a printout and he gestured her to

a chair while he grabbed a pencil and began to read out loud.

"'It takes years of hard work, training and physical conditioning, but for a few lucky young women, it all pays off when they are chosen to be Pasqualie Bravehearts.'"

He nodded. "Pretty good for a feature lead," he said, and read on.

"'I cried, I was so happy,' admits Cecily Briscoe, a nineteen-year-old dental receptionist who dances six hours a week at the Lillian Bail Academy of Dance and was chosen as an intern—a cheerleader who will train with the regular troupe, fill in when a regular is sick and take part in charity events. If all goes well, she'll be a full-fledged cheerleader herself next year."

He stopped reading and glanced up, "'If all goes well?' What does that mean?" He circled the phrase with his pencil.

"Oh, um, Cecily said they told her—"

"What were her exact words?"

Harriet fumbled open her notebook and flipped pages until she found what she was looking for. "'The cheerleader director said if I work hard and give a hundred-and-one percent, I'll be a regular on the troupe next year.'"

He nodded. "That's better. Use the quote. Try to stay away from vague language."

He glanced up to see how she'd taken his suggestion and was pleased to see her nodding, a furrow of earnest concentration creasing her forehead. She could take criticism without getting riled. Always a good sign for a budding reporter.

He finished the article, impressed at how good it was for a novice effort, and smiled at her anxious face. "Great job. I also want you to do a bigger piece. Something more personal."

"More personal?"

"I want a first-person account of your *own* experiences of struggling all those years to get where you are now. Your dream to be a Pasqualie High cheerleader and how you became one for the Braves."

Her face clouded even further. Those dimples had completely retreated, he noted. "I thought you wanted me to interview the candidates at the cheerleading trials and write about my experience as part of the team, not type up my teenage diary." She mimicked holding a book and writing in it. "Dear Diary. Got another zit today. Didn't make the cheerleading squad. Will boys ever know I exist?"

He chuckled. "You don't have to go into that much detail, but this story isn't about the other candidates anymore. It's about you."

He rose and came around the desk, squatting in front of her so he could look right into her eyes. "I want to know all about how you started, what it felt like when you didn't get picked on the high school squad, all the years of ballet and dance going to waste, how it felt to watch the less talented girls get their chance in the sun."

"You want my life story?"

"I'm looking for—"

"You're looking for I Was A Total Loser In High School. That's what you're looking for." She rose in one jerky motion, uncharacteristically graceless.

"What the…" He scratched his head. This didn't seem to be going quite the way he'd intended it.

She marched toward the door then turned to him. "You told me this article was about going behind the scenes as a Braveheart. What it's like to be one, what the other women are like, the tension, all that stuff. Now you're turning it into an analysis of what a miserable loser I was in high school."

"But, that's the power of the story. Look how far you've come. That girl who was overweight and overlooked in high school—"

"That girl was me. Is me. I'm still overlooked. Old weird Harriet. That's what they used to call me, you know."

"Harriet, you have to trust me. This series could win the *Standard* a journalism award. The *Star* won't be able to touch us. You'll be a big part of that."

She shook her finger at him. "I'm not going back to my miserable teenage years, so don't drag me back."

She stomped to the door and he watched, stunned, still in his crouched position in front of an empty chair.

"Hey," he called. "Did we just have our first fight?"

She turned a furious face his way. "We just had our last fight." And she was gone.

HARRIET WAS SO ANGRY she needed a good strong game of something brutal and competitive to work out her frustrations. Instead, she'd have to work at her desk copyediting.

She stomped back to her desk muttering and almost knocked Tess Elliot flying as she came around a corner like a speeding freight train.

"Oh, Tess. I'm sorry," she said as her colleague recovered her balance.

"Where's the fire?" Tess half laughed, then caught sight of Harriet's face. "What is it?" she said in a more serious tone.

Normally, Harriet wasn't one for blabbing her troubles, but she was so burning mad she couldn't stop the bitter words. "Steve Jerkface Ackerman. That's what's wrong."

Tess glanced right and left in the crowded newsroom and whispered, "bathroom," then put a surprisingly strong hand at Harriet's back and pushed her in the direction of the ladies' room.

Once inside, they determined it was empty and then Tess said, "What happened?"

For an awful second Harriet thought she might cry. Normally, she never cried, but lately it seemed that every time she entered the women's washroom she ended up an emotional wreck. Under normal circumstances she would never confide in a woman like Tess, a woman who had Homecoming Queen written all over her, but she was so upset she didn't care.

"You didn't go to Pasqualie High, but I did and so did Steve. I was the worst nerd you could imagine."

Tess nodded, clearly not finding the admission at all hard to believe.

"I mean, worse than now," she said earnestly, and it seemed that Tess struggled against a smile.

"You're not a nerd. You're an individual."

"Thanks," she said with real gratitude. "But Steve wants to do an article about my transformation from nerd to cheerleader. A first-person account of how the biggest loser in Pasqualie finally got to wave a couple of pom-poms in the air."

Tess's eyes widened. "You can't be serious?"

"I am. And worse, so is Steve."

"I know he's not too bright, but surely even Steve couldn't be that unfeeling."

"He's a man, isn't he?"

Tess snorted. "Silly me, I was forgetting. So, what are you going to do?"

"Well, I'm not kissing him again, that's for sure. And he can forget the second date."

"You've been dating Steve Ackerman?" Tess looked as though she couldn't believe her ears, which didn't do a thing for Harriet's ego, or her temper.

"One date." Harriet raised her index finger. "One. And it's the last one. Jerk."

"Do you want me to talk to him?"

"No. I'm hoping he'll come to his senses."

Tess leaned a hip against a sink. "I thought you'd be floating on air today, your first full day as a cheerleader."

"I thought so, too," she replied miserably, "but it's all a mess." Forgetting Steve for the moment, she explained about the hair and makeup.

"You want Caro," Tess replied. "That woman knows everything about makeup and hair."

"Oh, but I couldn't—"

Tess sighed and a frown pulled her brows together.

"I wouldn't say this to anyone, but you'd be doing her a favor. She needs to get out of the house and stop moping over Jonathon. Let me call her?"

"Well, if you think she'd want to..."

"I know she will. You have a lot in common. You can talk about what pigs men are."

9

HARRIET GRIMACED as she globbed a layer of foundation over the moisturizer that already felt sticky on her skin. Prior to becoming a Braves' cheerleader her makeup routine had been a flick of mascara over her lashes and a quick application of clear lip gloss to keep her lips from chapping. She'd also accumulated a little vinyl bag full of eye shadows, lipsticks and blushers she'd bought on various whims—most of which she now realized were the wrong colors and belonged in the wastebasket.

She'd had an exhausting trip with Caroline yesterday after work, and currently owned more cosmetics than she would have believed existed in the world.

Caro had been as thrilled about the shopping spree as Tess had predicted she'd be, taking Harriet personally to meet Darlene of Darlene's Skincare Den, the only qualified esthetician in Pasqualie.

Harriet watched from behind as the woman had bowed and scraped when Caro stepped through the door and couldn't have been more excited about teaching Harriet all about makeup.

"Gorgeous skin," Darlene, a redhead herself, said as she sat Harriet in a reclining chair that reminded her of one at a dentist's office and shone a bright light on her face. "What's your regimen?"

"Pardon?" Harriet asked, mystified.

"How do you care for your skin, honey?"

"Oh. I wash it every morning and before I go to bed with a bar of Ivory soap."

Darlene shrieked. "That's it?" She shot Caro a can-you-believe-this glance. "Oh, my dear, it's a good thing you came to me before you got any older." She tsked, and peered. "God gave you beautiful skin. Now it's your solemn duty to look after it."

Darlene's reaction reminded Harriet of the time she'd forgotten to feed her goldfish for two days. The aunts had made her feel like an animal torturer.

"I suppose you've never even had a facial."

Since Darlene supposed right, Harriet didn't bother to answer what was clearly a rhetorical question.

Darlene and Caro discussed her, almost as though she wasn't present. What she'd need for her skin care regime—it appeared she was going to have to add a few steps to her regular routine—and what colors and products would suit her best when she was performing.

While they messed about with her, Harriet had leisure time to fume some more about Steve's defection. How could he do this to her?

She'd e-mailed him her final copy of the cheerleader article and he'd responded that it was fine. Since then she'd barely seen him.

There were more important things in her life than discovering the man she'd had a crush on since high school was a grade-A jerk. There was day cream, night cream, a special cream to prevent wrinkles around her eyes, blusher, bronzer, seven kinds of lip goop, eyebrow pencil, lip liner, eyeliner… Between Darlene and Caro, Harriet ended up with more colored pencils than a children's art class.

Still, she had to admit it was a fascinating world. Since the aunts both believed beauty came from within, neither of them ever bothered much with cosmetics so she'd grown up without being exposed to makeup. Well, apart from that brief phase in high school when Harriet had taken a most unfortunate liking to grape-colored eyeshadow. Once she'd realized that instead of appearing sophisticated and exotic she looked as if she had two black eyes, she'd sensibly given up on the stuff.

Until now. Now she had an entrée into this exciting womanly world of cosmetics and her inner teenager was dying to try everything. It smelled wonderful in the shop, of mingled perfumes and herbal scents. Tiny pots and tubes winked at her from inside glass display cases, calling to her.

Harriet's first solo attempt at doing her makeup had her looking like one of the overpainted reject dolls down at Pasqualie Five-and-Dime.

The second application was better, though she could still have passed for a Saturday-morning cartoon character. By the third try they all agreed she looked pretty good.

Then Darlene sent her next door to Patty at the hair salon and Harriet got a stylish new cut that left her hair long, but gave it some shape, plus a lesson in different ways to wear it. Up, down, one side up, one down. With curls or straight. It was amazing what a woman could do with a tube of gel and a curling iron.

By the time Harriet left the hair salon, she and Caro

were having so much fun that they ran into Dave's Workout World. She bought some new workout gear, more of the style the other cheerleaders wore.

Emerging once again with a heap of bags, they grinned at each other. Caro bit her lip and said, "You know, if you want to go shopping for some regular clothes, I'm game."

As kindly as it was phrased, Harriet knew that what she was saying was, *Your clothes suck.*

Maybe Caro was right. But it was all too much change in one day. "Thanks, but I think I'm done for the day."

Besides, she'd spent most of her life dressing the way Lavinia and Elspeth had taught her to. Harriet was comfortable and it wasn't as if anyone was looking at her anyway, so she'd somehow never bothered to think about what she wore.

Then along came this cheerleader gig and suddenly she was showered in stardust and soon would be dressing in the sexiest outfit she'd ever seen. But it was still a uniform.

She glanced down at herself then at Caro. "I know I'm hopeless, but I appreciate you trying."

"You aren't hopeless at all. You have an understated style, but it suits you."

Harriet almost fainted. A former fashion model thought she had style. Style! She batted her fake lashes just to try them out. "Ow!" she cried, dropping a bag and slapping a hand to her face.

"What's the matter?"

"I poked myself in the eye with those false eyelashes Darlene stuck on me." She sighed as she stood in the middle of the sidewalk peeling off the lashes before she blinded herself.

So much for style.

"I THINK we want to go a smidge smaller here, and let out the bust a bit," said the costume fitter, who then nodded and stuffed a pile of pins into her mouth and started pinching fabric.

"Smaller?" Harriet almost shrieked. There was so much of her showing. Legs up to here, neck down to there, bare midriff, and the small amount of her that was covered, sparkled. The acres of flesh that weren't plastered with garish blue sparkles were mottled with a red flush of embarrassment.

"You were extracting a Hun's rabbit?" the woman mumbled through a mouthful of pins. At least, that's what Harriet thought she said, then she blinked and played word jumble games in her head until she made sense of the garbled words. *You were expecting a nun's habit?*

"Well, no. It's just so…small."

"If I had that boy I'd be bumping around naked." Blink. More word clarification. *If I had that body I'd be jumping around naked.*

Harriet couldn't think of a thing to say to that, so she said nothing. Rapidly, the woman's nimble fingers cinched, pinched and pinned the fabric until it was like a second skin. With sparkles.

Fortunately, the seamstress was almost out of pins when she next spoke, so her words were clear. "You'll be fine. You'll blend in with the other girls. Don't worry about it."

Don't worry about it. The woman was right. Harriet had wanted this, hadn't she? Wanted it badly.

She was simply grumpy because she'd risen two hours early so she could spend ninety minutes on her hair and makeup. Ninety minutes! She'd timed herself. It was ridiculous to spend that much time on her appearance. She hoped it was because she was slow and klutzy that it was taking so long. Surely when she'd had a bit of practice she could get her routine down to half an hour. Which was still twenty-five minutes longer than she was used to spending on primping.

She glanced at herself in the fitting mirror. Yes, she was glamorous and her hair was like something out of a shampoo ad, but she missed her five-minute beauty routine.

Straightening her shoulders, and accepting that all of Pasqualie was going to discover she had breasts, she decided to forget about the tinyness of the costume and concentrate on the enormity of her task. She had to learn all the cheers in two weeks. The squad was putting in extra practices so that she and the two spares they'd taken on could be brought up to speed, but still, it was an awesome responsibility.

"You all right, sugar?" Linda Lou, the runner-up to Miss Georgia Peach asked her, coming up from behind and slipping an arm over her shoulder. Linda Lou had been getting her own uniform touched up.

Harriet smiled and glanced at the pair of them reflected in the mirror. To a stranger, Harriet probably looked like one of the Bravehearts, which was more heartening than she could have imagined. But she'd stick out like a broken arm if she messed up her steps.

"I'm so scared I'll go left when I'm supposed to go right, or back when I'm supposed to move forward." She imagined the domino effect as one by one the blue sparkly women tumbled to the ground, each one rising to point an accusing finger at Harriet. She shuddered.

"Don't worry, honey. We all start out scared, but you'll pick it up in no time." She gave her shoulder a squeeze. "You're a natural."

Harriet tried to remind herself that she'd won the tryouts on her own merits, but she couldn't forget that, unlike most of the girls on the squad, she'd never actually *been* a cheerleader. And all her dancing and gymnastics had been performed in competition or fun meets.

She'd never had a whole lot riding on her before, and she felt as though one wrong move could land her on her far-too exposed, sparkly butt.

She forced herself to think positive as she changed back into her new workout gear and made her way to the rehearsal hall.

Now that she'd made the team, the other cheerleaders treated her as one of them. "Hey, Harriet."

"How ya doin', H?" and various other casual greetings were like balm to her wounded teenage soul.

The team practiced for three hours. They'd practice again on the weekend and within weeks she'd be on the field for her first game. She was a nervous wreck when she took her place, but soon she forgot her nerves as she tried to remember every step, move in harmony with the other girls and after a while, she started to enjoy herself.

For as long as she could pull this magic act off, she, Harriet Adelaide MacPherson, belonged to the in crowd. Of course, like any girl who'd read her fairy tales—and Harriet certainly had—she knew the clock would eventually strike midnight. But until the bell tolled, she would dance in her make-believe ball-gown.

In this new fairy-tale version of her life, there was even a handsome football prince who'd set his sights on her.

"Yo, Harriet," Rock Richards called as she packed up after practice. He swaggered toward her, fresh sweat dripping off his impressive biceps.

"Hello, Rock," she said, smiling at him shyly and dragging an oversize sweatshirt over her skimpy workout gear. Rock had a way of looking at her that made her feel as if her breasts had been painted in neon colors for his viewing pleasure. She forced herself not to cross her arms over her chest, trying to project the easy sexiness her fellow cheerleaders seemed to have been born with.

"Hey, Sugar," Linda Lou cooed as she sashayed past, dancing her fingertips along the back of Rock's tree-trunk neck. "How's things?"

Harriet could imitate the more enthusiastic Kelly, who took a running jump and leaped on Rock from behind, kind of like a baby ape might leap on its mother.

He patted, pinched or hugged every one of the girls, but for some unfathomable reason, Harriet held his attention.

"Can I give you a ride to Ted's?" Rock asked her. She blinked up at him, momentarily speechless. Probably his teammates had dared him to ask her to go with him, she decided when her faculties returned.

She'd never even considered going to the bar with the other girls. Harriet was, after all, a realist. She might be able to back flip, spin thirty times consecutively without getting dizzy and do the splits in either direction, but she had fourteen years of training in that stuff.

On "flirting in bars with men" she had not a minute's experience. Well, not firsthand experience, anyway. She'd watched plenty of other people flirt, but her dates had all been card-carrying members of Dullards International where the art of flirting was an elective no one bothered to study.

She was only human. Stupid dare or not, she couldn't resist showing up with Rock—knowing the *Standard* softball team was practicing tonight and might be there had absolutely nothing to do with her decision.

"I'd love to. Just let me change."

His gaze skimmed her. "You don't have to change. You look great. We all wear our workout gear there."

She smiled in true glee at the thought of walking into the bar on Rock Richards's arm where she might be spotted by her colleagues—one colleague especially who needn't think she was pining for him.

She felt a little foolish going out in so much clingy black Lycra, but Rock was right. All the girls wore outfits like hers to the sports bar. If she swallowed her bashfulness and went as she was, she might, for once in her life, actually fit in.

She grabbed her bag, Rock grabbed his and they were off.

Predictably, his car was a sporty black convertible with a very loud engine. She bit her lip before getting in, but decided she couldn't put on the plumage of a cheerleader and then act like a chicken. Squeezing herself onto the black leather passenger seat, she fastened her seat belt and hoped for the best.

He wasn't a wild driver, in spite of the car, so she was able to enjoy the cherry tree blossoms picked up by the headlights as they passed through town. Snuggled into her brand-new team jacket, she was plenty warm. Heck, even if it had been a hundred degrees outside she'd still have slipped into her team jacket.

She wondered if she'd feel shy with Rock and if she'd be able to think of anything to talk about. But he solved that problem when he cranked up the music until it almost masked the sound of the noisy engine. Harriet wasn't familiar with a lot of rap music, and decided there was no time like the present for expanding her musical horizons.

"What's the name of this group?" she yelled in Rock's ear, holding on to her hair as the wind whipped it about like a possessed blow-dryer.

"The Swollen Members," he yelled back.

"Oh," she said in a small voice.

That was pretty much the sum of their conversation until they pulled into the crowded parking lot.

The bar was exactly the same as it had always been.

It was Harriet who was different.

As she walked in on the quarterback's arm, she felt deliciously petite. And where, a few short weeks ago, she'd gazed in awe at the cheerleaders, she was now one of them.

The patrons hailed her and Rock as they entered the noisy bar and Harriet couldn't stop the grin from stealing across her face.

Of course, there wasn't much point being Cinderella waltzing in the arms of Prince Charming if there was no one to witness her transformation, so she glanced quickly around the bar to see if anyone from the *Standard* had made it yet.

Yes. There they were, at the same table they'd occupied last time. She noted a few bugging eyes and dropped jaws, then she encountered Steve Ackerman's gaze, and her smug balloon popped and shriveled.

He looked murderous.

Except it wasn't her he was glaring at with such heat she expected smoke to start billowing any second. It was Rock who held his attention.

Stunned, she glanced at Rock's face and found him staring back at Steve with a nyah-nyah-nyah-nyah-nyah-nyah expression. Then Steve's gaze shifted from Rock to her and she felt she'd let him down somehow. He gave her a quick nod of recognition, then went back to talking to Cherise, who was sitting across the table and giving him a whole lot more attention than she gave her crime beat.

Harriet was stunned. Surely the invisible battle she'd just witnessed, the flourishing of two testosterone-powered laser swords, wasn't for her benefit?

But when Rock put a meaty arm around her shoulders and dragged her, not to the table where the rest of the cheerleaders were sitting, but toward Steve, she wasn't so sure.

She tried to put on a relaxed, confident smile like

the ones the other cheerleaders wore, resisting the urge to cover herself somehow to hide her skimpy clothing. But it wasn't easy, especially now that she seemed to be the center of attention.

For once, being the invisible geeky girl seemed like heaven.

"Hi," she said in the direction of the table, but was unable to stop her gaze from coming to rest on Steve's angrily handsome face.

10

"WE MISSED YOU at the practice, Harriet," Steve said when they got closer.

Of course, he'd known she'd have to miss a lot of the practices, maybe even the tournament itself because of her cheerleading schedule, but it didn't make her feel any better to be reminded of it. And of how much fun she was missing.

"I'm sorry I couldn't make it. I'd still like to be on the team if you let me. I checked the schedule. I should be able to make most of the games."

He shrugged. "Up to you."

She couldn't believe how much she wanted a reappearance of the sweet guy who'd helped her get through her audition and who'd charmed her over Italian food, then kissed her while they were on the river walk.

Disappointed, she said a quick hello to the rest of the *Standard* table before she and Rock returned to sit with the cheerleaders and some of the players who'd also shown up.

Harriet sat quietly, taking it all in. She felt like a moth who'd accidentally stumbled into a butterfly colony. They were all so colorful and bright, flitting from here to there, topic to topic. She sipped a light beer and enjoyed the moment.

By eleven, she was yawning. She'd had too many early mornings and not enough sleep. When she rose, Rock stood with her. "Ready to go, babe?"

Only then did she realize that she didn't have her car with her. Rock had driven her. "Oh." She flushed. "I forgot. I can—"

"No. I'm ready to go," he said, squeezing around the table to her side.

"Well, if you're sure you don't mind."

"No trouble at all."

"I'll take you home. It's on my way." Where had Steve appeared from? she wondered as she took in his grim and determined expression.

Even as she opened her mouth, Rock said, with an edge, "I brought Harriet, I'll take her home."

"It's on my way," Steve insisted, taking her arm.

"Mine, too." Rock grabbed her other arm.

"I'm not a potluck casserole," she snapped, feeling the hot blush of embarrassment color her cheeks as all the other cheerleaders stared at the three of them.

Out of the corner of her eye, she was almost positive Rock's teammates were placing bets on who'd win the Harriet Tug-of-war.

She yanked both arms free and glared at the pair of them.

Rock stepped close enough to Steve that their chests nearly touched.

Steve narrowed his gaze and she saw with horror that his fists were clenched.

"She came with me, she's going home with me."

"I don't think so."

She rolled her eyes. "I'll take a cab home," she said and stalked toward the door.

"Why don't you drive me home, Steve?" Linda Lou asked, all fluttery and flirty, behind Harriet.

There was a short, tense pause. "Why don't I?" Steve said, sounding so happy at the suggestion that Harriet imagined she was already nothing but a faint memory.

Now that was the kind of tact that Southern women were famous for. Harriet should thank Linda Lou for salvaging an awkward situation. Except that for some bizarre reason she wanted to stuff a Georgia peach down the woman's pretty throat.

There was a flurry and rustle behind Harriet and then Rock was walking beside her as though nothing untoward had happened. "Sorry 'bout that," he muttered.

Harriet was so annoyed she felt she should jump into the cab that happened to be idling outside, if only on principle. But then she caught sight of Miss Georgia Peach and Mr. Jock Sports Reporter looking thoroughly cozy as they emerged from the bar and headed for his car.

Hmm. Why should she go home alone?

So she stuck to Rock's side as they crossed to his car.

They were silent on the way to her house. She didn't mean to be such a mouse, she simply couldn't think of anything to say to him. He didn't seem to mind. Besides, he had his music on again. She hoped desperately her aunts didn't make the same mistake she had and ask the name of the group.

When they pulled up in front of her house, he cut the engine, which made her dry-mouthed and nervous as she gazed at his calendar-hunk profile. "I, um, should go in."

"Aren't you going to invite me to come with you?" He seemed surprised, as though he were always asked in to women's houses, even on the first date. He leaned closer, until he was in kissing range.

A nervous giggle escaped her. "My two aunts are in their seventies. I don't usually have guests this late."

His eyes bugged out of his head and he quickly retreated to his own side of the car. "You live with two old ladies?"

She bristled in defense of her living arrangements. "They're my aunts. Yes, I live with them."

"Huh." He seemed to ponder this for a long time. She'd noticed he did a lot of pondering. He was either a very deep thinker or just slow. She was trying not to make a rash judgment. "You're kind of an old-fashioned girl."

Well, she thought, you can take a girl out of twin-sets, but you can't take her out of her own skin. "Yes, I suppose I am."

Another long pause, then a nod. "That's cool. So, do you want to…you know, get a pizza or something tomorrow night?"

She wasn't entirely certain she understood what he meant. "A pizza?"

"Well, doesn't have to be pizza. We could go to the steak house. You know. Dinner. You and me."

Surprise washed over her. "Rock, are you asking me out for a date?"

He flushed slightly. "Yeah."

She might as well know the truth now before she

ended up making a fool of herself. "Did someone put you up to this?"

"Huh?" His puzzlement was so genuine, she had to believe he was seriously asking her out. She didn't have a clue why, or what they were going to talk about when they got to this date. She was accustomed to seeing men who were at least as nerdy as she was, and had no idea how she'd handle a jock, who was one of Pasqualie's most eligible bachelors, but also a little conversation-impaired. If she wasn't so mad at Steve she could ask him for some ideas. Get some football trivia or something.

"I'm flattered, but, why me?"

"Well, obviously you're a babe." *A babe?* A handsome, successful man with two functioning eyes was calling her a babe? "And, I don't know." Another long pause ensued. "You're a nice kid."

The last part let some of the air out of her joy bubble, but she thanked him politely and accepted. She almost floated into the house thinking how nice it would be to date a man who didn't smell of formaldehyde, or who wanted to put her pathetic high school past on display for the entire town's amusement.

By the time she'd showered the gunk out of her hair, removed her makeup with a special cream and put on her night cream and eye cream and the lip balm that would prevent chapped lips, Harriet was beat.

It was heaven to think that it was a nonpractice Friday tomorrow and she wouldn't have to mess with her hair or a lot of makeup.

"HARRIET, are you eating properly?" Aunt Elspeth asked, a worried frown between her brows.

Since Harriet had just polished off a three-egg omelette, two pieces of homemade whole wheat toast and a glass of fresh-squeezed orange juice, she was amazed at the question. "Of course I am."

The crease didn't disappear from her aunt's brow. "But you're getting so thin. Isn't she getting thin, Lavinia?"

Her other great-aunt gazed at her over her reading glasses. "She looks fine. Don't fuss."

In fact, Harriet's body had become more taut and curvier, though she hadn't lost any pounds. "It's all the exercise, I think," she said.

"All that jumping around in skimpy bikinis would melt the pounds off anyone." There was a scolding note, but Aunt Lavinia couldn't disguise the pride in her tone.

"From the sound of things, that football quarterback certainly didn't think you were too thin."

Harriet blushed in spite of herself. "Rock. He's very nice."

"Mmm. We'd like to meet him, too, wouldn't we, Elspeth?"

"Oh, yes. So handsome in that uniform."

"Invite him in when he comes to pick you up this evening."

Harriet didn't trust Aunt Lavinia's benign expression for a second. She was pretty sure it was the same one Lavinia had used when asking a question of a student who obviously hadn't done their homework, but what could Harriet say? "All right."

AROUND MIDMORNING Steve called her. Her heart gave a funny bump when she heard his voice.

"Harriet, can you come in here for a minute?" he said. "I need some help writing the cutlines for your story."

"Sure," she said, still delighted that her very first feature article with her byline was coming out in the weekend edition.

She couldn't keep the excitement out of her voice. Everything seemed to be happening at once. She was about to fulfill a girlhood dream and become a cheerleader at the ripe old age of twenty-three, and she was now going to fulfill the first step of a career dream.

Her aunts would be so proud they'd burst.

Harriet all but bounced into Steve's office.

He glanced up and his eyes widened.

"What is it?" she asked, wondering if there was something embarrassing about her appearance that no one else had bothered to tell her about in the two hours she'd already been at work.

"I can't get used to it," Steve said. He removed his glasses, rubbed them on his polo shirt and slipped them back on. "One day you're a glamour girl, the next you're back to being Harriet again. Hard to keep track."

She experienced the oddest sensation, as though her body had suddenly dropped a few hundred feet and her stomach was plummeting to catch up. She glanced down at her dark green tartan skirt and the beige wool sweater Aunt Lavinia had brought her back from Edinburgh after attending a recreation of the battle of Culloden.

"I always look like this for work."

"I know. I guess I thought you'd keep the fancy hair and…I don't know. The new image."

"No." She tried for a bright smile. "This is me. Old weird Harriet."

Steve pushed up his glasses, his forehead creasing. "Hey, I didn't mean… I think you look good…" He flushed and fiddled with a pen on his desk. "I'm making a total mess of this. Look. I want to apologize for the way I acted last night."

"You do?"

"Yes. The thing is, I've been thinking about you a lot. Do you want to play squash tonight? Grab some dinner after?"

"Tonight? Have dinner with you?"

Amusement twinkled in his clear gray eyes. "I know you eat."

"Of course." She shuffled her feet, wondering if there was some new hidden camera show she didn't know about, entitled "Make a Fool of the Dorky Girl." "I already have a date tonight."

"Oh." Steve appeared truly disappointed.

She didn't want him to get the idea that she wasn't interested in him, when she'd worshiped him from afar for years, and, even if he was clueless about her feelings, he'd apologized. So she added eagerly, "But I'm free tomorrow night."

The amusement was back in his eyes, remarkably intelligent eyes for a man with a reputation as a dimwit. Maybe it was the glasses that made him look intellectual.

Why hadn't she bitten her tongue in two rather than act so eager?

But he didn't laugh. "Tomorrow works for me. Do you want to go for a hike first and really work up an appetite?"

Her forehead wrinkled. "But we'll be all dirty. I know, why don't I bring along a picnic instead of going to a restaurant?"

"Sure, great." He beamed at her, then his face clouded. "You're not thinking of carrying a picnic basket are you?"

She giggled. "For a hike? Of course not."

He sighed with obvious relief. "A girl I knew once packed a picnic for what I thought was a hike and it was in a huge—" he sketched a large rectangular shape with his hands "—basket with prissy straw handles. There was a red-and-white checked table-cloth inside and wineglasses. I kid you not."

Well, if he was looking for wineglasses and ging-ham he ought to take Aunt Elspeth out for the day. "I was thinking tuna fish sandwiches and lemonade. In a backpack."

He sighed blissfully. "Harriet, you are my kind of woman."

Her heart skipped a beat, even though she knew he was joking. And yet, the crazy thing was, she *was* his kind of woman. They both loved sports and the news-paper business and they understood each other. Well, considering Steve's idea for the story that would have embarrassed her in print, he didn't know much about her, but she felt she knew him well.

He wasn't a man who wore his heart on his sleeve, so only someone who really listened to him and knew about lost dreams could understand that he'd always have a small regret about not becoming a professional athlete. She decided to put the other matter aside. She had a week or so to work on him before the second article—the one about her—came out.

"Great." She beamed at him. She couldn't believe the kind of luck she was having lately. Two dates with two different men over the weekend, and no call for the turkey baster.

He tapped his fingers on his desktop then said, "I know it's none of my business, but is it Rock you're seeing tonight?"

"Yes." Probably, she should have been a bit more coy and acted as she imagined any other Braves' cheerleader would act when asked the same question. Of course, that would involve hair-flicking and eye-batting, neither of which she excelled at.

"You won't be the first woman we've ever gone to battle over," he said grumpily.

Fight over her? She had to bite her lip to stop from laughing with delight. If, in this brief moment in time, she was to be fought over by two of the hunkiest hunks in Washington state, she was going to enjoy every blessed second of it.

Besides, it was obviously time to put away her teenage notions of herself. She wasn't a nerd anymore. But whether it was Caro's advice about attitude or simply her own self-confidence now that she was a Braveheart, she felt attractive and interesting. And if two men were smart enough to see that there was more to her than tartan, then maybe she could even get in on the game. "Who usually wins?" she asked.

He chuckled and leaned back in his chair. "Depends who wants to badly enough, I guess." His expression was warm when he glanced at her and without thinking she flipped her hair over her shoulder, watching him watch the gesture.

Then it hit her. She'd just flicked her hair. She was flirting, that's what she was doing. Enjoying every second of it, too.

A warmth suffused her body, and suddenly she remembered the day Steve had given her that hickey. She recalled the feeling of his lips against her skin, the way he'd smelled when he got close, so clean and all-male. Then she remembered that wonderful walk on the riverbank when he'd kissed her. She licked her lips, soft and dewy from the cream she religiously applied each night.

His eyes followed the movement of her tongue over her lips and suddenly his office felt small and warm, as though someone had cranked up the thermostat. Inside the wool sweater, her skin felt prickly, and so very aware of the man in front of her.

Silence lengthened and she had a strong intuition he was thinking about their one shared kiss, as well, and the fact that he'd promised her more kisses on their second date. He cleared his throat. "So, where's he taking you tonight?"

"Dinner." The word came out soft and husky.

Steve rolled his eyes. "Typical. No imagination."

She was glad, for poor Rock's sake, that she hadn't mentioned the pizza versus steak house debate.

"Oh, yes," she said, continuing to think about this supposed contest the two men were waging over her, and deciding to enjoy this extraordinary situation. "There are extra points for imagination."

He laughed. "So now you're doing the scoring?"

"Isn't it usually the woman who determines the

winner of these contests?'' She could not believe she was coming up with this stuff. She was flirting with a very attractive man and oh, Lord, but she was enjoying it.

He rose and came around the desk toward her. As much as she liked this teasing side of her that was emerging, she wasn't at all sure what was coming next. ''The woman always determines the score,'' he said softly.

He'd reached her now, and his hands settled on her shoulders, warm and confident. She wanted to close her eyes and sway into him. But, in the first place, she didn't think work was the place for this. And in the second, it wasn't fair. She narrowed her gaze. ''Are you trying to steal a few points during Rock's inning?''

He threw back his head and laughed. ''All's fair.''

''We are on *Standard* time, you know.''

His hands left her shoulders, and she wanted them back. Her skin was still warm where he'd touched her. ''Right. Here are the photos from the tryouts. I thought we'd use these ones.''

HOURS WENT BY and still Harriet couldn't stop the thrill that crept up her spine every time she thought of that first article with her name on it. She worked late and tried not to feel bad about letting Steve down for tonight. She'd bake some cookies in the morning to go with their picnic, she decided.

She barely had time to rush home and comb her hair and brush her teeth before Rock arrived, promptly at seven.

The aunts were hovering like two darling, fluttery

white butterflies. Harriet was all ready to step out the door when her date rang the bell. She glared at her aunts firmly. "No funny business. You can make one remark each."

"Come in," she said to Rock, who looked muscular and commanding even in jeans and a sweatshirt.

He stepped inside and she introduced Lavinia and Elspeth. As they each shook his hand she thought they looked like delicate china teacups next to a lump of granite. For the first time it occurred to her how much Rock's name suited him. He was huge and hard and his muscles certainly seemed rock-hard. He was also unlike every man she'd ever gone out with, and she could tell from her aunts' expressions that they weren't quite sure about him. Rock didn't come from Pasqualie, so they didn't know his family or his history.

She didn't need a quiz about his likes and dislikes at school to give away the secret that Rock was no genius.

She thought again about Steve and the gleam in his eyes. Maybe he didn't quote Shakespeare or recite the periodic tables for light conversation, but she had to wonder if he was really as thick as his reputation suggested.

However, she wasn't going out with Steve tonight, she was going out with Rock, and her aunts were not going to spoil her date. She glared at them one at a time, hoping they'd be good.

How much trouble could they make with one line? Aunt Lavinia wouldn't have time to grill him on his knowledge of civil war battlefields and Elspeth couldn't express her gratitude to a man for taking Harriet out on a date, as she so often did.

But after twenty-three years of experience, Harriet still underestimated them.

"Thank you so much for inviting Harriet out today," Elspeth said with a gracious softness, as though her niece were a shut-in going on a charity outing.

Harriet tried not to cringe. That was Elspeth's one line down. One to go.

"Come to tea next Sunday," said Aunt Lavinia, in her clear, crisp tone. "Three o'clock."

Even as she glared at her other aunt for that unbelievably underhanded use of her one line, Harriet started to protest, "I'm sure Rock has—"

He flashed his chick-eating grin. "Tea, huh? Sounds great." He'd made a common mistake. He'd fallen for their charming-eccentric-elderly female line. He couldn't imagine how wrong he was.

Afternoon tea on Sunday with the aunts was as traditional as a church service and more formal than teatime at Buckingham Palace. An invitation was like military inspection and woe betide the young man whose boots weren't polished to perfection, or whose knowledge of Petrarch's sonnets was rusty.

Rock seemed almost not to recognize her at first, then, after the front door shut behind them, looked her up and down with his protuberant blue eyes and winked.

"I like that whole schoolgirl thing you've got going. It's a turn-on."

She smiled weakly. *Schoolgirl thing?* This was her normal wardrobe, but she didn't know how to tell him that, so she smiled politely and said nothing.

Since Steve had asked her out, and explained about the rather flattering rivalry, she hadn't liked to ask him for a lot of football trivia to help the conversation along on her date with Rock, so she planned to wing it. She'd seen a lot of the games, and figured she could keep asking Rock about himself. Men seemed to like that.

"Is the Texan Grill okay?" Rock drawled. "They have a thirty-six-ounce steak I like, and the place kind of reminds me of home."

"Absolutely," Harriet replied. She'd been there before. The decor was Texas cowboy, the portions huge and the staff mostly made up of students from Pasqualie University.

Harriet needn't have worried about conversation lagging. She learned that he missed Texas. "Does it ever stop raining up here?" he complained.

"It's not raining tonight," she reminded him, although the sky had been so thick with clouds earlier that she'd tucked a folding umbrella into her bag.

"It's going to."

He didn't only miss the weather in Texas, it turned out Rock missed his family and he hoped to be traded to his home team.

They talked about the Pasqualie Braves and its chances this year and Rock's plans for the future and she decided she'd made assumptions about him, too, based purely on external cues. In fact, Rock was a nice guy as well as a studly quarterback. All wrong for her, but a nice guy all the same.

She glanced at her watch a couple of times thinking she needed to get an early night in if she wanted to bake cookies and pack a lunch before Steve came for her at nine. When she realized she was being rude enough to dream about one man while out with another, she forced her attention back to the man who treated dessert like dim sum. "I love their pecan pie," he said to her over the dessert menu. "And I better have a little mud pie. And if there's strawberry ice cream, I'll have some of that. And maybe some chocolate ice cream, too. How about you?"

"I'm pretty full, but the cheesecake looks good."

"Why don't you have some and we'll share?" He grinned at her and she couldn't help but laugh.

"Um, Rock, about Sunday tea—"

"I can't wait."

"But my aunts are—"

"Hey, I'm great with little old ladies. We'll have fun."

She realized she couldn't stop this man when he was running with the ball any more than a rookie linebacker could.

11

STEVE HAD HIT the jackpot. A trip back to Pasqualie High had unearthed a stash of pure gold. He rubbed his hands with delight trying to decide which of the ''before'' photos to use in his feature spread on Harriet.

He couldn't believe how far the newest Braveheart had come from the girl in these photos. It was difficult to even recognize the Harriet he knew, with her clear skin, sexy, athletic body and inner confidence, from the dorky gal in his photos.

Even though he'd had none but the most minor role in her transformation, he was as proud of her as he would be if he'd coached her to victory. She was a beautiful woman who didn't have to emphasize her looks. She was an inspiration for the girls of Pasqualie, and he wanted them all to see that.

He gazed at the array of photos in front of him, thinking maybe his Cinderella headlines were all wrong. What he had here was the duckling turning into a swan. He chuckled softly. And she'd been a particularly homely duck.

He was partial to the picture where she was grinning at the camera, proudly holding up a trophy she won during the school chess tournament. Her braces reflected the flash and you could see she had part of her lunch stuck in the silver metal.

But there was also the photo of the girls' field hockey finals. There was Harriet, red in the face, hair sticking damply to her face, her too tight uniform lovingly outlining every roll of puppy fat.

He chuckled, deciding to use both, and to keep the backups in case he had extra space. This was going to be one of the best features he'd ever done and was about to blow the *Star*'s sports section out of the water in the upcoming journalism awards.

He loved coming from behind to win, whether in a battle for newspaper awards or in a contest of athletic skill.

And that's what Harriet had done. He picked up the "after" photos: the pictures Eric, the *Standard*'s best staff photographer, had taken at the cheerleaders' training practice. This Harriet was a different woman. Sexy, voluptuous and toned. What dorky and unappreciated teen wouldn't be inspired by seeing how Harriet, the biggest nerd in high school, had fooled everyone and turned out to be a sexy, gorgeous cheerleader.

Ever since their hike last Saturday, he'd been more determined than ever to show the world what they'd overlooked. She was funny, open, sweet and made some of the best oatmeal chocolate-chip cookies it had ever been his pleasure to wolf down.

He hadn't had to wait for her on the trail, not that he would have minded, but her strong legs ate up the ground. He would have happily ended the day in a restaurant, but sitting in the dirt, sweaty and enjoying the outdoors had been more fun for him, and he suspected for her, also.

They were already planning their next wilderness outing, and he couldn't wait. With Harriet so busy with practices, and showing up yawning at work, he was taking things easy. As much as he wanted to move in aggressively to steal Harriet from under Rock's nose, he also realized his heart wasn't in the game this time. He wanted Harriet to choose him— the four-eyed, dented-skull, failed pro athlete over the twenty-twenty-visioned, lead-headed, successful pro football player.

Steve wanted it as much as he'd ever wanted anything.

He wondered how Harriet would feel when she discovered that he'd gone ahead and made her the subject of an entire two-page spread? After her squeamishness when he'd first broached the subject, he'd decided to keep the article a surprise. She was embarrassed about being in the limelight, he could tell. But these pictures would show her what little resemblance existed between the swan she was now and the gangly duckling in the "before" pictures. All she needed was the encouragement he could provide and she'd see herself as the exciting, successful woman he saw.

Grinning to himself, Steve imagined her excitement. The quiet little overlooked girl from high school was getting her moment in the sun.

The layout was a secret for now. She was still working on the second of her own first-person stories, which he'd edit and run as a sidebar.

He didn't want this sounding like something that

should be on the Feature page, though. He glanced at the field hockey photo. He'd get a quote from the coach, Margaret Gaynor, about what a great athlete the young Harriet had been.

Perfect.

But a phone call to the school yielded the unwelcome information that Harriet's coach wasn't in Pasqualie anymore. No, the school secretary said, she had no idea where the woman had moved to.

It was just his bad luck that while the coach had moved on, the school secretary hadn't. He tried to charm her on the phone and didn't get far. Usually he was good at sweet-talking women, but he had a feeling Mrs. Channing still remembered that unfortunate incident during senior year, involving Steve, a water hose and the principal's car.

The funny thing was he and Harriet were in the same school for two years. She'd have been a sophomore the year he was a senior. He didn't remember her at all, but then it was a pretty big school.

"Is there a phys ed teacher I could speak to who would have known the coach?"

"No. They keep changing," the secretary said, grumbling.

"There must be someone who knows how to reach her?" Steve didn't know why, but all of a sudden it seemed desperately important to get someone from her high school days to admit publicly that Harriet had been a hell of an athlete.

Maybe he was taking this whole thing too far, but he wanted it on the record that she could have been as terrific a cheerleader in high school as any of those bouncy blondes he remembered.

"Well, I seem to recall that the field hockey coach was pretty good friends with one of our retired teachers who still lives in Pasqualie," Mrs. Channing said.

"Who?" Steve grabbed a pen and paper. This was more like it. Maybe Mrs. Channing didn't remember the waterlogged car incident after all.

"Lavinia MacPherson."

Steve gulped and felt himself pale. "Miss MacPherson? The history teacher?" His voice bounced like that of a nervous adolescent. Just the thought of Miss MacPherson was enough to make a grown man regress to sweaty palms and an unstable vocal register.

"That's right. Would you like her phone number?" At that moment he knew Mrs. Channing hadn't forgotten him at all and his punishment for flooding the principal's car wasn't over yet.

"No, thank you. I have it," he said, with an assumption of calm. "I don't suppose anyone else might—"

"Not a chance."

Steve put the phone down slowly. He'd known, of course, in some vague part of his brain, that one of Harriet MacPherson's two maiden aunts might well be the woman who'd terrorized her history students for several decades. Of course, you had to respect Miss MacPherson. He doubted there was a single graduate from her years at Pasqualie High who couldn't recite the Gettysburg Address flawlessly and who at least understood the rudiments of the Civil War.

He found himself muttering, "Four score and seven

years ago, I attended Pasqualie High,'' as he dug out Harriet's phone number.

When he was connected with Miss MacPherson he took a deep breath and prayed his voice would sound manly. ''Miss MacPherson, this is Steve Ackerman at the *Standard*. I'm not sure if you remember me—''

''Of course I do, Steven,'' she interrupted, sounding as commanding and formidable as ever. ''How nice to hear from you.''

''Thank you. I'm a sports reporter at the paper.''

''Yes, I know. I see you still hide your light under a bushel.'' He could have sworn he heard a note of humor in her voice. He sure didn't remember that from high school.

Maybe being miles away, at the other end of a phone line, made him bold, for he answered, ''And you're still pretending to be a crotchety old spinster?''

There was a silence and he wanted to bang himself silly with the phone receiver. He'd killed his one chance at getting ahold of Harriet's former coach, not to mention ever being allowed to darken Harriet's door again. Surprisingly, the next sound he heard wasn't the phone slamming down, but a long chesty chuckle.

''I've read some of your stories. Your prose is clean and elegant. I'm disappointed to see you waste your talent on the sports page.''

She'd read his stuff? The most frightening woman in Pasqualie had read his articles? He gulped with fear at the notion and contemplated the possibility he was about to experience his first case of writer's block. ''I like sports,'' he said at last, feeling as though his literary efforts were perfect for lining a bird cage.

"Obviously. And what is the purpose of your call?"

Oh, right. "I'm working with your niece, Harriet…" What was the matter with him? He was acting as though she had twelve nieces living with her and he had to help her distinguish them. He had to get a grip.

"Yes, I know."

"Well, as part of the feature we're writing, I'd like to interview her former field hockey coach for some quotes on what a fantastic athlete Harriet was in high school."

"Really?" Her voice lilted with surprise. "Does Harriet know you're hoping to interview Margaret?"

"No. That part's kind of a surprise. I'm planning a two-page spread on Harriet's amazing success in becoming a Braves' cheerleader."

"I see."

There was another pause. Unable to see Miss MacPherson's face, he had no idea what her pause meant.

"May I have Mrs. Gaynor's phone number?"

"Mmm? Oh, yes, of course." A moment later she was reading out the number.

"Thank you," he said, delighted to have got through the ordeal so easily. But, just as in high school history classes, Miss MacPherson didn't let him off the hook that easily.

"You've been a good friend to Harriet these last few weeks, and I'd be delighted to see you again. Come for afternoon tea. Sunday after next. Three o'clock."

She might have retired, Steve thought bitterly, but

she hadn't lost her domineering ways. There was no "Would you like to come?" no "Is it convenient?" Not so much as an implied question mark. It was more like a command performance.

Afternoon tea with Miss MacPherson was a treat he'd look forward to the way he'd look forward to a lobotomy. Without anesthetic. Come to think of it, the way the woman teased and forced a person's brain out of them was probably quite similar to the frightening procedure.

"I can't wait," he said, feeling as if he already had a whole scone lodged in his windpipe. He hoped Harriet would help him get through the tea. Or better still, help him get out of it.

He hung up, then had to roll his shoulders a few times and indulge in a little imaginary sparring before he was ready to pick up the phone and talk to another retired member of the Pasqualie High faculty.

He got through right away to Mrs. Gaynor, the woman who'd coached Harriet's field hockey team. "Oh, yes," she said cheerfully. "I remember Harriet. Excellent speed and great playmaking ability."

"Did you know she wanted to be a cheerleader?" he said.

The ex-coach snorted. "This is off the record, but Harriet was too good an athlete to waste her talents leading cheers for boys." The way she said the word *boys* made him feel like a small, unwashed varmint, as though he and the rest of his sex were unworthy.

His high school memories were getting fonder by the minute.

However, he wasn't going to get the quote he wanted by arguing with his source, so he merely said,

"But, according to Harriet, she tried out for the cheerleading squad and was never chosen."

"She also led the girls' field hockey team through their greatest season. We almost made the state playoffs." She sighed noisily. "There aren't many young women with Harriet's focus and abilities."

When Steve hung up, he had a couple of good quotes about Harriet's dedication and athleticism. It was a great start.

He also had been reminded of a fact he'd forgotten. The cheerleading competition at Pasqualie High had been run by the students. Now, wouldn't it be great to interview some of the women who'd been instrumental in keeping Harriet off the team? He'd love to get them eating crow in print.

12

HARRIET BLOTTED HER FACE with a cold, wet towel in what had become her sanctuary—the ladies' room.

Since she'd suddenly become a gutsy go-girl type, she seemed to be spending an awful lot of time in here.

She sank back against the white tile walls, swallowing another surge of nausea, and glanced at her watch. She might as well just hang the darn thing from her bangs, all she did was glance at it every five seconds and calculate how much longer she had until her very first game as a Pasqualie Braves' cheerleader. Six hours, twenty-eight minutes and…nine seconds.

She'd never been so nervous. She'd been too keyed up to eat breakfast or lunch, which she imagined was the only reason she hadn't tossed her cookies.

She took a good hard look in the mirror. Who was she kidding? She was Harriet. Old weird Harriet. The girl who kicked butt at field hockey and could hit a baseball farther than most men.

But she wasn't a cute little fluffball of a cheerleader, for goodness' sake. She felt like a freak, an Amazonian ape-woman next to the Miss Almost Georgia Peach and Cecilia Briscoe, the nineteen-year-old dental hygienist with the sparkling teeth and cavity-free personality.

Harriet was overcome with dread. What if she stumbled? What if she fell?

This wasn't field hockey where you could fall face-first into the mud, get up, run harder and play with more conviction and still score a goal.

This was cheerleading. Falling face-first into the mud was not an option.

What if she forgot the routines?

She felt like slapping herself. She wouldn't forget the routines. She'd practiced and practiced until she could do them in her sleep.

She pulled the first one up in her mind and stared at herself in the mirror as her eyes went from blank to desperate. What was the first routine?

"Don't panic," she said to herself, swallowing nausea yet again.

If she assumed her first pose, imagined herself in her uniform, she'd be fine. She blew out a breath and moved to the center of the bathroom floor. She struck her pose, and pasted a bright smile on her white, terrified face.

The music. She needed music. She started humming their first number, snapping her fingers to the rhythm. Good. This was good. If she remembered the music, the moves couldn't be far behind.

Her feet remembered before her mind. Run forward, smile at the crowd, bend at the waist, back up, turn and immediately into a layover. At first her muscles felt stiff and achy, almost as though she were coming down with the flu, but as she felt her confidence grow, she relaxed.

The crowd was roaring in her head. Back flip to handstand. And hold it...

She was so absorbed in her routine she didn't notice the door open. There she was, upside down, with her skirt flipped over, her Jockeys For Her on display for the entire newsroom.

She heard the voices first and glanced up through her stiff arms to watch Cherise and Tess walk into the bathroom together. They were so surprised they stood there, holding the door wide open. Behind them, the others in the newsroom turned to see what Cherise's scream was all about even as the interruption startled Harriet so much she was knocked off balance and tumbled in a heap of tartan skirt, red hair and classic-cut cotton panties. In pink.

For a moment there was stunned silence. Tess pulled the door shut and the three women stared at each other.

Cherise spoke first.

"Go team!" she said, raising her fist in a rah-rah gesture.

Twenty minutes later, fed up with herself and her own humiliation, Harriet sucked it up as best she could, pulled her shoulders back and walked out of the bathroom.

It was one of the hardest things she'd ever done.

She eased open the door and slipped out into the newsroom. It had never seemed so huge, or so full of people.

She waited, already blushing fiercely for the teasing.

Nothing.

Everybody was busy on the phone, tapping away at a computer or away from their desks.

In fact, it was suspiciously quiet. She glanced left and right as she made her way to her desk, but it was as though no one had seen her practically mooning everyone, as though Cherise hadn't spread the embarrassing story.

But Harriet wasn't falling for the deceptive calm. There'd be something on her desk.

Sure enough there was something on her desk.

A teddy bear. A brown furry teddy bear wearing a child-size Braves' T-shirt and holding a note. The note read, "Two, Four, Six, Eight, who do we appreciate? Harri-ate! Harri-ate! Rah, Rah, Rah!"

Even if she hadn't recognized Steve's handwriting, she'd have known the bear was from him. It had a round red mark on its neck.

Her teddy bear was sporting a hickey.

Her vision misted as she realized how much Steve's support meant to her.

She vowed at that moment, as she picked up the teddy bear and hugged it to her, that she wouldn't let down her team, she wouldn't let down Steve Ackerman, who had helped her realize her dream. And she wouldn't let herself down.

Her nerve-clenched muscles started to uncramp and her stomach settled.

Throughout the rest of the day she glanced at her bear whenever she felt nervous, and it helped.

Tess came by as she was getting ready to leave. "I wanted to wish you good luck. Mike and I will be at the game tonight. We can't wait."

"Thanks," Harriet said breathlessly. "Sorry about the bathroom earlier."

Tess twinkled at her. "That's okay. You have great legs."

"I can't believe no one said anything."

Tess looked as though she couldn't decide about something then glanced at the bear and back at Harriet.

"It was Steve," she said.

"Steve?"

"Uh-huh. He said if anybody said one single word to embarrass you, he'd personally kick their ass."

Harriet's jaw dropped. "Steve did that?"

"Yes. And he was holding a lethal teddy bear at the time so everyone believed him."

Harriet hugged the bear to her once more. "I can't believe he did that."

Tess shook her head. "He's got a major crush on you, Harriet. Get with the program."

"Oh, he does not. He's just being nice to me because I'm so hopeless."

"Listen," Tess said, leaning forward so she was right in Harriet's face. "You get out there and show them all what you've got or I'm going to kick *your* ass. You got that?"

"You are?" Harriet couldn't help grinning. She must have had three or four inches of height and forty pounds on Tess and all of it was muscle.

"Well..." Tess hesitated, scanning Harriet from top to toe. "I'll make Mike do it."

STEVE COULDN'T SIT still. He couldn't hang around and shoot the breeze in the press box with the other sports reporters and he couldn't go out and hang with the crowds at the stadium as he sometimes did.

He was too nervous. This was Harriet's first game and he wanted her to succeed so badly it hurt.

One part of him knew she was ready for this and he'd helped her make her dream come true at last.

The other part of him was worried sick she'd fall or trip the rest of the team up or do something that would humiliate her so much she'd never take a chance again.

So he paced.

Imagined the worst.

Dreamed of the best.

Paced some more.

He'd tried to see her before she left the office, to wish her well in person, but she'd gone early. He hoped she was all right. He wished his press pass would let him into the women's dressing room. Well, he'd wished that many times, but this was the first time he'd wanted to go back there to help someone out. He remembered how he'd inadvertently helped her when she'd been so scared at the cheerleader trials. What if she needed him?

He paced some more. At least she had the bear. She knew he was thinking of her.

It seemed about three ice ages had come and gone before the announcer started his patter. Steve scanned the stands. Had they ever been as packed with fans as tonight? Had the word gone out that there was a new cheerleader or what?

"And now," the announcer boomed, "the ladies who put the Heart in our Braves, ple-ee-ease welcome your Bravehearts!"

Steve must have watched the cheerleaders hit the field a hundred times, but never before had the spectacle made his palms sweat or his mouth turn dry. Harriet was out there somewhere. Was she as nervous as he?

It didn't take him half a minute to pick her out as the blue, sparkly lithe bodies bounced, skipped and danced their way onto the field all waving, shaking their blue-and-silver pom-poms, all smiling.

Harriet would have drawn his gaze even if he wasn't looking for her, he was certain. Her smile, her bright hair, the sparkle of her personality were unmistakable.

He paced some more as the uniformed football players jogged out to applause. Their opponents also jogged out to lesser applause.

And for the first time since he'd been involved in sports, Steve couldn't care less about the game. All his attention and focus were on the cheerleaders. On one cheerleader in particular.

He barely kept track of the plays, and realized with a pang of horror that he'd have to catch the late-night sports show on TV before he could file his own story.

But Harriet was out there and he was much too busy watching her smile and wave and cheer with the other gals to have an eye to spare for the team they were cheering on.

For the first two minutes he sat there white-knuckled, his stomach in knots. Then, miraculously, he realized it was going to be okay.

Once more, he'd underestimated Harriet, and, he suspected, she'd underestimated herself. She was incredible. As full of life as athleticism, her muscular body in utter harmony with the music, the other cheerleaders, but most important, with the crowd.

If ever there was a woman who was living her bliss, it was Harriet at this moment.

In a small way he was part of her success and so he clapped and hollered so loud when the cheerleaders performed that the other cynics in the press box eyed him askance.

Of course, the Braves won. It seemed to Steve that Rock was playing the best game of his life, no doubt to impress Harriet. After the game, he sprinted down the stands to hang around and congratulate her, but Rock had the home field advantage. In the time it took Steve to flash his press pass and walk onto the field, the uniformed giant had ambled over to the cheerleaders, beelined for Harriet and grabbed her for a kiss.

Steve slowed, though he was close enough to hear Harriet's squeak of surprise. She laughed and he heard her congratulating Rock on a great game.

Despite one concussion too many, Steve could figure out that he wouldn't appear to have an advantage over Rock on today of all days. When he congratulated Harriet, he intended for them to be alone.

HARRIET FELT HER PULSE start to calm for the first time since the game began. She was more elated than she'd been at the tryouts. This really was her dream come true, cheerleading in front of a stadium full of fans. She'd never had so much fun in her life.

Her teammates had helped her through a couple of tiny glitches, and congratulated her for doing such a great job her first time. And here was Rock, the big man himself, giving her a sweaty kiss and a hug.

But where was Steve? He'd been there all the way and she wanted to at least thank him. Over Rock's shoulder she thought she saw him walking away. She felt an impulse to run after the man, but the idea of racing across the field in her flashy blue outfit to accost a man who might turn out to be a stranger was more than she could contemplate.

Besides, if it *was* Steve, why hadn't he come over to talk to her?

"I'm sorry?" she asked Rock, realizing he'd said something to her and she hadn't taken in a word.

"Earth to Harriet. What time do I have to be there on Sunday?"

The guy who'd looked like Steve had been swallowed by the crowds now, and her stomach felt hollow with disappointment. "Rock, it's really nice of you to agree to come to tea, but please don't think you have to. I'll tell my aunts you have to practice."

He smiled down at her, making her feel very much the little woman. "We don't practice Sunday, Harriet."

She smiled at him, keeping her lips closed so he wouldn't notice that her teeth were clamped together, and gave herself a moment to let the irritation pass before she spoke. "I know, Rock. I'm suggesting a small white lie."

He looked at her in concern. "You can't lie to a pair of little old ladies. It isn't nice."

Much as she appreciated the sentiment, calling her aunts "little old ladies" was like suggesting a diamond was coal that had passed its prime.

Her argument fell on deaf ears until she gave up.

Rock wanted to come. She was puzzled until he explained why. "Honey, coach likes us to put in our hours of community service. If I can spend a couple of hours bringing joy to a pair of elderly women, then I've done my bit. And I can claim the hours and get out of that charity pitch-and-putt tourney with the Boy Scouts." He shuddered.

She was momentarily diverted from his total misunderstanding of her aunts. "Don't you like Boy Scouts?"

"Oh, yeah. Don't get me wrong. I like them fine. But they all try to prove something. Like they're almost as big and tough as me. It's kind of like that big guy that gets all the little guys running after him."

"You mean Gulliver and the Lilliputians?"

"No. I was thinking of Shaq O'Neal."

Harriet stifled her smile. "I'm not sure the Scouts wouldn't be easier on you. My aunts are lovely, but they…"

"Don't you worry. I even got them presents. We'll do fine."

She'd done her best to keep him away and failed. He really wanted to come to tea.

It wasn't that she didn't like Rock. She did. He was a nice man and he'd flattered her senseless with his attention. But he wasn't the man she wanted in her life.

As far as she was concerned, the "game" Rock and Steve had supposedly been playing was over. But—and it was no surprise to Harriet—now that the prize had been won, the victor seemed to have lost interest in claiming her.

13

THE DOORBELL RANG and Harriet was able to put one worry away. At least Rock was prompt. It was two minutes past three according to the clock in the hall, which kept perfect time. Harriet always suspected it knew it would be punished if it became sloppy and unpunctual so it never dared disobey.

"He's here," she called with what she hoped was casual ease even though her stomach was quaking.

She waited for her aunts to breeze into the hallway and then she opened the door to Rock.

He walked in and said hi to Harriet.

She'd warned him to dress nicely, and he was in clean khakis and a golf shirt.

"How ya doing, ladies?" he said to the aunts in a loud voice.

Aunt Lavinia extended her hand, but quickly pulled it back and the three women stared at Rock's huge ham hands. They held bright blue Nerf footballs dotted with sparkly stars. "These are honorary Braves' footballs."

He held them up as though they were dumbbells and began squishing them rhythmically. "Great for squeezing," he bellowed in a voice so loud all three women winced. "Helps prevent arthritis."

He must think all old people are deaf, Harriet

thought in horror as the afternoon began to look like one giant shouting match.

"He's the sort of person who shouts at foreigners, no doubt," Aunt Lavinia said quietly behind Harriet, who was very much afraid she was right.

He presented each of the aunts with her blue Nerf football, beaming when they politely thanked him. "No, no. You try it." And he stood there expectantly until Aunt Elspeth, who hated to hurt anyone's feelings, obligingly gave the blue foam a few quick squeezes.

"That's great!" said Rock, and he grabbed her upper arm and pumped as though he were a human blood pressure cuff. "Good muscle tone," he said heartily, and winked.

He turned to Lavinia and Harriet hastily stepped between them before her aunt's sarcastic tongue carved him into blue-and-silver ribbons.

"Shall we go in for tea?" she trilled like a society hostess on fast forward, pushing Rock through the dark oak double doors with their leaded glass panes into the elegant living room.

Well, the aunts called it the living room. It was a parlor, really. With dainty velvet settees, small occasional chairs and round footstools—each lovingly embroidered by Aunt Elspeth—the room reminded Harriet of something from Victorian England. The settee and chairbacks were protected by starched linen antimacassars, also embroidered by her industrious aunt.

Rock took a step into the room and Elspeth's collection of Royal Doulton ladies wobbled, their full-skirted china gowns dancing and their pretty porcelain heads seeming to shake in disbelief. Lavinia called them sentimental knickknacks, but since Elspeth did the dusting, she was allowed to keep them. Harriet hoped the statuettes survived the afternoon.

This was Elspeth's room, as was the kitchen, in the same way the library with its vast collection of first editions was Lavinia's.

Just as Harriet had the whole basement for her assorted sports equipment, activities and junk.

Rock gulped and some of his confidence seemed to drain as he skirted an antique cabinet crammed with crystal treasures, setting the whole thing tinkling. Harriet often felt large and gangly in this dainty room, but she had nothing on Rock.

Still, he did his best, managing to right himself with the quick agility of an athlete when a footstool tripped him up, before gratefully sinking into the tapestry wing chair that was the largest seat in the room.

By the time he sat, a lot of his cocky sureness had deserted him, she noted with no surprise. The room had that effect on pretty much everyone under seventy.

It was like being in an ancient library or a sacred church. You felt as if you should whisper and keep your knees pressed together.

Then the two aunts, dressed in their Sunday church dresses of starched linen in muted florals, sank daintily to their accustomed seats. Harriet, wishing she were in another state, sat in her usual spot, the wing chair across from the one Rock occupied.

''Would you care for a sherry?'' Lavinia asked Rock.

''Sherry, well now, I—'' His eyes searched the

room frantically and she imagined he was looking for a girl named Sherri. She stifled a nervous giggle.

Poor Rock. This was dreadful and her aunt Lavinia was looking far too much like the spider who'd caught the unsuspecting fly in her web. Harriet did her best to help him out. "We have both dry and sweet sherry. My aunts usually have a glass before tea."

"Right. Sherry. Yeah, sure."

He was obviously beyond the dry or sweet distinction, so she took pity on him and poured him a glass of the dry. Lavinia also took dry and Elspeth preferred the sweet. Since Harriet hated sherry, she had nothing.

She handed the aunts their small crystal glasses first, then gave Rock his. The sherry glass almost disappeared in his meaty grip. He glanced up at her like an animal caught in a trap, then tossed back the wine as though it were a shooter down at the sports bar.

She felt a pang of compassion as she thought of all the delicacies to come. Rock was a steak house kind of guy, not an afternoon tea type. She should have worked harder to talk him out of this, she realized as she tried to imagine how he'd make out with the menu.

He'd be all right with the homemade Scottish short-bread, which Aunt Elspeth had prepared in the special mold with the thistle imprint. But he was going to have to face scones, too. With clotted cream and strawberry jam.

After a suitable interval for sherry quaffing, Elspeth disappeared to make the tea. Harriet would normally help her, but she didn't dare leave Rock alone with Lavinia.

She gave her great-aunt a glance that begged for pity, but Lavinia was too happy to have a fresh Sunday afternoon victim, one she'd never taught, to worry about Harriet's futile eye daggers.

"Are you a university man, Rock?"

"Why, yes, ma'am. I got a scholarship to Dimmit College in Texas."

"Really? It's not a school I'm familiar with. Did you win an academic scholarship?"

He chuckled as though she'd made a joke. "No, ma'am. A football scholarship."

"A football scholarship." Aunt Lavinia's opinion of athletic scholarships was well known. She thought it a poor excuse to waste valuable teaching resources on persons who cared nothing for learning and wanted only to throw a ball around a field for their life's work.

"That's right." He must be recovering his confidence since he was bellowing again.

"And did you actually attend classes at this institute of higher learning?"

"Aunt Lavinia taught history here at the high school for many years," Harriet threw in, hoping Rock would take the hint.

But, he didn't.

"I attended enough classes to graduate, sure," he shouted. "But—" he winked at Harriet "—I usually found a cute girl to help me with my homework."

"Are you a plagiarist?" Aunt Lavinia asked in a clipped tone.

"No, ma'am. My major was kinesiology. That's the science of movement."

Harriet felt helpless to protect Rock, hoping his

own thickness would deflect most of her aunt's verbal arrows. But, in fact, obviously realizing he was prey not worth hunting, Aunt Lavinia seemed to have given up.

"I'll help Elspeth with the tea," she said, rising grandly and sending Harriet a glance that clearly said she could do better for male companionship. "Excuse me."

Normally, Lavinia would never abandon a guest that way, and Harriet stared at her aunt in shock, but the older woman explained softly as she went by, "I've got to rescue the Royal Crown Derby."

Harriet had to agree it was a good idea not to serve Rock with their usual special-guest china. Poor Rock could turn bone china into bone dust faster than he could score a touchdown.

If he'd been a handkerchief kind of man, Harriet imagined Rock would pull one out of his pocket and mop his brow as her aunt left the room.

He smiled weakly at her. "She's quite a gal."

"Yes," Harriet said. "I'm really sorry about this. I tried to warn you."

"Well, I gotta say, the little Boy Scouts are looking better all the time."

"If you want to leave, I could tell them you've got a headache or something."

"A headache? What would that do to my reputation? I head-butt two-hundred-pound linebackers all the time. I can't go around saying I got a headache to a couple old gals. I'll look like a sissy."

"I'm sorry. I wasn't thinking." She had to give him marks for courage.

She heard the aunts on the way down the hall with

the tea trolley. In any case it was too late for Rock to escape. Or for her to escape this excruciating afternoon.

"Here we are," Elspeth said brightly, bringing in the antique tea trolley with the silver tea service, the tiny sandwiches of salmon and watercress, the shortbread and the scones with her homemade strawberry preserves and the clotted cream.

Next to Rock, everything seemed so miniature, from the second-best teacups to the spoons.

"Cool," said Rock. "Doll-size sandwiches."

"Please," said Elspeth, passing him a napkin and the serving plate of sandwiches.

"Thanks, ma'am," he said, and placed the tray of two dozen tea sandwiches on his lap.

Harriet tried to get his attention but it was too late. He'd already picked up an egg sandwich and shoved it into his mouth and was choosing a salmon sandwich chaser. "You shouldn't have bothered cutting them up so small. I usually eat about three triple-deckers at a go." He swallowed and thumped his stomach. "Lot of me to feed."

Elspeth managed to carry on without a hitch, and Harriet had to admire her aplomb. "How do you like your tea?" she asked him, her hand hovering over the cream jug and sugar bowl.

"Tall glass. Plenty of ice," he mumbled.

"I'll get him some iced tea," Harriet said, jumping up for an excuse to escape. At least the china was safe.

Since she had a feeling that one glass of iced tea wouldn't be enough, she brought in a whole pitcher and put it on a small tray by his elbow. After that, they mostly just watched Rock eat. He demolished the plate of sandwiches in about two minutes.

Elspeth had offered Lavinia and Harriet the scones and the shortbread, with a silent glance of apology at the lack of sandwiches. They drank their tea hot, in small delicate cups, while Rock glugged iced tea until the gallon pitcher was nearly empty.

Then he spied the scones.

His eyes lit up and he turned to Elspeth. Harriet expected him to ask what they were, but instead he said, "Did you make these?"

"Why, yes."

"For a lady who makes such teensy sandwiches, you sure make a decent-size cookie." Whereupon he helped himself to one and chomped it as though it were an oatmeal cookie.

And he kept eating the "cookies" until the plate was empty.

"Please," Elspeth said faintly. "Try my shortbread."

"I don't get much fancy stuff like this," he admitted, taking her up on her offer with alacrity.

"It's nice to see a man with a good appetite," she said as he finished off the last shortbread.

"The all-you-can-eat smorgasbord place always puts the Closed sign up when they see me coming," he boasted as he pressed the last crumbs off the plate with his finger and then licked it clean.

"Really?"

"Ha, ha. No, I'm joking. But they threaten to. I always pay double, but I still don't figure they make much money off me or the other guys on the team."

"Well, there's a lot of you to feed," said Aunt Elspeth.

"All that bulk and not a single viable brain cell," Aunt Lavinia murmured into her teacup.

"That's what I say. There's a lot of me to feed and a lot of me to love." He winked broadly at Harriet.

"It was so nice you could come," she said to him. And, feeling Aunt Lavinia ought to be punished for inflicting this tea on them all, said, "It's nice for my aunts to have a visit before their Sunday-afternoon nap."

"Right," he said, rising. "You ladies have a nice sleep and thanks for the home baking. Great stuff." He then shook their hands and Harriet walked him to the door. Never had she made the trip more thankfully.

At the door, Rock turned to her. "So. I'll see you at practice?"

"Yes, absolutely."

But he didn't leave. He shifted from foot to foot then said, "Look, Harriet. You're a real nice girl, but I was sort of going out with Linda Lou before you came along, and—"

Harriet's eyes bugged open. "You stopped seeing Linda Lou for me?"

Rock's gaze shifted away and he looked acutely embarrassed. "I guess I should have told you. I don't want you thinking—"

She was so flattered she felt like kissing him. "Oh, no. I perfectly understand. I'm all wrong for you and Linda Lou's perfect. I'm just so…" She grinned at him. "Good luck. And thanks." Then she rose on tiptoe to kiss his cheek.

Getting dumped had never felt so good.

She returned to the parlor and Aunt Lavinia said, "Well, Harriet, I hope our guest next Sunday has a better idea how to behave."

"Who's coming next Sunday?" she asked as she helped load the empty dishes back onto the tea trolley.

"A former student of mine, and a friend of yours. Steve Ackerman."

Harriet almost dropped the empty scone platter. "You invited Steve Ackerman for tea?"

"Yes."

"Oh, Aunt Lavinia, how could you? He'll think you're pushing me at him."

"Nonsense. I invited him because I've always thought he was an interesting young man."

She stared at her great-aunt in dismay. "Other seniors take up clogging or crochet. Why did you have to take up bachelor-baiting?"

14

"STEVE, you can't come to tea on Sunday." Harriet roared into his office Monday morning like a plaid steam engine, huffing and red in the face.

"You mean I'm uninvited?"

Oddly enough he felt disappointed. He'd sort of looked forward to seeing Miss MacPherson again. He'd been terrified of her in high school, well, everyone had been. But he'd respected her, too. He had a feeling she'd seen through him as no other teacher had. "What did you tell Miss MacPherson about me?"

Harriet blinked at him as though he were crazy. "No, it's not that. Of course Aunt Lavinia wants you to come. She needs a new sacrificial lamb, but I only found out about it yesterday. I swear she was keeping the invitation from me deliberately. I can't let you do it. You don't know what she's like."

Steve thought back to history classes at Pasqualie High. "Oh, yes. I know what she's like." But if Miss MacPherson hadn't entirely cowed him in his teens, she was unlikely to manage it a decade later. At least, he hoped not. Especially in front of Harriet.

"It's only tea, Harriet. I think I can get through it without making a fool of myself."

"Ha," she said darkly, and he wondered what her aunts did to men who showed up for tea.

"Hey, want to catch a movie tonight?" he asked her.

She shook her head. "I've got cheerleading practice. We're learning some new routines so it's every night this week."

Disappointment smacked him. "How about lunch?"

"I'm working through lunch hours so I can get off early for practice." He'd think she was avoiding him if he didn't see the wistful expression in her eyes and the dark circles of tiredness under them.

He rose and walked around the desk until he was close enough to touch her. "You were fantastic in your first game."

She blushed rosily. "Did you really think so?"

How could she have any doubt? "I was hoping we could get some time together this week so we could celebrate properly."

Between cheerleading practice, softball practice and the evening events he had to cover, it was a busy time of year for both of them. The only consolation was that if Harriet didn't have time for dating then Rock must not be seeing her, either.

Steve had been thinking about her all morning since he'd been working on the layout for her spread in the Sunday paper. Somehow, someway they were going to have to find some time to spend together.

"Nothing could keep me away on Sunday. At least I'll get to see you," he said.

She blushed adorably, as he'd hoped she would,

and began to fiddle with a button on her sweater. "I miss you, too," she said quietly.

"Well, one way we can spend some time together is working on the two-page weekend feature all about you," he said, deciding to spring his surprise early.

"Pardon?" she squeaked, as bowled over as he'd imagined she'd be.

"I thought you'd be too shy to boast about your accomplishments so I wrote a feature piece about you and I've got some great photos. Come here. Let me show you my surprise." He'd thought at one point that he'd let her read the feature on Sunday along with everyone else in Pasqualie, but he was too excited. He wanted to see her face when she saw the full spread all about her triumph.

"Surprise?" She looked at him with shy excitement and he wished there weren't so many people nearby or he'd kiss the breath out of her.

Instead he took her hand and led her around his desk to take a look at the layout.

A gasp escaped her when she looked at what he'd done. "No!" she cried.

He thought at first it was a gasp indicting modesty, but one glance at her face showed him the expression of someone in the middle of a horror movie. "What do you mean, no? What's the matter?"

"What's the matter?" she shrieked. "It's like a terrible nightmare." She touched the photo of herself with the baby fat and groaned. "You went to the high school and got these."

He was proud of how hard he'd worked to show the old Harriet, with the photos culminating in the glamour shot they'd taken of her posing in her new uniform. "Yep. And I interviewed your field hockey coach and a few teachers who remember you. Got some great stuff."

But she didn't seem as thrilled as he was. "What are you calling it? 'Geek To Pinup Girl'?"

"'Cinderella Keeps Her Eye On The Ball,'" he told her, not without pride. "It took me a while to come up with the perfect headline. Don't you like it?"

"Like it? It's the cruelest thing anyone's ever done to me." She turned to him, her eyes dark with hurt, and he could see she was fighting tears. "I thought we were friends."

What was wrong with her? "I hope we're more than friends. You're not that girl anymore. Can't you see that?" He pointed to the glam shot. "This is you now. Girls in high school who aren't part of the in crowd will look up to you. They'll believe in dreams again, they'll believe that if you could achieve this success after being overlooked all your life then they can, too."

She shook her head, her eyes wide and bright, her face flushed. "This isn't about me at all. It's about *you.*"

"What are you talking about?" A flash of irritation surged through him but he tried to laugh. "News flash. I never wanted to be a cheerleader."

"No. You wanted to be a quarterback, but you were kept off the field because of your concussions. Instead of being the big man on campus, the team quarterback, you got teased and called four eyes. You're using this feature about me to vent your own high school grievances."

"That is about the most stupid thing I've ever heard in my life," he all but spluttered, wondering why a ball of lead seemed to have lodged itself in his chest. "You're being ultrasensitive."

"I'll never be able to live this down. I can't believe you'd do this to me," she said, backing out of the room rapidly. Since she looked like a woman fighting tears he didn't even try to stop her.

"I'm sure when you calm down you'll see I'm right."

"You're an insensitive ass."

Ouch. That stung.

"Does this mean I'm no longer invited for Sunday tea?"

She paused and turned. He waited for another verbal assault, but she gazed at him, hurt and anger pulsing from her in waves. "Oh, you're invited for Sunday tea. It's the best punishment I can think of."

HARRIET BARELY SLEPT all week thinking about the feature that Steve was putting in the Sunday paper. She was beyond the how-could-he-do-this-to-me stage and had moved to the how-soon-can-I-move-out-of-town stage of embarrassment.

She'd considered throwing a hissy fit and marching into the managing editor's office to demand the story be stopped, but she didn't. She had a fatalistic attitude that this final blow would give her the guts to leave her aunts and shake the dust of Pasqualie off her feet.

She didn't know how to warn Lavinia and Elspeth. What could she say? For all she knew they might think it was exciting to look at old pictures of Harriet as the dorky geek she'd been in high school. Steve certainly did.

In fact, she realized, as she dragged herself out of bed Sunday and forced herself to the barre for her morning exercises, they'd be as tearfully proud of her as they'd always been. The fact of their uncritical love and devotion had her eyes misting.

But she still planned to leave town.

There must be copy editor jobs all over the place. She was certainly good at her job and it was time to accept that she had to go elsewhere for people to see her as she really was.

Maybe, when you'd always been the odd one, the strange-looking girl with the old-fashioned upbringing, you had to leave your home and go to a big anonymous city before people would accept you.

She sighed as she leaned into a stretch.

But then, who was she really?

Her gaze found the framed Bravehearts glam shot on her dresser. Was she the woman with the curled hair and heavily made-up face smiling at the camera from inside her teensy, sexy blue and spangly costume?

Her inner cheerleader shouted, *Yes!*

Harriet had to agree that surprisingly attractive woman in the glam shot was a part of her. A part no one but Harriet had known existed until recently.

Finishing her stretches, she went to the closet to pull out her clothes for the day and was confronted by acres of tweed and plaid and demure woolen sweaters for fall and winter, dainty cotton and lace sweaters for summer. There were her Laura Ashley print summer dresses and her neatly arranged flat-heeled schoolgirl shoes.

But the woman who wore those comfortable old friends was also part of Harriet. The oldest and most secure part.

And the impatient woman whose beauty regimen took less than five minutes was delighted.

She hadn't taken Caro up on her offer to go clothes shopping. Why?

Why wouldn't she seek the advice of a former model, a woman who always dressed in the height of fashion? Why wasn't she running out and choosing clothes for the woman in the glam photo?

She slumped to her bed as the truth hit her.

Harriet Adelaide MacPherson liked the person who lived inside the fusty twinsets and the Mary Janes.

She liked the comfy way her clothes felt, like a warm hug from a loved friend. And she loved spending more time living than she did in the bathroom fussing with her hair and makeup.

In fact, she liked who she was.

For all the years she'd spent looking up to the pretty girls, the popular girls, the cheerleaders, Harriet had overlooked something important.

She was just as special in her own way.

As epiphanies went, it wasn't going to make the evening news. Although, with a chuckle, she realized her "transformation" had made the sports section of the Pasqualie *Standard*. Oh, well. The joke would be on Steve Ackerman when the woman whose transformation he'd so painstakingly documented didn't change at all, but discovered how much she liked herself as she was.

Perhaps she should demand a retraction. She could almost see the story now.

The *Pasqualie Standard* made an error in its Sunday edition. Miss Harriet MacPherson was incorrectly identified as having made over herself from mousy nerd to glamorous cheerleader. In fact, Ms. MacPherson has decided to remain a mousy nerd, and will put on the glamorous cheerleader uniform only to fulfill the terms of her contract with the Pasqualie Braves.

Ms. MacPherson is still a nerd. The *Standard* apologizes for suggesting she be anything else.

And so it was with a lighter heart that she prepared to face the daily paper and whatever furor it would cause.

Today, Steve was coming for tea. He might as well witness firsthand the true Harriet. Not so old, not so weird Harriet. And if he wanted a cheerleader who was glamorous all the time, she could give him some phone numbers.

She came down the stairs in a long print skirt, white blouse and black loafers. Her hair was neatly brushed and held back by a black hair band.

"Good morning, dear," Elspeth said brightly, putting a plate of French toast in front of her, cooked to golden-brown perfection with a light dusting of icing sugar. A jug of real Vermont maple syrup and a bowl of multicolored fruit salad stood in the middle of the table. Harriet accepted her tea with thanks.

Aunt Lavinia had her nose in the paper, as always

in the morning, no matter how Elspeth nagged that it was bad manners.

A quick glance allowed Harriet to gauge her slow but steady progress through the paper. She was almost through the international news section. After that there were four pages of local news, then sports.

Harriet said nothing, merely ate her breakfast and chatted with her aunt Elspeth. Harriet was resigned to the newspaper article, but she hoped it wouldn't hurt her aunts' feelings on her behalf.

The paper rustled as Lavinia turned each page, reading each and every article and most of the ads before turning to the next. She threw out the odd comment which didn't make much sense without the context.

"Ridiculous man. What was he thinking?" she asked at one point.

A minute later she snorted softly. "Oh, yes. Blame it on the feds. Always a convenient target, aren't they?"

At this she glared at Harriet over her glasses, and, used to her aunt's idiosyncrasies, Harriet nodded, blaming the feds for she knew not what.

"This mayor and council get sillier every week."

Okay. Local news. Soon she'd get to the article about Harriet.

A page turned without comment.

Then another page. Harriet could barely eat her breakfast. It wasn't nerves exactly cramping her stomach. She simply didn't want the two women who'd raised her to be upset by the feature, or to see how much it had hurt their great-niece.

The page rustled as it turned, and Aunt Lavinia

uttered a small cry. It could be delight or distress, Harriet wasn't sure which. She glanced up, worried, but it was delight creasing her aunt's face in a broad smile.

"Why look at this, Elspeth. Two whole pages about our Harriet."

Elspeth jumped up, leaving her half-eaten French toast cooling on her plate. "Oh, let me see, let me see."

Harriet didn't bother joining it. She knew exactly what they were looking at and the less she saw of those awful pictures the better. But, if the aunts weren't upset, she decided she'd live down the stupid article as best she could while searching for a job in another town.

Living down Steve's betrayal—he who of all people should have understood how she felt—would be more difficult. Oh, well, she reasoned, he was coming to tea today. That should be ample punishment for his crimes.

15

THE DOORBELL RANG and Harriet tried to control the fluttery feeling in her stomach. It was merely annoyance about the article, she told herself, and disappointment that a man she'd liked could do such a rotten thing to her.

Well, that and the horrible feeling that history was about to repeat itself. Afternoon tea had been bad enough last week with Rock, but she didn't think she could survive a second ordeal of that magnitude such a short time later.

When she opened the door, Steve was looking nicer than she'd ever seen him. He wore dress pants, a crisp white shirt and a sports jacket. A dazzle of light caught her eye and she dropped her gaze to find he'd polished his shoes.

He sent her a charming smile that made her wonder if he'd forgotten everything she'd said to him about the feature, and she tried with all her heart to remember how mad at him she was.

"Come in," she said stiffly, trying not to notice the flowers.

Were they an apology?

Would she accept them?

But no, the flowers weren't even for her. With a "Thank you for inviting me," which sounded so sincere you'd think he'd been pining for years for the chance to have afternoon tea with a couple of batty old ladies and their spinster niece, he stepped into the house and offered Aunt Elspeth the bouquet.

"Oh, how lovely," she said, pinkening to almost the same shade as the roses. "How kind of you."

She was so delighted Harriet felt one part of her anger with Steve thaw.

One tiny part.

Then he held out a bag to Aunt Lavinia and Harriet held her breath thinking of the Nerf balls of last week.

Lavinia sent her a glance that suggested she was thinking of Nerf balls, too, but as her hand closed around the bag, the shape of a bottle became clear, and she, too, cried out with delight as she pulled out a bottle of her favorite sherry.

"How did you know?" Lavinia stared at Harriet who shook her head and they all turned to stare at Steve.

"Investigative reporting," was all he'd say. There was only one liquor store in a town where most everybody knew everybody, it couldn't have been that hard to discover what Lavinia liked to drink, but it was still thoughtful. Harriet only wished he'd been as interested in her wishes when he'd created that awful feature. She'd still refused to glance at it, and tried to forget it. The aunts had taken several calls from their various friends congratulating Harriet on her success.

She couldn't get out of town fast enough.

"Well, you turned out to be good at something then," Aunt Lavinia said in a tart tone, as if to make it clear she couldn't be buttered up so easily.

Still, Harriet had to give Steve top marks for effort.

They adjourned to the living room and, though Harriet hovered anxiously, ready to rescue breakables or to guide Steve through the obstacle course, he managed with grace and finesse to navigate the room and then sank gracefully into the chair Elspeth indicated, the one Rock had occupied the week before.

"Do you prefer a dry sherry yourself?" Lavinia asked him, waving her hand at the bottle he'd brought.

"Thank you. Yes."

Harriet took her first comfortable breath since he'd arrived, and soon the three sipped from the crystal sherry glasses while Harriet tried not to twist her hands in her lap.

There was a pause, and Steve asked Elspeth about her garden. Score another one for Steve. Harriet stood quietly to put the flowers in water, confident the subject of Elspeth's garden would keep the conversation going for at least a quarter of an hour. Well, it would go on forever, but Lavinia tended to snip gardening conversation in the bud. Harriet groaned softly at her own bad pun while she cut the ends of the flowers and arranged them in a vase.

She couldn't have been five minutes, but it turned out she'd wasted too much time. She returned to the living room with the flowers and almost dropped the vase on the floor when she heard Steve say to Elspeth, "I loved the gardens when I was in Virginia last year on vacation."

Harriet tried to make a frantic shushing movement with her hands, but only succeeded in slopping water over the edge of the Waterford vase.

She and Elspeth exchanged helpless glances.

He had to mention Virginia!

Lavinia, who'd been tapping her toe, straightened and brightened immediately.

"Were you anywhere near the Shenandoah Valley?" she asked.

Harriet shook her head, trying to send Steve a message that he should on all accounts say no. He either didn't see her or ignored her.

"Yes," he said. "I passed right through it."

Elspeth made a small sound but Harriet was silent, waiting for a repeat of the last time she had a male guest for tea.

She might as well leave town, and the sooner the better if she ever had a hope of having a serious relationship with a man.

Even moving out and getting her own place wouldn't be drastic enough. So long as tea could be bought in Pasqualie and so long as Elspeth could still see to make scones, Harriet's future as a spinster was assured. Unless she started dating an expert in Civil War history.

Ha, she thought. As if.

"It's an area I'm quite familiar with myself," said her aunt. The woman had a Ph.D. in Civil War history and if Steve didn't know it after having her for a teacher he was a bigger dolt than anyone had given him credit for.

Harriet was beyond trying to save the day. Now that the magic word *Shenandoah* had been uttered, nothing would stop Aunt Lavinia.

Nothing.

"I'll put the tea on," said Elspeth in a faint voice.

"I also visited the Fredericksburg and Chancellorsville battlefields,'' Steve announced cheerfully, blundering into disaster like General Lee on his way to Appomattox.

Aunt Lavinia's eyes began to twinkle and Harriet suddenly felt as though she had missed some crucial exchange between her guest and her aunt.

''They're quite a sight, aren't they, the battlefields?'' her aunt said in a friendlier tone.

Steve glanced at Harriet almost in apology and she realized he'd deliberately ignored her when she'd tried to help him.

''Yes. I found the trip…emotionally moving. Richmond, Petersburg, Manassas, somehow standing there brought the history to life. I haven't forgotten the lessons you taught us, and I kept reading and studying after high school. It was great to finally see the area.''

The old woman might be cantankerous, but Harriet loved her and she wasn't about to watch Steve make a fool of her by pretending to have knowledge he didn't possess. What had he done? Clicked on Civil War Battlefields on the Internet?

Faking an interest in the Civil War to butter up Aunt Lavinia was as shameless as using loser photos of her in high school to sell newspapers. She decided it was time to put smarmy Steve Ackerman in his place.

''They call Virginia the Mother of Presidents, don't they?'' Harriet asked.

''That's right,'' said Lavinia in her schoolteacher tone. ''Eight presidents were born there.''

She flicked her aunt a quelling glance and turned to their tea guest. ''I can never remember them all. Can you, Steve?''

It seemed both her aunt and Steve had caught on to her, for they glanced at her with almost identical expressions of smug amusement. Ha, see how smug Steve felt when he made a fool of himself the same way he'd made a fool of her in the paper.

"You want me to name all eight?" he asked her with mild surprise, as though she were the dummy.

"Yes."

"Don't you know any of them?" She could have sworn he was laughing at her, but she refused to be drawn.

Of course she did. She'd lived with Lavinia MacPherson for twenty-three years, as he very well knew. "They've slipped my mind."

"Miss MacPherson," he said with an amused glance at her aunt. "This is like the cobbler's niece having no shoes."

"Never mind your jokes. Do you know them or don't you?"

He sighed, almost as though he were in pain, and she felt momentarily abashed for exposing him in front of her aunt.

"Yes," he said. "I know them."

"Perhaps you'd be kind enough to share your knowledge?" She found herself mimicking her aunt's teacher tone and hoped it scared him speechless.

Obviously he could tell at a glance she wasn't letting him off easily so, with a sigh, he said, "Washington, Jefferson, Madison, Monroe, Harrison, Tyler, Taylor and Wilson." He glanced at her and must have seen her shock. "That's organized chronologically. I can do it alphabetically if you prefer. Harrison, Jefferson—"

"No. No. I believe you."

Aunt Lavinia chuckled. "Did you major in history at university?"

"No. I majored in journalism but I have a minor in history."

"Summa cum laude, I hope?"

Once more he looked sheepish. "Yeah."

Her aunt roared with laughter. "I used to get so cross with you pretending to be thick as a brick. I'm certain people in this town still see you that way."

"Yes." He glanced at Harriet. "I think you're right."

"Well, I think you'd have made a wonderful historian, but I suppose writing for newspapers is your passion."

"No. Sports is my passion. Writing about it helps me stay in that world."

"I have to say, you bring a certain elegance to the sports section that's sadly lacking in most newspapers. Your piece on Harriet was very well written."

"Aunt Lavinia, please," Harriet protested, already blushing. Of course her aunt didn't know she and Steve had fought over the spread, but it was the last thing she wanted to hear discussed. And she never, ever wanted to see the stupid thing in her life.

But Aunt Lavinia could never be stopped if she had something she wanted to say. "I thought the headline was most apt. 'Dream Comes True For *Standard* Copy Editor.'"

Harriet's eyes widened. That wasn't the headline she'd pitched a fit over. What about Cinderella?

Steve turned and stared right into her eyes. "It was the headline that told the story best."

"Excuse me," she said, jumping to her feet. "I'll help Aunt Elspeth with the tea."

She raced to the kitchen and, ignoring Elspeth and the tea trolley, grabbed today's copy of the *Standard* and fumbled through the pages searching for the sports section. She almost flipped past the feature because she was looking for those awful pictures of herself. She got to the end of sports and worked backward, a ray of hope illuminating her heart.

By the time she got to the headline Aunt Lavinia had referred to, the ray of hope became a beacon. There was no mention of Cinderella, the headline was exactly as her aunt had said.

There was her official glam shot, but he'd replaced the high school geek photos with pictures of her on the field with the rest of the cheerleaders. She'd become accustomed to seeing newspaper photographers on the field, so she hadn't noticed that the *Standard*'s camera had focused on her. Steve must have given him specific instructions at the last game.

Staring at herself—one of a group of other happy athletic women—doing what she loved, she thought she'd never been happier. She scanned the first few paragraphs of Steve's story. It mentioned her dream, the tryouts and her triumph. There were quotes from the cheerleader director, some of the other cheerleaders, even, she noted with a grin, Rock Richards. "Great gal. Terrific athlete," he was quoted as saying.

She scanned the rest of the article and found not a word about high school.

"He changed it," she said to Elspeth, her voice choking on her emotion. "He rewrote it!"

"That's nice, dear," answered her aunt, who was elbow-deep in Crown Derby china and not really listening.

With a lightened heart Harriet helped Elspeth with the tea trolley. She couldn't believe how snarky she'd been to Steve. He must have wondered why.

Well, she'd make it up to him just as soon as she could.

Of course he drank his tea hot, and, from his demeanor, one would think he drank out of dainty Crown Derby cups every day instead of slurping coffee from a huge mug that advertised baseball bats.

He managed the scones—including the clotted cream and strawberry preserves—like a pro, and complimented Elspeth on her shortbread, which was the only thing in the world that she was vain about.

And to Aunt Lavinia he spoke intelligently and with insight.

Harriet's toe started to tap with impatience. She and Steve needed to go somewhere private and have a serious talk.

Now.

STEVE COULDN'T KEEP the grin off his face when Harriet practically hauled him out of the house the second he'd finished his tea. Of course, he had accepted the second cup knowing perfectly well she was dying to smack him in the face with his summa cum laude.

He'd barely said his thank-yous before she was dragging him by the hand out the door.

"I need to walk off all that rich food and I know Steve will want to join me," she said in a voice that brooked no refusal. Not that he wanted to refuse her anything, least of all time alone together.

"Thanks again, Miss MacPherson," he said, feeling his arm almost pull out of its socket with Harriet's impatience.

"I think it's time you called me Lavinia. I have a feeling we'll be seeing quite a lot of you," she said, and then she winked at him.

He damn near fell down the neatly painted steps at the front of the house. Miss MacPherson had just winked at him. Still, she was right. If he had his way they'd be seeing an awful lot of each other.

"You bet, Lavinia," he said, and winked back.

"Well, well, then you must call me Elspeth," said the younger sister.

"It would be my pleasure," he assured her.

"Would you come on!" Harriet exclaimed with a tug.

He sprinted down the steps and, taking a firm grip on her hand, started walking down the street. "You know," he said, "one day, I really want to see you back flip this yard."

"Well, it will be a cold day in Hades before that happens," she informed him in a snit.

He glanced at Harriet and his heart squeezed. Her hair was picking up sparks of light, glowing fire, reminding him of her redhead's temper. Her cheeks were flushed and her eyes sparkled.

Her outfit couldn't have been more demure and that suited him just fine. He loved knowing that she packed a serious centerfold's body beneath those girlish clothes.

"I can't believe you lied to me," she sputtered as

soon as she'd walked off some of her anger—at least he hoped she had.

"What are you talking about? I never lied to you."

"You let me believe you were a dimwit."

"I let anyone believe that, but only because they make assumptions. I kind of thought you were onto me anyway."

"I guess I was," she said, and he loved her incurable honesty. "But you didn't go out of your way to let anyone know you were smart."

He sighed and figured if anyone had a right to the whole truth, Harriet did. He turned her toward a convenient elm tree at the end of the street. Its leafy canopy offered a nice sheltered spot where they couldn't be seen unless a car passed, which wasn't all that frequent an occurrence in this quiet older neighborhood.

"Harriet," he said, "I've learned so much from you."

Her beautiful sea-green eyes widened with suspicion, but also eagerness. "You did? What did you learn?"

"This is going to sound so corny, but you taught me how important it is to be true to yourself."

She smiled up at him and her off-kilter tooth called to him to shut up already and start kissing her. "Really?"

He picked up a fiery curl and twirled it around one finger. "In high school when you were a nerd, and I admit you were, I should have been a nerd, too. I had bad eyes and a gigantic IQ. But I didn't want to be some smart geeky guy in the library."

He sighed heavily. "I wanted to be out on the field

playing football—well, anything really. There wasn't a thing I could do about my eyesight, but I was smart enough to work the academic system so I always did okay, but never so well that I called attention to myself. You know?''

Harriet shook her head, puzzled, and he realized it had never occurred to her to hide her gifts.

''Anyhow, it wasn't until I got to college that I realized my mistake. So I let the monster out of the closet, aced college and then came back here. I guess I never thought that everyone would still think I was a dumb jock. But they did, and I suppose I was busy enjoying my own private joke.''

She sighed softly.

''Are you disappointed?''

''No. I'm so happy. I want to have intelligent conversations with the man I love, not just—''

She gasped as though the words had slipped out without her knowledge or consent.

He touched a hand to the smooth, warm skin of her cheek, thinking he'd never heard words that sounded so good. ''I love you, too.''

She cocked her head, a worry line appearing between her brows. ''Are you sure it's not Harriet the cheerleader you love?''

''Well, of course I love Harriet the cheerleader,'' he almost yelled. ''She's terrific, who wouldn't love her? But I also love Harriet the serious writer. Harriet the woman who seems to belong to every clan and wears all their plaids with pride. Harriet the woman who stays with her aunts because she loves them. You're a whole and individual woman and I love everything about you.''

The way her smile widened and her eyes misted he had to think she believed him. "Even my temper?"

He swallowed. "Even that. In moderation."

She giggled happily. "The spread in the paper was great, by the way. I never saw it until Aunt Lavinia mentioned the headline and I knew it wasn't the same as the proof I saw."

"So that's why you were looking so mad at me. I thought it was because I showed up with presents for your aunts but nothing for you."

She blushed adorably. "No. Of course not."

When she tilted her chin up just so and her eyes dazzled him with their brilliance, and her scent lured him, he could think of only one thing.

"I do have something for you," he said, dropping his voice and leaning closer.

She must have got some hint of his intention from the way his arms trapped her against the tree trunk.

"You do?" she asked softly, her pink tongue sliding along her bottom lip in a nervous gesture that was about the sexiest thing Steve had ever seen.

"Harriet," he said, realizing he even loved her name, "I have a hickey with your name on it."

If he'd gone down on bended knee with a four-carat engagement ring, he didn't think she'd have reacted so blissfully.

"I've been hoping you'd do that again," she said, lifting her chin higher to give him access.

"I've been thinking about doing it again ever since that first time. Oh, there are a lot of things I've been thinking about doing with you."

"Well," she said breathlessly, "quit dawdling and let's get started."

He traced his index finger down the length of her creamy throat, watching smugly as a shiver of excitement rippled across her silky skin. He thought he had control of the situation, but the minute he touched his lips to her throat he was lost....

Play the Romance Crossword Game

and get...

2 FREE BOOKS

and a

FREE GIFT...

YOURS to KEEP!

Scratch Here!

Yes!

to reveal the hidden words.
Look below to see what you get.

I have scratched off the gold areas. Please send me my **2 FREE BOOKS** and **FREE GIFT** for which I qualify. I understand that I am under no obligation to purchase any books as explained on the back of this card.

▼ DETACH AND MAIL CARD TODAY! ▼

311 HDL DRT4   111 HDL DRUL

FIRST NAME   LAST NAME

ADDRESS

APT.#   CITY

STATE/PROV.   ZIP/POSTAL CODE

Visit us online at
www.eHarlequin.com

ROMANCE	MYSTERY	NOVEL	GIFT
You get **2 FREE BOOKS** PLUS a **FREE GIFT!**	You get **2 FREE BOOKS!**	You get **1 FREE BOOK!**	You get a **FREE MYSTERY GIFT!**

Offer limited to one per household and not valid to current Harlequin Duets™ subscribers.
All orders subject to approval.

© 2001 HARLEQUIN ENTERPRISES LTD. ® and TM are trademarks owned by Harlequin Enterprises Ltd.   (H-D-04/03)

The Harlequin Reader Service® — Here's how it works:

Accepting your 2 free books and mystery gift places you under no obligation to buy anything. You may keep the books and gift and return the shipping statement marked "cancel." If you do not cancel, about a month later we'll send you 2 additional books and bill you just $5.14 each in the U.S., or $6.14 each in Canada, plus 50¢ shipping & handling per book and applicable taxes if any.* That's the complete price and — compared to cover prices of $5.99 each in the U.S. and $6.99 each in Canada — it's quite a bargain! You may cancel at any time, but if you choose to continue, every month we'll send you 2 more books, which you may either purchase at the discount price or return to us and cancel your subscription.

*Terms and prices subject to change without notice. Sales tax applicable in N.Y. Canadian residents will be charged applicable provincial taxes and GST. Credit or Debit balances in a customer's account(s) may be offset by any other outstanding balance owed by or to the customer

If offer card is missing write to: Harlequin Reader Service, 3010 Walden Ave., P.O. Box 1867, Buffalo NY 14240-1867

BUSINESS REPLY MAIL
FIRST-CLASS MAIL   PERMIT NO. 717-003   BUFFALO, NY

POSTAGE WILL BE PAID BY ADDRESSEE

HARLEQUIN READER SERVICE
3010 WALDEN AVE
PO BOX 1867
BUFFALO NY 14240-9952

NO POSTAGE
NECESSARY
IF MAILED
IN THE
UNITED STATES

Nancy Warren

A Cradle for Caroline

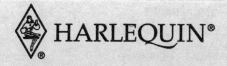

HARLEQUIN®

TORONTO • NEW YORK • LONDON
AMSTERDAM • PARIS • SYDNEY • HAMBURG
STOCKHOLM • ATHENS • TOKYO • MILAN • MADRID
PRAGUE • WARSAW • BUDAPEST • AUCKLAND

Dear Reader,

A Cradle for Caroline was conceived when I was visiting my in-laws, Roy and Lois Reynolds, and they told me about their friend Fanny, an eighty-year-old bartender. I knew at that moment I had to put Fanny in a book, and what better part for her to play than the much-loved mother-in-law of my heroine?

I have never met the real Fanny, but I thank her anyway and hope she likes my fictional Fanny, who was a treat to write. *A Cradle for Caroline* is about family and friends and the importance of both in our lives.

Writing this book reminded me that I couldn't do what I do without the support and cheerleading I get from all my family. You guys are the best!

I've thoroughly enjoyed writing about the fictional people of Pasqualie, Washington. Thanks for coming along.

Happy reading,

Nancy

Books by Nancy Warren

HARLEQUIN DUETS
78—SHOTGUN NANNY

HARLEQUIN TEMPTATION
838—FLASHBACK
915—HOT OFF THE PRESS

HARLEQUIN BLAZE
19—LIVE A LITTLE!
47—WHISPER
57—BREATHLESS

For James, who first made me a mother.
I've loved every minute of our time together.

1

"AND WHAT IS THE SECRET to being chosen Miss Pasqualie Motors two years in a row?" Caroline Kushner asked in her professional interviewer's voice, keeping to herself the suspicion that being the daughter of the sponsor might have something to do with the great honor being bestowed on Brooke Billingston.

But, as her editor had explained to Caro, Billingston Motors was a big advertiser with the *Pasqualie Star,* so they turned a blind eye to nepotism.

Take that, Jonathon, she thought gleefully as she imagined the publisher of the rival *Pasqualie Standard* and stickler for journalistic integrity, reading his soon-to-be-ex-wife's byline in the paper he called "a muckraking tabloid."

She could now add muckraker to her résumé, along with former high-fashion model and former wife. Well, not quite former, she didn't have the divorce organized yet, but it wouldn't be long. She forced down the nausea that rose every time she thought of Jon and the mess he'd made of their marriage—and since she couldn't stop thinking about it, she felt as if she had a permanent case of the flu.

If it were mere pettiness that had her working for Jonathon's despised rivals, she'd consider being ashamed of herself. But the truth was, she needed the distraction.

Not that she was getting much distraction from Brooke Billingston. The high school senior gushed in incomplete sentences where the *ums, likes* and *ya knows* vastly exceeded any sense. Caro took a few notes for form's sake, but she'd end up fudging the girl's quotes, reminding herself again of ad revenues at the *Star*.

Leaving the Billingston home in the affluent west side suburbs of Pasqualie, Washington, she headed downtown for her next interview. She'd scheduled her day this way to give herself a treat after the Billingston puff piece.

Fanny Kushner was turning eighty. The birthday itself wasn't that big a deal, but Fanny's occupation made her birthday news, for she was about to become Pasqualie's first octogenarian bartender.

Fanny'd been tending bar since World War II. She'd buried two husbands, raised four children, and probably listened to more problems than the local priest, minister and rabbi combined.

Fanny could make everything from a pink lady to a black Russian with her eyes closed and her martinis had been known to make grown men weep.

Everybody loved her, including Caro. Even though Fanny was soon going to be her ex-mother-in-law.

Fanny had conceived Jonathon when she'd thought she was too old to get pregnant. Her first three children were almost grown, she'd been a widow for ten years, and along came Hector Kushner, who always said he fell in love with her martinis, then the woman who created them.

Jonathon was born less than a year after the wedding.

Caro figured that was part of his problem. He was almost an only child of older parents, and he'd ended up an odd combination of his earthy, unpretentious mother and a wealthy, elegant father who'd died happy knowing his only son was settled at his old alma mater, Harvard, in his old faculty, law.

Would Hector be as happy had he known Jonathon would dump law for journalism and move back to Pasqualie to buy the *Standard?* As she drove east toward Fanny's Roadhouse, Caro wondered what Mr. Kushner would make of his family now.

Would he have approved of Jon's marrying her? Or would he be delighted they were splitting up?

Why was she thinking about Jon? It was making her sick to her stomach again. Must be the weather. Damp weather always depressed her.

She walked into Fanny's and the depression

lifted immediately. The jukebox belted out K. D. Lang and she smelled the cedar paneling, fresh beer and a hint of pine from the cleaner Fanny used. Fanny had higher standards of hygiene than a hospital; Caro didn't think she'd ever been in a tavern that was as spotless. Or as much fun.

They'd agreed on a two o'clock meeting, since that was Fanny's slow time in the bar. The busy lunch crowd would be back at work and it was too early for the after-office cocktail hour. Still, a few shift workers and the shiftless hung out nursing beers. She heard some good-natured ribbing then the clap of pool balls from the back room.

Fanny stood behind the bar polishing glasses. She glanced up the minute the door opened, and a big smile lit her face. "Well knock me down and steal my teeth if you don't get prettier every day."

Caro laughed. She couldn't help it. Fanny could cheer a corpse. Jon's mother had been a beauty once, and you could see the remains of her looks still in the eyes, faded to baby blue now, but which Caro suspected had once been the same deep azure as Jonathon's.

Nobody had ever seen a gray hair on Fanny's head in all her eighty years. That was just about the only color they hadn't seen, though. Today her permed hair was red.

Not auburn, or titian or strawberry-blond—it was crayon red.

The old woman's matching crimson lips grinned

wide, pinching the wrinkles in her cheeks together like twin accordions. Her earrings, shaped like chunky artist's palettes, took up the crayon theme.

"I like the new do," Caro said.

They exchanged a loud smacker across the bar. "It's the only way I can ever get anybody to look at me. Especially if something young and pretty like you comes along."

Caro smiled at her, feeling older and more used up at thirty than Fanny did at eighty. She pulled out her notebook. "Ready for your interview?"

"Why don't you go back to modeling?"

"Because I'm thirty. My glory days were ten years ago."

The old woman snorted. "Thirty. Older than dirt." She addressed her comments to the glass she was polishing. "She's a baby, and still a skinny little thing."

"So." Caro plunged into her first riveting interview question. "How does it feel to be eighty?"

"I lied." Concern lit the older woman's eyes and she put down the gleaming glass to peer into Caro's face. "You don't look gorgeous. You look like somebody shot your puppy."

A lump formed in her throat and she swallowed it down like a stuck pill. "Fanny, I—"

"Not as miserable as my Johnny, though. When are you two going to patch things up?"

"Fanny," she said as gently as she could, reminding herself this woman was eighty years old and needed to be treated carefully, "we're getting a divorce."

It was as if one day had been shuffled into the middle of her life like a nasty joker in a deck of playing cards. On that day, she and Jon had visited the fertility specialist in the morning who'd given them the bad news that Caroline's chances of conceiving naturally were slim to none. That evening she'd come home after work, already miserable, to find one of the *Standard*'s sales managers, Lori Gerhardt, all but naked in Caro's own bed and Jonathon looking ready to join her. She'd capped off that memorable day by packing a bag and moving to her friend Melanie's.

The bartender's colorful expletive didn't sound as if it came from a frail old lady. "That boy's wheel is still turning, but the hamster's dead. Hasn't he crawled across glass yet to beg your forgiveness?"

"How does it feel to be eighty, Fanny?"

"Like I should call God 'Sonny.'"

This wasn't quite the angle Caro was going for. Maybe she'd make up an answer for question number one. Still, Fanny's expressions were as colorful as her hair. She'd have to remember to include a few. She doggedly went on to her second question in her best interviewer's voice. "I bet you've got some funny stories from your years behind this bar. Care to share a few?"

"You coming to my surprise party?"

Caro dropped the notebook in defeat. She'd heard most of Fanny's anecdotes over the years anyway. And she felt no surprise that Fanny knew about her party. It was more of a mystery why Jon had thought he could keep a secret from the one-woman info booth for the goings-on in town.

"I received an invitation," Caro said carefully. In truth she hadn't decided about going to the party. She was torn between wanting to be there for Fanny and not wanting to be anywhere near Jonathon.

"Hmm." Fanny picked up another already gleaming glass and polished it ruthlessly. "What am I going to do in a fancy restaurant with a bunch of stuffed shirts?"

"You don't fool me. You *married* a stuffed shirt."

"Gave birth to one, too. My eggs must have got too old. Don't you wait until you're middle-aged to have kids. Specially if Jon's going to be the father. You've already got one stuffed-shirt gene."

Fanny didn't know Caro's egg carton had come up empty. She and Jon had tried to conceive for over a year with no luck. Fanny's words were like bullets, piercing Caro's sensitive skin. Maybe if she'd been able to get pregnant he wouldn't have… No, that was ridiculous. She had a shelf full of self-help books at home that she'd practically memorized for occasions like this, when melancholy hovered. She sucked in a deep breath and reminded herself of her mantra.

I will look forward to the future, not back at the past.

She was taking charge of her own happiness.

A woman on the brink of freedom and a new life.

A woman who wanted to throw herself against her former mother-in-law's wrinkled bosom and sob her heart out.

JONATHON KUSHNER had a problem. Well, he had several problems, but the most pressing was how to organize an eightieth birthday bash for his mother when she never took a night off from work.

Caro would know how to do the thing, if she were speaking to him. And that just brought up the most major of his problems.

Caroline.

"Morning, Mr. Kushner." The cheery greeting of one of the summer interns from Pasqualie University's journalism program interrupted his thoughts. He forced a pleasant smile to his face and answered automatically.

Caroline, whom he'd loved deeply and faithfully for the five years of their marriage—whom he still loved in spite of everything—thought he was a philanderer. The idea that she could think so little of him, so little of their marriage, made him furious every time he thought of it. Since she'd stormed out on him and refused to listen to reason a month ago, he'd given her time to come to her senses, only to have her tell him she was going to house-sit for a few weeks for a friend while thinking about her "options."

Options were for the stock market, not a damned marriage, and if Caro was running away at the first hint on trouble, she wasn't the woman he'd believed her to be.

He strode to his office, trying to haul his mind back to business, back to the rising price of newsprint, the national advertiser who was thinking of moving from newspaper to TV.

When he passed her desk, his assistant, Lillian, handed him a bundle of messages. He flipped through them rapidly, automatically sorting them into call-back order and working out which calls could be palmed off onto other members of his staff.

There was one from his mother, and that, naturally, went to the top of the pile.

He dialed her home, where he knew she'd be this time of day. When he had her on the phone, he said, "Well? Did you find somebody you trust to tend bar so I can take you out for a quiet birthday dinner?"

Jon already had the most expensive restaurant in town booked, the champagne ordered and an elegant sit-down menu chosen. Everybody who was anybody in Pasqualie would be there. He longed to get his mother off her feet for one night so she could be waited on instead of her doing the serving.

"I haven't had a chance to think about that, yet," she said airily, and he heard his own teeth grind. Her birthday was a week away. How was it so difficult to get her to take one night off from slinging beer?

"Mom, I'll hire another bartender for the night," he said with the strained patience of a man who's said the same words a thousand times.

A most unladylike snort answered him. "One person couldn't do what I do. Specially not if it's a man."

"Fifty bartenders then. I want to watch you sit down and enjoy yourself for once."

There was a pause and he hoped she was figuring out whom he could hire to replace her for one single evening. "You haven't asked me what I want for a birthday present."

That's because he'd already bought her a cruise. She was in her golden years, she should be relaxing more. But he'd play along. "What do you want for your birthday, Mom?"

"Why don't you come down to the Roadhouse this afternoon and we'll talk about it. Take a late lunch and drop by when I'm not so busy."

He checked his calendar. "How's two-thirty sound."

"Make it two."

He sighed. He might be a busy executive and

she might be a golden-ager, but she still called the shots. And he loved her so much he let her. "All right. See you at two."

He checked furtively to make sure no one was approaching the open door of his office and eased open his top drawer. He slid out a file marked Correspondence and stared down at the picture of Caro, the one he used to proudly display on his desk that he now had to sneak glances at, as though she were a banned substance.

Which she should be given the way his heart rate spiked and memories spun like dreams, simply from staring at a photograph of her cool, beautiful face.

He narrowed his eyes. If she thought this crazy situation was going to continue very much longer, she was vastly mistaken. She'd found him in a horribly compromising position, he'd give her that. And somebody other than him had blabbed the story all over town, which hadn't helped. Caro was entitled to her pique. He could have withstood yelling, tears, tantrums, even a whack over the head with a frying pan. But he'd never believed she'd simply walk out on him. He knew the last few months had been the worst of their marriage, but that didn't mean they couldn't work through it.

Almost a month had passed since that fateful day and he'd waited long enough for her to come to her senses. He was going to have to take matters into his own hands. Tonight he'd start plotting a strategy—which was as good a way as any to while away another empty evening in his all too empty home. He'd tried to make Caro stay in the house, but she'd refused it with the same contempt she'd refused to listen to his side of the story.

Now he hated that house. It had too many empty rooms for the kids he and Caro had hoped to have. The picture of a butternut cradle she'd clipped out of some designer baby magazine was still hanging on the fridge and he hadn't had the heart to take it down.

Besides, he wasn't nearly finished with Caroline.

Having decided to take a more active role in bringing one stubborn woman to her senses, he was able to turn his thoughts to business.

He worked straight through to early afternoon and managed to make it to the Roadhouse by ten after two.

He pushed through the doors, took two strides into the dim bar and stopped, feeling as if somebody had swung a baseball bat into his solar plexus.

Caro was there, straight and elegant atop a bar stool, with the graceful posture that had once helped sell everything from tanning lotion to designer clothes. Her long legs were crossed, showing a hint of shapely thigh, her blond hair smooth and gleaming, her back a graceful curve. She'd always been model-slender, but the thought flashed through his mind that she'd lost weight in the past few weeks. She seemed a little bony.

They'd always had a kind of sixth sense around each other, their sex sense they called it back when they were speaking to each other. She hadn't turned around, but she knew he'd just walked in. He could tell from the way her shoulders tightened imperceptibly and her fingers clenched the pen she was holding, writing something on a steno pad.

Her tension told him that bumping into each other was as much of a surprise to Caro as it was to him.

"Mother, don't try to play matchmaker." He couldn't keep the irritation out of his voice as he stalked up to the bar.

2

_____

"WELL, WHO STOMPED on your petunias?" asked his mother—at least Jonathon assumed that woman with the scarlet hair was his elderly parent.

He advanced on her with a glare.

She glanced from him to Caro and back again. "Gotta get something from the back." She scuttled behind the swinging door into the kitchen so fast she left a jet stream behind her.

Caro turned to face him. "Hello, Jonathon," she said in that cool, sexy voice of hers with just a hint of huskiness that always reminded him of lava flows beneath an ice field.

He knew her secrets. He knew that beneath her cool, refined exterior she was a woman of passion. She almost got away with appearing unaffected by his presence, except for the slight pinching of her lips.

He got to her, all right. As much as she might try to pretend otherwise, he got to her.

He almost asked whether she'd known he'd be here, but only a stupid man would think anything so preposterous given that she'd refused to see him since she'd left home. He was many things, but stupid wasn't one. He didn't cheat on his wife, either, but he seemed to be the only person in Pasqualie who believed that, with the possible exception of his mother.

Caro certainly believed he was an adulterer, in spite of his pleas that she listen to reason. In spite of his love.

He was awfully tempted to grab her by her slender shoulders and give her a good shake, but his mother would come charging out of the kitchen, five feet two inches of vengeful fury, and hit him over the head with a broom, so he stifled the impulse and pulled up a bar stool beside Caro's.

His wife immediately flipped her notebook closed and started to rise. "I think I've got everything I need," she said.

Without thinking, he placed his right hand atop her left, which felt foreign without his ring on her finger. "Stay," he said.

He felt her tremble, and then he watched, fascinated, as her fingers formed a claw. He felt as though he were in one of those science documentaries where the unwary narrator is attacked by the most placid-seeming animal.

As he'd guessed, she wasn't nearly as immune to his presence as she pretended. It wasn't much to build his future hopes on, but, at the moment, it was all he had.

"I can't stay," she said coldly.

"My mother may be crazy enough to dip her

head in fire-engine paint, but she loves you. That's why she pulled this stunt. Can't you at least spend five minutes in my company?''

''For what purpose?''

Ooh, she could really get to him. ''We were married for five years. Maybe she thinks we have things to say to each other.''

She had a way of staring at a man that made him feel as though his heart had been sliced out with a diamond blade. It was part of the arsenal she'd needed during her modeling days when she got hit on all the time, but she'd never used it on him until recently. If she hadn't already cut out his heart by leaving him without so much as a good fight, it would really hurt. As it was, he was numb.

''We have nothing to say to each other.''

''I have plenty to say, but you've refused to listen. Not quite the same thing.''

She rose with queenly grace and he stopped her once more, not by touching her this time but with a comment that was a stroke of inspiration. ''I need help planning Mom's birthday party. Could you at least spend a few minutes of your precious time on that? Or does the woman who treated you like a daughter mean nothing to you now that you've dumped the son?''

Sitting at the bar with the smell of beer and peanuts in his nostrils, as though he didn't have a score of urgent tasks back at the office, he watched her struggle with this request. He'd deliberately switched off his cell phone so he could argue with his mother in peace, little realizing it would also leave him free to argue with his wife in peace.

"What do you want me to do?" she asked him at last, resuming her perch on the stool beside him.

What did he want her to do? He watched her lips move as she said those simple words and he had to bite back the urge to tell her he wanted her to move back in with him and stop being a fool.

"I want you to convince her to leave the bar for one night on her birthday." He glanced at the kitchen door, but he figured if his mother were eavesdropping, the neon glow from her hair would give her away.

"Leave the bar." Caro's forehead crinkled. What was wrong with everybody? he wondered.

"Of course, leave the bar. I've booked the whole of Le Beaumari for the evening. We're having a sit-down dinner with champagne and all of the movers and shakers of Pasqualie will be there. But first I have to convince the woman who is celebrating her eightieth birthday that she can take a single night off work. You'd think I was asking her to do a striptease for a bunch of bikers. No, scratch that. She'd far rather do a striptease for bikers, if I know my mom, than take a night off."

It might have been a ridiculous thought. For all his mother's bluster she was a pretty straight arrow, but it won the first smile he'd coaxed out of Caro since she'd walked out on him. "Why won't she take the night off?"

"She says there's no one she can trust to watch the bar for her."

"I could do it. Do you think she'd trust me?"

He forced himself not to grind his teeth, but it wasn't easy. "You're coming to the party."

"I really don't think—"

"Not for me. For my mother. I notice you haven't RSVP'd. I'm counting on you to be there."

She glared at him. "All right."

Caro tapped her pen on the cover of her steno pad. What was she doing with that thing anyway? Taking dictation for his mother? Hardly seemed likely. His mother wasn't one for letting anyone do a task she could perform herself, and besides, Caro didn't take dictation.

Steno pads made great reporter's notebooks, though.

He jerked his head up and stared at her. Was she working on something for the paper? He snorted to himself. Oh, yeah. That was going to happen. She'd stopped helping with the fashion section on the *Standard* the minute she left him.

Caro turned to him and took a resolute breath as though she'd made up her mind about something.

"She doesn't want that kind of party, Jon."

He was floored, not only by her statement, but by her use of his nickname. He hadn't realized, among all the things he missed about her, that that was one of them. But it was the part of her statement that went before "Jon" that he had to deal with now. "What do you mean, she doesn't want that kind of party?"

"Fanny loves it here in the bar. This is where she'll want to spend her birthday."

He knew Caro must have lost her mind to throw away their marriage. This just proved it. "You think she'd rather spend her eightieth birthday in a smoky bar slinging draft and dishing up nachos than in an elegant restaurant eating *foie gras?*" His voice rose and he dropped it before he could bellow his surprise into the kitchen.

Caro sent him one of those pitying, men-are-so-unevolved looks. "Your mother is not the *foie gras* type. You are."

"Are you saying I'm planning this party for myself?" He could barely believe how insulting she was being when he'd knocked himself out trying to give his mother something really special.

"Yes." The simple word, delivered with cool amusement made him want to act as childish and unevolved as she could possibly think him.

"I think most thirty-two-year-old men would be a lot happier hanging out in a dive like this, slinging back longnecks and scarfing cheeseburgers than dressing in a tux snacking on smoked salmon and champagne." He didn't even like champagne. Of course, he had made certain his favorite brand of single malt was stocked at Le Beaumari.

"You're not like most thirty-two-year-old men," she said, her brows rising slightly.

He groaned as the truth slapped him in the face. "I'm not, but my mother is."

How could he have failed to see the obvious? No wonder his mom had been so skittish about leaving the bar for a night. He dropped his head into his hands.

"I blew it, didn't I?"

"Yes," she agreed. "You blew it." It wasn't fair. It simply wasn't fair. No sooner did Jonathon act like the arrogant, faithless man she knew him to be, than he switched gears on her and revealed the nice guy she didn't want to remember.

It was tough to hold her pride together when he was around, to stop herself from dropping to the floor and hanging on to his ankles so he couldn't be rid of her.

Why did he have to keep looking at her with those dark blue eyes? Sending secret messages that were so hard to ignore?

"I wanted to give her something special."

"And you will," she assured him, determined to help him, not for his sake, but for his mother's. Amazingly, Fanny had refused to take sides in the breakup. She'd promised Caro in her no-nonsense way, soon after she'd moved out of the home she and Jonathon had shared for half a decade, that she wouldn't try to interfere. And, bless her, she never had.

Until today.

The outside door swung open and in ambled a couple of guys who looked to be finished an early shift on the road crew. They headed straight for a table and one sat. The second, stretching his back as though it ached, approached the bar and his brows rose when he saw there was no one behind it.

Fanny didn't reappear, though Caro knew she had a close circuit TV monitor in the kitchen. Presumably she was busy watching her favorite new soap opera—Caro and Jon—and had no intention of coming out front.

Jonathon must have figured out his mother's strategy for he glared toward the camera hanging from the ceiling above the bar, waited a minute, and glanced at the customer shifting from work boot to work boot. Jon muttered something under his breath and rose, raising a hinged portion of the bar and slipping behind.

"Hi," he said, as though he weren't in a designer suit, "What can I get you?"

"Where's Fanny?" asked the customer, a small frown pulling down the corners of his mouth.

"She's in the kitchen. She'll be out in a minute."

"Who are you?"

Caroline's lips twitched as Jon tried to work out how to answer that one. He shot her a half-amused, half-frustrated glance and went with the simplest of truths. "I'm her son. I'm helping out."

"Okay. Give me two Miller drafts." The burly customer narrowed his eyes and glanced from Jonathon's stylishly cropped hair to his designer suit, and Caro had the feeling he was tempted to lean right over the polished mahogany bar to check out her ex-husband's shiny shoes. She could have told him they were handmade in Switzerland. Jonathon had a thing about quality. "You know how to pull a draft?" the customer asked doubtfully.

"Sure thing." He'd worked summers in the bar from the time he was old enough to drink to the time he finished college. He looked unlike any bartender she'd ever seen, but she had to admit, he pulled a great draft. She had a feeling he put a little extra flourish into the procedure simply to impress the big guy.

He took a crumpled bill, made change, and didn't so much as turn a hair on his millionaire head when his customer handed him a couple of coins by way of a tip. Even though Jon was beneath contempt as a human being, she had to give him credit as he dropped the coins into a communal tip jar.

"While I'm here, can I get you something?" he asked Caro.

She was about to refuse, but stopped herself, feeling witchy. "Yes, thanks. A Singapore sling." It was the most complicated drink she could think of and she settled back, not because she was remotely thirsty or wanted to drink alcohol in the middle of the afternoon, but because she wanted to watch Jonathon bungle.

Of course, he didn't.

Her irritation rose as he built her a Singapore sling as smoothly and competently as he did everything, until, in record time, she had a perfectly layered drink. She watched his long-fingered hands hesitate, then choose a purple plastic sword. "To match your dress," he said.

She wanted to hit him. What was he doing noticing her lavender linen sheath? He stabbed a maraschino cherry with the sword and she fancied he'd done something very similar to her heart.

He placed the drink, each perfect layer shimmering, in front of her, and grabbed a draft for himself.

As Jonathon knew perfectly well, she didn't drink much, and when she did she preferred a glass of dry white wine.

"How is it?" he asked her politely as he came back around to reclaim his seat beside her. A quick glance showed a mischievous twinkle in his eyes.

She sipped her drink. Having only the foggiest recollection what a Singapore sling was supposed to taste like, this one seemed to fit the bill. "It's very nice, thank you."

While she'd watched Jonathon prepare the drinks, she'd had leisure to think more about

Fanny's birthday celebration and the more she thought about it the more certain she was that her ex-mother-in-law wanted to be right here for the big day.

"Can I make a suggestion?" she asked him.

"You know how to make a better Singapore sling?"

She shook her head. "I was thinking about Fanny's party. Why not have it here?"

He blinked at her, drank beer, and blinked at her again. "Have her eightieth birthday party in the bar where she *works* every night of her life?"

"I think this is where she wants to be. If she won't go out to the party, bring the party to her."

"But, I can't ask people...like Rose and Walt Elliot, the mayor and councilors to a bar."

"Then they're not your mother's friends," she said a touch acidly. "Any friend of your mother would be happy to come to this place. If they're too snobby to be seen here, then they're too snobby for your mom."

It was so simple, she couldn't believe he was having trouble grasping the concept, but he still stared at her as though she'd lost her mind. She leaned closer, which was a mistake because she caught a whiff of his aftershave, the same brand he'd worn ever since she first met him. Drinking it in made her dizzy.

Her reaction annoyed her enough to make her blunt. "You are the snob. Not your mom."

His jaw clenched and his eyes grew a shade colder. "I'm not a snob."

"You're the worst kind. A snob who doesn't realize he is one."

He practically spluttered, "I went behind the bar and served drinks, didn't I? Would a snob do that?"

"Yes." She could see he was not taking her opinion all that well. Tough. The truth hurt sometimes.

"A snob would stop his mother working at a roadhouse when everyone knows he could afford to fund a very comfortable retirement."

She laughed out loud. The first time she'd done so in his company in months. "It would take more than you to stop your mom from doing whatever she pleases."

"Would a—"

"Look," she interrupted. "You asked me for my advice and I'm giving it. Host the party here."

"And make my mother pour the drinks for the whole town? That sounds like a big treat for the old girl."

If he didn't know how much of a treat that would be for his mother to sling beer for the bigwigs of Pasqualie, he was further out of touch than she'd realized.

"She doesn't have to do the serving. You could hire bartenders and waitstaff to serve food, but this is her place—I'm certain she wouldn't want to leave it. Do this for her.'' She touched his sleeve impulsively, then wished she'd cut off her arm before doing anything so foolish.

Under his sleeve was one of the arms that had hugged her so often, beaten her at umpteen games of tennis. Attached to his arm was his hand, the hand that had held hers through movies, walks, and touched her in so many ways.

She pulled back as though she'd been burned, wrapped her fingers around the cool glass and took a sip of her drink, tasting of fruit juice and rum. She swallowed, but it didn't sit well and that must have shown on her face.

''Why don't I get you a glass of wine?'' he said softly beside her.

''No. This is fine.''

He blew out a breath. ''I've booked everything. Already sent out the invitations. It won't be easy.''

''I gave you my opinion. What you do with it is your business.''

''Oh, don't get salsa on your tail feathers, I know you're right.''

She laughed a second time in surprise. ''Don't what?''

He seemed startled at her reaction until he realized what he'd said, then he grinned ruefully. ''One of Mom's. I can't believe I said that.''

He was so nice when he was human, and actually admitted he'd screwed up, that she couldn't help but warm to him. With a gasp, she realized how stupid she was being and then made a show of glancing at her watch. She gasped again, this time because of the time.

"I have to go," she said, jumping up. "I'm late for my next appointment." She scrambled for her purse, gesturing to her barely touched drink. "I'll leave some money for that."

He waved her away. "I've got it."

She wanted to argue, but being in his own mother's bar she'd end up losing and looking foolish, so she forced a pleasant smile to her face, hating to be indebted to him even for a drink she didn't want. "Thank you."

Amusement lit his eyes once again. He knew her too well. "You stopped me making a big mistake for Mom's birthday. Consider one barely sipped cocktail a thank-you."

She inclined her head and reached for her pen and notepad.

"What are you? A roving stenographer?" he asked as she snatched up her things.

"No," she said, feeling a delicious thrill. She couldn't believe with all the friends they had in common that no one had blabbed. And that Jon didn't bother to read the competition. Mentally, she kissed every one of their friends for their discretion so she could watch his face when she told him the news herself. "I'm a reporter."

His head jerked back and his eyes blinked open

in surprise. "A reporter? I don't recall seeing any of your stuff in the *Standard*."

Oh, she was enjoying this. She was really enjoying it. Maybe it didn't revenge her for finding a next-to-naked woman in bed with her husband, but it was a start. "I don't write for the *Standard*," she informed him with relish.

"But what—"

"I write for the *Pasqualie Star*."

"What?"

She ignored the wrathful shout, turned to hide her grin of triumph and scooted out the door.

She really did have to hurry or she'd be late for her next appointment. She was writing ad copy for Pasqualie Taxidermy. The owner already had a slogan in mind—you snuff 'em, we stuff 'em.

3

JONATHON TOOK two furious steps after his wife.

"You can't stop her, Jon. You'll only look like a fool." His mother's voice stopped him cold. She was right, and, when he took a second to think about it, storming after Caro to throw a big-boy temper tantrum would accomplish nothing.

There could be one reason and one reason only why she'd take a job with that tabloid and that was to get back at him.

When he had time to cool off, he'd appreciate her tactics, as a fencing opponent might appreciate a good hit. And he'd have leisure to indulge the probability that if she was full of negative emotions toward him, at least she wasn't indifferent.

So he turned slowly on his heel, ignored the burly workmen who'd both half risen—drawn in by Caro's helpless look as so many men were—and stomped back to the bar.

He pulled out his wallet. "I owe you for a draft and one Singapore sling."

"Who had the sling?" Fanny asked as she waved at him to put his money away.

"Caro." Even through his fog of fury that she

was working for the *Star,* he had to chuckle. "I guess she didn't believe I could make one."

"You're rusty," said his mother sternly, eye-balling the drink as a jeweler might study a diamond. "Too much grenadine."

He leaned forward and ruffled her absurd hair. It was as soft as a baby's and as red as ketchup. Why couldn't he ever love an ordinary woman? "How would you like to spend your birthday here?"

She glanced at him, an expression of smug delight crossing her face. "I don't know how you manage without Caro in your life."

Frankly he didn't know how he managed life without Caro either. But he was going to have to figure it out soon. Or get her back.

He preferred the second option.

He ought to return to the office, but, while his mother had been spying on them from the kitchen, she'd also put together his favorite Reuben sandwich, so he settled back to finish his beer and to eat while visiting with his mom. Maybe not a lot of mothers were interrupted by strange characters who came to get change for the pool tables, or to fetch a beer, but she was who she was.

He left feeling better. Still not happy his ex was at the *Star* of all places, but not seething with frustration. However, once he'd put out a couple of fires back at the *Standard,* he picked up the phone.

"Mike Grundel," came the voice of his oldest friend.

Mike was the news editor of the *Star* and he'd raised muckraking to an art. He'd recently exposed a nasty secret development deal that had caused a local developer to move most of his business out of town. Of course, Mike had worked with Tess Elliot, who'd turned out to be one of the *Standard*'s best reporters, so it wasn't all his doing.

But his old buddy was going to pay for keeping the fact that Caro worked for the *Star* from his childhood friend. "Can you manage a squash game tomorrow morning?"

"Yeah. Sure."

Jon had considered getting all the info about Caro and the *Star* from Mike tonight, preferably by force, but Mike spent most evenings with his fiancée, Tess.

He and Mike had fallen into the habit of early squash games at his club, alternating with boxing bouts in the mildew pit Mike insisted on frequenting. Since they'd never grown out of the kill-or-be-killed mentality they'd developed as kids, conversation during play was not an option.

"Can you swing breakfast afterward?"

"No problem."

"I'll book a court for six-thirty. And I'm warning you, I plan to take your face off."

There was a short pause. "Any particular reason?"

"I saw Caro today. On assignment."

"She finally told you. Good."

"Yeah." He could blast Mike about how *he* should have told him first, but that might sound like sniveling. Taking Mike's face off was better.

"IT'S A GREAT HONOR to be chosen Miss Pasqualie Motors," Caro whined the words out loud in a valley-girl voice as she typed them into her computer amid the noisy chaos of the *Star* newsroom.

"Congratulations, I didn't know you were a competitor," said Mike Grundel on his way past her desk.

She shot him a dirty look. "Very funny. I'm trying to sound like an eighteen-year-old airhead," she said, frowning at paragraph one of her story. She'd been on paragraph one for half an hour, unable to concentrate after her recent visit with her ex.

"You're making up quotes?" Mike's easy humor vanished. The *Star* might not care about serious journalism, but Mike sure did. As news editor he was a stickler for getting the facts right and his no-holds-barred style of reporting was famous. In his book, making up quotes would be right up there with robbing a bank, perjury or assault—worse, probably.

While Mike would break a lot of rules to get a story, he was scrupulous about reporting it.

She held up a hand to stop the lecture she could see building. "Talk to Mel. She told me to do it."

Mel was the managing editor and, ever since Mike had been promoted to news editor a month ago, the two of them had been indulging in loud and colorful disagreements several times a day. It kept the troops entertained and seemed to afford the combatants untold delight since they went after each other so often.

Mike stood by her desk a bit longer. He picked up a pen, clicked the top a couple of times and replaced it. She wondered what was coming next.

"I'm playing squash with Jon in the morning."

She dropped her gaze to where her fingertips rested on the keyboard. "You don't sound too happy about it."

"He told me he was going to take my face off for not telling him you were working here." In spite of the fact that he and Jon habitually lobbed insults, she could tell he felt guilty.

She sighed. "I never asked you not to tell him, but I'm glad you didn't. It was great being the one to drop the news."

"Tess and I promised each other we wouldn't get in between you two or the next thing you know we'd be having a rumble. Boys against girls."

It wasn't tough to imagine Mike in a rumble, but the image of the rest of them going at it was silly enough to make her smile. "Please don't let our mess cause trouble for you, too. You've got a wedding to plan."

"Yeah. I still feel bad about not telling Jon."

"You could always let him win tomorrow," she suggested.

He snorted. "I feel bad, but not that bad."

She laughed, then said, "I'm sorry you've ended up in the middle of this. Really sorry."

"I hate it. You know that, don't you? I..." He screwed his eyes shut as though in pain. "I care about you two."

In spite of her heavy heart and a pricking behind her eyes, Caro smiled up at him. "Tess is good for you. You just expressed a feeling."

STREAMING WITH SWEAT and feeling as if he'd bashed out not one iota of his frustration, Jon stepped into the shower thankfully and let the water pound his stretched and tired muscles.

He reminded himself it wasn't Mike's fault Caro worked at the *Star,* nor was it his responsibility to tell her almost ex-husband about her movements. Still, a man had loyalties to a childhood friend, didn't he?

He tried to tamp down his justifiable resentment as he strode into the club restaurant.

The waitress had barely filled Jon's cup and placed the stainless-steel carafe on the table when Mike arrived, his shoulder-length hair still damp. He wore his most disreputable sweats. Jon knew it was his way of giving the finger to "the establishment." They'd been friends too long for such behavior to surprise him or the staff and members at Pasqualie Lawn and Tennis Club. Mike kept it up anyway, more from habit than anything, Jon suspected. Or maybe to emphasize to the world that he might be marrying into one of the town's wealthiest and most established families, but it wasn't going to change him.

Mike must have been thinking something along the same lines as he sank into the seat opposite Jon's and poured himself coffee. "Next time we'll go to my club." He shot a glance of pure devilment at Jon.

"For a free dose of athlete's foot," he said, recalling with loathing the smell of mold in the change room of Mike's boxing club. The place ought to be condemned, but guys like Mike loved it. "If I want to see that many tattoos in one place I'll hang out at a biker bar."

"Same difference. You'll still end up beaten to a pulp," Mike told him cheerfully. "At least at the club you get a helmet and mouth guard."

"Couldn't you at least find somewhere clean?"

Wet hair flicked his shoulders as Mike shook his head. "Your trouble is you're a snob."

"That's what Caro said," he told his old "buddy," glaring at him as he did so. "Right before she dropped the surprising news that she's working for my competition—*your* paper."

Mike picked up a menu and opened it and Jon fought the impulse to pull it from his hands and whack him over the head with it. The hunter-green leather folder wouldn't do Mike's thick head any harm, but the gesture would make Jon feel better.

"I had nothing to do with hiring her, you know. That was Mel."

"I can't believe she'd stoop to that...that... tabloid."

Mike glanced up, a half-humorous, half-warning expression on his face. "Hey, I work there and we're still friends."

"I'm not living with you!"

"Don't want to rub salt into the wound, but you're not living with Caro, either."

Jon drank his coffee, hot and black and bitter. "I can't believe she's being so stubborn. I'd no more cheat on her than I'd cut off my right arm."

"It's no fun for any of us. I'm glad Caro told you. I didn't think it was my place to blab, but I hated not telling you. So it's out now and we all stay friends, okay?" Mike's head tilted at a belligerent angle that reminded Jon of how many hours he spent boxing. But few people knew him better. Jon understood the aggressive gesture masked how awkward Mike was feeling with the situation.

He forced himself to relax. This whole mess wasn't Mike's fault. "I'm warning you, if you and Tess ever have troubles don't ask me for help."

A short bark of laughter reached him. "With your track record, you're the last guy I'd ask."

Jon couldn't help himself; he laughed, too.

They spent a moment with the menu and both chose the signature breakfast: three eggs, bacon, sausage, hash browns, toast, the works.

Once they'd placed their order, Jon leaned across the table and asked Mike, "How is she doing really?"

"Ask Tess. Chicks know stuff like that. She looks great, writes decent copy. I think she likes what she's doing."

Mike fiddled with his silverware, which made Jon suspect there was something unpleasant coming.

"Maybe I shouldn't tell you this, but Mel's thinking of hiring her the next time a full-time reporting job comes open."

"How do you know?"

"Because I recommended her for the job."

Jon felt as though he'd been sucker punched and he wished they were at the boxing club so he could use his fists on his former friend. "You recommended my wife to work full-time for that... that..."

"It's a tabloid. It's not the *Satanic Daily Bulletin.* Maybe we don't cater to snobs like you, but the regular people like our paper fine, thanks."

He wanted to tell Mike that Caro wasn't like those tabloid readers, she was a *Standard* woman, but that would only make him sound like more of a stuck-up jerk.

"Why did you recommend her?" He wouldn't have expected his worst enemy to pull a stunt that would hurt him so much.

"She's terrific." Mike gazed at him as though

he were toying with him. "Believe me, your loss is our gain. Ah, I mean, your paper's loss."

"But Caro was working on bringing us up to speed on our fashion section. You don't even have a fashion section."

"If you ever stooped to read our paper, you'd know she's working on human-interest features. She loves talking to people and they open up to her. She's amazing at that. Didn't you know?"

It appeared he hadn't. Of course, he'd seen how well she did at cocktail parties and she always seemed at ease with his friends, no matter how pretentious they might be—and some of his classmates from Harvard law gave the term new meaning—but he never thought of her as writing features.

It hadn't occurred to him that she'd want to. Or, if he were brutally honest with himself, that she'd be capable of it.

He was aware that he and Mike had broken their unwritten, unspoken rule not to talk about Caro. Mike had been there for him at the beginning, offering uncritical friendship when he'd needed it. But Caro and Tess were best friends, so a dual friendship had worked out well once Tess and Mike got together. Unfortunately it was doomed to disaster when Jon and Caro split up.

Now, he was more careful around Mike, and Caro was the reason. He accepted it on the assumption that Caro and Tess were also just as cautious when it came to conversations about him.

He wanted to pour out his guts and to tell Mike how much he missed his wife and how much he wanted her back. Instead, he attacked his meal with gusto and refused to whine.

Along with his bacon and eggs, he'd digested this new information. Caro was a feature writer, was she?

As he'd worked on his strategic plan to get his wife back last night, he'd stalled at the first move—how to get her in his vicinity for an hour just so they could talk.

If she wouldn't come to him for the asking—which he knew she wouldn't—he wondered if the *Star* would be interested in doing a feature on a certain project he was working on. And he knew just the reporter for the job.

He realized he was hungry and gave his attention over to the food, doing his best to put Caro temporarily out of his mind, and steering the conversation into calmer waters. "You have to admit this is the best bacon and eggs to be had in Pasqualie."

"You are so out of touch," Mike replied, clearly equally happy to change the subject. "Big Ed's Diner. Three eggs, half a dozen slices of bacon, toast and coffee. $2.95."

At least some things in his world stayed constant, he thought as he rolled his gaze. "I'll give Ed's best breakfast *under three bucks,* but nobody beats the hungry-man breakfast here at the club."

And lately he'd been having a lot of meals here.

It was a convenient excuse to himself and anyone he ran into that he was grabbing a meal after his workout, but the truth was, he was working out *so* he could eat here. He hated eating at home all alone, and his mom's bar wasn't a place he could stomach every night of the week. Going to a restaurant alone was all right once in a while, but he was determined not to act pathetic, so he usually organized business dinners.

"I want to ask you something," Mike said through a mouthful of eggs.

"Sure."

"This is kind of weird, but you're the only one I want."

"You're right, that's kind of weird."

After shooting him a don't-push-me glance, Mike said, in his surliest street-fighter tone, "I want you to help me find a tux for the wedding."

Jon choked on his coffee. Mike must be deeper in love than even he had guessed if Tess had talked him into a tuxedo. "I'm honored."

"But will you do it?"

Mike was running a finger under the frayed neck of his T-shirt as though imagining being choked by a tie.

"Of course," Jon said. "I'm thinking John Travolta in *Saturday Night Fever*." In case there was any doubt in Mike's mind what he meant, Jon struck the famous pose, index finger pointing to the ceiling.

Mike snorted. "What I wear, you wear, buddy. You're the best man." He sighed noisily. "I can't believe Tess talked me into a monkey suit."

Privately, Jon didn't think Tess would have any trouble getting Mike to do or wear whatever she wanted, but he kept that thought to himself.

"Tess is bugging me to get them ordered. She already has her wedding dress and Caro's maid-of-honor dress is being made."

"Matron of honor. Caro's married," Jon said automatically.

"Yeah, whatever." A frown crossed his face. "Are you two going to be able to stomach each other?"

"I hope we can put aside our differences to celebrate the wedding of our dearest friends." Privately, Jon was filled with glee that Caro would have to deal with him. He hadn't thought much about Tess and Mike's wedding, but being reminded that he and Caro were the chief attendants at the wedding gave him a perfect opportunity to contact her. They'd have to work together on wedding-related activities, and he'd be her escort for the big day.

He smiled to himself.

Maybe he'd rethink step one of his strategic plan.

He'd always been lucky at weddings.

4

CARO RAN for the phone, dripping water on the faded Persian rug of her friend Melanie's town house. Originally, she was only going to take care of the plants while Melanie was on vacation, but when Caro had discovered Jon was cheating, the town house had provided a refuge until she could organize her future.

The towel she had clutched to her chest left her just this side of indecent as she grabbed the receiver.

In the old days she'd leave the phone if she didn't feel like answering it, but since she'd started freelancing she'd become its slave. The phone was her lifeline to a job and a world outside. Both of which she needed right now.

"Hello?" she said, grabbing a dish towel from a black wrought-iron rack in the kitchen to dab the drips off her face.

"Were you in the shower?" an amused male voice asked.

She pulled the towel tighter around her chest and sank on wobbly legs to one of the breakfast bar stools.

"Jonathon."

She didn't care that he couldn't see her; she felt ridiculously exposed and vulnerable in nothing but a towel.

Who else knew her so well that he could guess her predicament when she'd spoken one word?

"Well, were you?" He still sounded amused, but his voice had dropped to a huskier tone, the one he adopted to tease her when they were together. Water dripped to the hardwood floor, but she didn't have the coordination right now to wipe up the puddle.

"What do you want?" She heard her own voice soften as images from their happier days crowded her mind. If he was here right now, and they were still married, that towel would hit the floor in seconds. The thought filled her with a longing to turn back the clock that was so fierce she had to grip the kitchen countertop.

"I can't begin to tell you all the things I want. Why don't I come over there and show you?" He wasn't teasing. His tone was serious and pulled at her to respond.

Oh, how she wanted to.

Then, as she felt herself weakening, an image of Lori Gerhardt, the woman who'd been Jon's advertising sales manager, rose up in front of Caro, as lifelike as the day she'd found Lori naked in her own bed—with Jon getting ready to join her.

No. She reminded herself. She wasn't being

completely accurate. Lori hadn't been naked. She'd worn a G-string.

"If you're feeling lonely, I'm sure Lori Gerhardt would be happy to oblige you," she said with frigid politeness.

"Lori Gerhardt took a job in Houston, as you very well know. And, for the thousandth time, there was nothing going on between us!" He'd dropped the sexy teasing and sounded furious. Which made her so mad she wanted to break something. Preferably over his pig head.

"You didn't call me to talk about old history, I hope."

He blew out a breath, something he always did when he was frustrated. "No. I called because we're both standing up for Mike and Tess. I don't want to spoil their day so I thought we should get together first."

"What are you talking about?" Gooseflesh spread along her upper arms and shoulders and she rubbed the chilled skin with the end of her towel.

"I think we should spend some time together before the wedding, clear the air, so we don't embarrass ourselves and ruin our friends' wedding."

She almost laughed. Jon had always been a man of creative ideas. "Are you suggesting we make a date to yell at each other and throw things?"

"If that's what it takes so we can be civil to each other, then yes."

"I'm not sure there's anything that can make me

civil to you,'' she told him honestly. As hard as she'd tried to put her marriage in the past and move forward with zenlike tranquility, she only had to think of Jon and rage boiled within her.

''Then you should tell Tess you can't be her matron of honor.''

''Bridesmaid,'' she snapped. ''And I most certainly will be there for Tess on her wedding day, just like…''

There was a pause, and he finished the sentence she'd begun. ''Just like she was for you.''

She blinked rapidly. She would not remember her beautiful wedding to Jonathon and all the hopes and dreams they'd had, and she wouldn't cry. Her job now was to pull herself together and to figure out what she wanted to do with the rest of her life.

''Don't worry, Jon. I won't be uncivil to you. I'll simply ignore you.'' She wondered how he'd take that. He wasn't used to being ignored by women. The idea of him being stuck with a date who wanted him living on the other side of the solar system was mildly amusing.

She could never pay him back for the pain he'd caused her, but she wasn't above a tiny spot of revenge. If she had to spend the better part of a day and evening with him, she'd do it with style.

Jonathon would be escorting an iceberg.

She was delighted her best friend Tess wanted her to be her bridesmaid. It was unfortunate that Mike had the bad taste to be friends with Jon. Although they'd been friends since they were kids and played on the same Little League team, she always found it hard to imagine the scrappy street kid and the well-to-do preppy becoming best friends.

Remarkably they had. And more remarkably they'd stayed friends over the years while Jon went to Harvard and Mike went to the school of hard knocks as he was so fond of telling everyone.

If Mike wouldn't dump his childhood friend because he'd cheated on his wife-to-be's bridesmaid, she supposed she couldn't completely hate him for it. She'd suggested to Tess that someone else stand in her place, but her friend had insisted she wanted Caro, so she'd agreed.

The wedding was only a couple of weeks away. She hoped the fact that she and Jon were getting divorced wouldn't jinx Mike and Tess's future. She didn't think it would, but she was just superstitious enough that she'd held off visiting her lawyer until after the wedding.

A *brrrp* caused her to glance down to where her cat, Cyclops, winked her one good eye at her, then licked at the puddle with her delicate pink tongue.

"I've got to get ready for work, Jonathon. So, if you've nothing else to talk about, I have to—"

"There is something else." She gritted her teeth and waited for him to start in on her about her new job, but, amazingly, he didn't.

"It's about Mom's birthday party."

Cyclops had abandoned the puddle of water and started licking Caro's big toe. The sandpapery tongue made her squirm, but she wouldn't pull away. After finding the small cat, one-eyed, matted and mewing plaintively in her backyard, Caro had taken her in and given her a home, then brought her to Melanie's when she moved. In the last few awful weeks, Cyclops had helped her as much as she'd helped the homeless stray. She had a feeling they had quite a bit in common, both being defective and abandoned.

She pulled her mind away from her misery and tried to concentrate on Fanny. "Yes?"

"I wanted to thank you." Jon's voice sounded almost hesitant. "You were right. I've canceled Le Beaumari and I'm going to do the party at the Roadhouse."

"That's great, Jon." Her voice came out warmer than she'd intended it. She wanted Fanny to have a special party, for she was a special woman, even if she had spawned a womanizing heartbreaker.

"I know it's a lot to ask, but I was wondering if you'd help me with the party. Now I've got to start from scratch and I've only got a week."

She paused to think about it, wishing she could tell him what he could do with his party, but it was for Fanny, after all. Besides, it was her advice that had caused him to change his plans. "I'll do what I can," she said at last, "but I'm doing it for her."

"I appreciate it. We've got all the guests to

phone about the change of plans. Caterers to book.''

She nodded, even though he couldn't see her. ''Decorations. A cake. A live band would be nice.''

''Yes. It would. I'll get back to you when I have more details.'' He was cold and clipped, as businesslike as though she'd been an advertiser who owed the paper big bucks. Ha. He should be groveling at her feet.

Once she hung up, she bent to pick up the cat, a much heavier bundle than when she'd found it hanging around her back door, skinny, frightened and alone. ''We're just a couple of abandoned strays, aren't we?''

Cyclops purred and snuggled under her chin. Since they'd adopted each other, the cat had begun to groom itself meticulously and her coat was soft where it touched Caro's skin above the towel.

''WHAT AM I GOING TO DO?'' Caro wailed to Tess after summoning her friend with an SOS call to meet at the out-of-the-way Mexican restaurant they patronized when they wanted privacy.

Once settled into the Naugahyde booth, she realized she was starving and since she wanted everything on the menu, ordered the Fiesta plate.

Tess blinked at her. ''I've never seen you order anything but a taco salad.''

''I'm expanding my horizons. And starving,'' she admitted, grabbing for the basket of tortilla chips and salsa in the center of the table while Tess watched her in amazement and sipped iced tea. Some days the thought of food made Caro queasy and other days she pigged out. It must be stress. In between scarfing chips, Caro relayed her excruciating conversation with Jonathon almost word for word.

Her friend had been blessed with classic good looks, but since she'd found love she'd bloomed. There was a new warmth and approachability to her that Caro loved.

Tess put down her tea and leaned forward, almost whispering. "I can't believe he suggested a shouting-and-throwing-things session. That sounds so...Mike."

She was right of course. Mike was the kind of guy who blew up even when he wasn't particularly mad, as she'd discovered from the daily temper-fests between him and Mel. "Well, it's a phenomenally stupid idea."

"You never did have a let-it-all-hang-out emotional scene. You must be the only couple in America who could break up without a single yelling match."

Caro sniffed. "I wouldn't stoop to that level."

Tess looked as though she wanted to say something, then changed her mind. She shook her head. "So why does he want to host a screaming match now?"

"He says it's so we'll be civil to each other at your wedding."

"You two are always civil." Tess reached for a chip from the rapidly emptying bowl. "If you ask me, that's part of the problem. What's he really afraid of?"

"That I'll embarrass him as a date, I suppose."

"So, bring your own date."

Caro stared at her friend for a stunned moment. Tess had an almost regal air that made you want to watch your language around her. Normally she was meticulously groomed, but today, her short blond hair was tousled and her blouse sported a wrinkle or two, as though she'd scrambled this morning to get to work.

Caro felt momentarily depressed that she was so perfectly coiffed and unwrinkled. Nobody was keeping her in bed late in the mornings. Tess's matter-of-fact strategy echoed in her head until she repeated it out loud. "Bring another date?"

Apart from the satisfied expression of a woman happy in love, Tess also had a gleam of mischief in her eyes. "Why not? We asked you two to stand up for us, it doesn't mean you have to show up and leave together."

For a long delighted moment, Caro imagined the look on Jonathon's face when she walked in on another man's arm. "That is such a great idea. I can't believe I didn't think of it."

"Well, start thinking."

Her glee dimmed rapidly. "Who would I bring?

All I could scrape up would be pity dates, and Jon knows all the same people I do."

Tess shook her head. "You need the big guns for this one. A movie star would be best." She tapped her fingers on the varnished wood tabletop. "I interviewed John Cusack last year for a movie he was promoting. I still have his publicist's phone number."

Caro just stared at her.

"Come on, we're brainstorming. Every gorgeous man on the planet is up for consideration. Oh, I know." She leaned forward, her big blue eyes sparkling with excitement. "Didn't you do a charity fashion show with Hugh Jackman? What about him?"

Caro shook her head, trying not to laugh. At least she was starting to feel better. "One—he's married. Two—Australia is a long way from Pasqualie. Three…" She thought hard. "There is no three. He's the perfect date, except for One and Two."

"When you were modeling you hung out with all those beautiful people. There must be someone."

"Rupert Everett was a lot of fun."

"We're trying to make Jon jealous here. What about one of those male models with their six-pack abs and stunning biceps."

Tess put her head in her hand. It had been such a long time since she'd dated anyone. And as spectacular as a lot of the male models had been, there was no one she'd ever been close friends with, except for…

She jerked upright and snapped her fingers. "I've got it. Andre Giardin."

"Never heard of him." Tess was obviously still daydreaming about movie stars.

"You'd recognize him if you saw him. He does a lot of magazine work. He's gorgeous in a real man way, funny, charming and—"

"Gay?"

"Not gay. Married."

"Does Jon know him?"

Caro grinned, suddenly filled with enthusiasm for this faux-date idea. Jon had ripped her heart out of her chest and stomped on it. Now he seemed to think all he had to do was call and she'd come crawling back. What he needed was a taste of his own medicine.

"No. Jon doesn't know him. Andre and I worked together a lot in New York, but after I moved here and got married, I didn't see much of him. He also got married, had a couple of kids."

"Where does he live now?"

"Somewhere in Oregon. We're working on the Fashionistas for Animal Rights show in Seattle. That's what made me think of him."

Tess raised her eyebrows. "You're modeling?"

"Sure."

"But you never model anymore."

"I decided to do this one because it's a cause I

believe in. I wish we'd had a chance to get that animal shelter up and running before Jon and I split up.''

Tess nodded. ''That was a wonderful project and you were both so keen. Couldn't you still go ahead?''

''The land belongs to the *Standard* and it was already rezoned by council especially for the refuge. To start all over again without Jonathon...'' She shook her head slowly. ''Right now, I simply don't have the energy. But I can take part in the Fashionistas for Animal Rights, at least, and scoop myself a dream date for your wedding.''

''This Andre sounds perfect. Will he do it?''

She shrugged. ''He's always enjoyed practical jokes, and if somebody needs a lesson, yes, I think he'll do it. Besides, I introduced him to his wife. He owes me.'' Caro laughed. ''I love it.''

Tess laughed, too, but not so heartily. ''You're sure about this?''

''What do you mean? This date was your idea.''

''I know, it's just that you and Jonathon...''

''Are finished.''

''But you're both... I don't know...interested in each other.''

Caro felt a flash of something she couldn't name. Somewhere between hope and fury. ''Does Jonathon ask you about me?''

''Only every time I see him.''

''What do you tell him?''

Tess rolled her eyes. "What do you think I tell him? I'm your friend. I tell him you're doing great. Never been happier, blah, blah, blah. You wouldn't believe the lies I tell."

"I *am* happy." Caro grabbed hot sauce and squirted it all over her enchiladas.

"And I'm a brunette."

Caro sighed. "Well, I'm as happy as I can be right now." She sucked up her negative emotions and pulled her shoulders back. "I'm facing the future, not revisiting the past."

Tess leaned over and touched her wrist. "I know."

"And it absolutely and totally sucks," she said, gripping her friend's hand.

"I don't think of myself as a cruel woman, but I'd like to take Lori Gerhardt apart."

Caro shook her head. "I've been reading a lot of self-help books lately. They say you have to put the blame where it belongs. Lori was simply an enabler, but Jon chose infidelity."

"Then how come she was next-door-to-naked and he was fully clothed when you found them together?"

It was too painful to contemplate, so she mostly didn't. Except at night sometimes when she couldn't sleep and the scene rose in front of her in every hideous detail.

"He couldn't fire her, but Jon got her that job in Houston and made her take it, you know."

"Moving forward, not gazing into the past," Caro mumbled, and stuffed another enchilada in her face.

There was a pause. "I guess your new career is about the future. How's it going?"

Caro glanced up at her friend, grateful for the change of subject. "I love it. Thanks for not telling Jon about my work with the *Star*. I bumped into him at Fanny's and he just about swallowed his tie when I told him."

"If it makes you happy that's great. But are you sure you're not working for the *Star* merely to drive Jon crazy?"

"No. I'm working at the *Star* because I love it. Driving Jon crazy is a side benefit."

5

"CARO, CAN YOU COME IN here a minute?" the *Star*'s managing editor bellowed through her doorway as Caro passed.

When she'd first started freelancing for the paper, she'd been appalled at the way Mel managed the news department. Caro had thought the *Standard* newsroom was chaotic, but it was an oasis of calm next to this place.

After years of modeling and being a corporate wife, she felt she could handle a smartmouth and a loudmouth, but unfortunately, Mel possessed both.

However, in her short time here, Caro had come to accept it was simply Mel's way.

She usually got her assignments from the features editor, but occasionally Mel would assign her a piece. Caro always trembled slightly in the older woman's presence. But she took comfort in knowing most everyone did.

"Yes, Mel," she said, keeping her voice deliberately at a normal level, though she had no idea why she bothered. Mel wasn't one to notice a good example, much less follow it.

''I've got something—'' She broke off when Caro entered her office, running her gaze up and down Caro's length. Too used to Mel's odd behavior to fidget, Caro stood still, raising her brows slightly in a gesture that had repressed many a man eager to get the fashion model out of her high fashion as soon as possible.

''Is that another new dress?'' Mel mostly wore pant suits that were pretty much interchangeable. She looked about the same every day. Her bleached cropped hair was always mussed from her habit of running her hands through it while she was thinking, and her lipstick was always worn down to a thin line around her lips from her smoking addiction. She got most of her exercise jogging back and forth to the closest outside door for a smoke break.

''No. I've had it a couple of years.''

Mel ran her fingers through her hair and Caro tried not to wince. ''It was bad enough when Tess started hanging around here to smooch with Mike. I don't think the place can take too many high-society types.''

''Is that why you wanted to see me?'' Caro was half amused. What was she supposed to do? Toss out her wardrobe and start showing up in jeans and a leather jacket?

''No. I've got something better to do than worry about what people are wearing. So long as you turn in decent copy you can come to work nude for all I care.'' She gave a short bark of her trademark laughter. "No. Then the guys would never get any work done. I insist on at least a G-string."

Caro stiffened. The term *G-string* brought back the afternoon when her seemingly perfect life had turned out to be a total sham, and Jonathon a lying cheat.

Mel cleared her throat and mumbled something, which only embarrassed Caro more. Of course everyone in town knew all the sordid details of her breakup. She wondered why she even stayed on in Pasqualie with nothing but bad memories and a population that knew her most intimate humiliation.

"I've got an assignment for you," Mel said briskly, staring at a sheet of paper in her hands.

Pulling her mind back to the present, thankful once more that she had work to keep her thoughts off her troubles, she asked, "What is it?"

"Sit down."

That was odd. Mel never invited anyone to sit. She wasn't one for idle chitchat and wasting time.

Caro searched behind her for a chair, located one under a pile of old newspapers, which she pushed to the floor, and sat. The fake leather seat squeaked in protest as though it wasn't sat on very often.

Mel was running her fingers through her hair again. Absentmindedly, she pulled a cigarette from a dented pack and stuck it in her mouth. She didn't light it; even she'd given up trying to fight the city's no-smoking bylaws.

"I have a story I think might interest you," she mumbled around the cigarette. "A wildlife refuge right here in Pasqualie."

"What?" How could such a project be happening without her, when she'd conceived the idea. She'd organized fund-raisers, bullied and cajoled Jon into giving up a chunk of land the *Standard* owned out past the building that housed the printing press. When he'd bought the building it had come with a huge parcel of land, and she thought he'd actually been quite pleased to give some up for a good cause.

"Think of the great P.R.," she'd teased.

"I am. I am," he'd retorted, but at the time she'd believed they shared a common cause.

Since a recent municipal corruption scandal had been exposed by Mike Grundel and Tess Elliot, the mayor and council were now sticklers for following every law, statute and bylaw to the letter. The wildlife refuge could go ahead only if its founders ensured that the refuge was self-supporting and wouldn't need to be bailed out by city coffers. Jon had gone one better, promising that the *Standard* would take responsibility for the refuge—as a corporate charity, backed by him personally.

It was the day they'd found out the project could go ahead that she and Jon had last made love. The next day she'd come home from work to find Lori gyrating on her three-hundred-thread-count Egyptian cotton sheets. Then Caro and Jon had split up and the last thing on her mind—or presumably his—had been the refuge.

She wondered who had picked up the dropped ball. Tess's mother, Rose Elliot, was one of the volunteer board members, as was Jeremy Dennis, the director of Bald Is Beautiful, an organization dedicated to preserving bald eagles in the area.

Was it one of them who'd continued to work on the project?

She and Jon had also recruited a schoolteacher, since they believed the refuge offered educational opportunities for local schoolkids. A member of council sat on the board, as did a couple of members at large from the community. Any of them could have resurrected the idea, but would it have killed them to give her a call?

She immediately felt ashamed of herself for being so small-minded as to feel offended they'd gone ahead without her. For all she knew this was a completely different group working on another refuge. All that mattered was the shelter. She and Jon had become known as the people to see in town if you came across a wounded or orphaned animal. Between them and their veterinarian they'd nursed injured eagles, orphaned bear cubs, and any number of deer, squirrels, rabbits and small birds hit by cars. Some they couldn't save, but a gratifying number were back swimming, flying or running in their natural habitat.

Aware that Mel hated editorializing, she didn't

squeal, "That's great," as she wanted to, but merely nodded, flipped open her notepad and said, "Go on."

Questions were racing through her head. Who was behind this new effort? Would they be able to use the *Standard* land? Might she be able to volunteer in some capacity without affecting her credibility as an impartial journalist covering the story?

"There's not much to tell. I wish we didn't have to cover the story since Jonathon Kushner's involved, but then we'd look like immature weenies." She dragged on her unlit cigarette. "I hate that."

"Jonathon?" Caro stared at her, thinking if she wanted to act like an immature weenie she darn well would. And, depending on where this conversation was going, she felt an incipient weenie attack coming on.

There was a pause during which she heard the background soundtrack of a busy newsroom—keyboards clacking, voices on phones or chatting. Footsteps jogged past Mel's open door. Somebody was late for something. Wherever they were going, Caro passionately wanted to join them, and jog side by side out of here.

"So we need to do a story." Mel stared at her expectantly.

"Are you suggesting I cover this story?"

"Yeah." Mel made a merry-go-round of the

word, dragging it out to four syllables and covering her complete vocal register.

Caro refused to lose her cool. She leaned back and crossed her legs. "What aspect of the story did you want me to cover?"

"What aspect? This isn't a Mideast peace deal, hon, it's an animal shelter. You go out there, interview Kushner and give me five hundred words by Thursday."

"But Jonathon and I are separated."

"So what? That lowlife Marco Desudrio is my ex, but I still buy my corned beef from his deli 'cause it's the best in town."

"Jonathon and I aren't...on those kind of terms."

Mel leaned forward and took the cigarette out of her mouth. "Honey, take my advice. Pasqualie is not New York, where you could live your whole life and never see your ex. You either need to get yourself on *those* kinds of terms, especially if you're planning to stay in the news business, or else get out of town."

Caro knew that. She simply hadn't decided yet what she was going to do, and she resented being pushed.

"Did Jon put you up to this?" He was doing it deliberately, she knew it in her gut. This whole animal shelter was nothing but a pathetic excuse to make her life miserable.

More miserable.

"A press release put me up to this." Mel's lips thinned, emphasizing the thin red line that remained on the very extremities of her lips.

Caro had often wished for the courage to give her some makeup advice, but she knew she didn't have that much in stock. And today, the only thing she noticed about Mel's lips was that she didn't care for the words coming out of them. "Couldn't you assign the story to someone else?"

"Of course I could. But only one person on my staff knows all about the project. Only one person gives a rat's ass about saving a rat's ass. And that—" she poked the cigarette in Caro's direction "—is you."

It was undeniably true, but Caro refused to be manipulated quite so easily. "Isn't there someone else I could interview about the shelter?"

"Jon's the president of the shelter society and he's the one who okayed the land deal. Plus it makes the *Star* look mature and noble interviewing a rival publisher."

A flicker of reluctant amusement had Caro's lips quirking. Mel was so easy to read, which Jon had no doubt banked on. "And if I interview anyone else we'll look like a bunch of immature weenies?"

"I knew you had brains underneath all those designer labels." She handed Caro a press release and said, "It's all set up for three o'clock today. Jonathon's office."

"Not at the site?" The last thing she wanted to

do was skip into Jon's office. She hadn't been near the place since the split.

"There's nothing at the site. Talk to Jon about faking something out there for our photographer, but the meeting's set up at his office."

"Very well. I'll do the interview by phone."

"Don't push me! If you care so much about those animals, you should want to get a nice article in our paper. We'll put a thumb-sucking blurb at the end telling people they should contribute blah, blah, blah. I hate those."

The list of things Caro would rather do than interview her husband at three o'clock today was so huge she could paper the earth with it and still have enough paper left to go to the moon.

She'd been conned. But where Jon, and no doubt Mel, knew they had her was that she would do a lot more than see her ex-husband if it would help save animals.

Still, if she had to see Jonathon again, she'd like time to choose the outfit. No one knew better than an ex-fashion model what messages clothing could send. She must have something in her closet in Drop-Dead.

"MR. KUSHNER, Mrs. Kush—" He heard a mumbled exchange of female voices and then, "Um, *Caroline* to see you."

"Send her in," he said, hoping his voice didn't betray his delight.

He hadn't been certain she'd come. Not all the

Mels or wounded animals in the world could make Caro do something she didn't want to do. And nothing, but nothing, would make her change her mind once she'd made it up, as he'd discovered in the most painful way possible.

She walked in and, as she'd done the first time he'd seen her, she made him blink with surprise that any woman could look so flawlessly gorgeous outside of a movie screen or glossy magazine. "You get more beautiful every time I see you," he said, taking pride in the fact that she was his, forgetting for the moment that she wasn't.

She gave him the look she usually reserved for slime and pervs and pulled out her notebook. "Shall we get started?"

He sighed. "Have a seat." He indicated the round table and chairs in one corner, thinking it would be easier for her to take notes. She sank gracefully into a chair. But then, she did everything gracefully. She flipped open her notebook and he saw that she'd come prepared with a list of questions.

As Caro glanced at them, he wondered who she thought she was kidding. Years in the newspaper business had taught him to read upside down. He could see the series of neatly penned questions in her even, curved handwriting, and immediately suspected that she'd scribbled and crossed out and fussed over them and then rewritten her list. She'd obviously decided to pretend he was a stranger and that she was coming into this story cold.

He settled back, prepared to let her interview him. While she was doing that he'd have the luxury of staring at her, which he'd missed. When she finished the interview he hoped she'd be relaxed enough that they could talk.

It annoyed him to have to manipulate his own wife into a conversation, but this impasse was becoming ridiculous.

Lillian had strict orders that she was to hold all calls and to admit no one while Caro was with him. She was enough of a friend that he had no doubt she'd throw herself bodily at anyone who tried to interrupt the interview.

He had all the time in the world, knew they wouldn't be distracted, and they were on his turf, all according to his carefully crafted strategic plan.

"Why did you decide to open an animal sanctuary?" She read the question then gazed up at him and it felt as if his heart hiccuped. It wasn't her beauty this time that caught him off guard, but the expression in her eyes. It was cool and remote, and he'd known and loved her for long enough to recognize the hurt and anger smoldering under the blue ice.

She already knew the answer to her question; it was because she, Caro, had wanted it. She'd seen that the local animal shelter was full to overcrowded with abandoned cats and dogs and had no room, never mind resources, for wild animals that were injured or orphaned too young to fend for themselves.

Jon used to laugh and say saving orphaned animals fulfilled her baby urge, but after almost a year of trying to get pregnant, they'd stopped with the jokes.

Their lovemaking had been timed to her biological clock—not the one that said it was the time in her life to have a child but the one that said, "I'm fertile for the next forty-eight hours. Go. Now." It could sure take the fun out of sex.

He shook his head to scramble his thoughts into some semblance of order, "I wanted to do something..." he said, wishing he could offer some gesture to prove to her that he still cared for her, an act that would break through her angry refusal to face the problems in their marriage. No. He'd promised himself to ease into all that. She was still gazing at him and he wanted to tell her that if she expected any sense out of him she should look the other way. He couldn't stare into her eyes and not remember...not want—

"You wanted to do something..." she prompted.

"Right. The committee and I decided to go ahead and get P.W.R., that's Pasqualie Wildlife Refuge," he said as though it might be news to her, "up and running before summer."

"Why now?" she asked. She wasn't looking at her notes but at him, and he'd seen her next question was about community support. The "why now" had been off the cuff. So she felt left out, did she? Maybe if she'd returned any of his calls she'd have known the committee was meeting again.

Since she'd departed from her script, he decided to depart from his, as well. Keeping his gaze on hers, he said, "Just over a month ago, we got the approval from the city to go ahead."

He still remembered how excited they'd been when they got the news. He and Caro had made love that night even though she'd been a day or two away from prime fertility and, according to the books and charts, they should hold off, saving Jon for stud service at the peak. But they'd got carried away and it had been how it used to be, before getting pregnant had turned into a giant chore and source of constant stress.

She'd glanced at him that certain way she had and one thing had led to another. It had been the most fun they'd had in months.

CARO STARED AT JONATHON, knowing he was remembering their last night together. Her body eased imperceptibly forward as she remembered it, too. His eyes darkened as sexual awareness hovered between them, and her lips parted on a sigh.

Then pain clouded her vision as she recalled the following day when she'd come home to find another woman in her bed.

Why had he fooled around? Was it because they'd become so baby focused? Or was it because they'd learned she was infertile and he wanted greener pastures?

While she puzzled over questions she refused to ask, Jonathon sat across from her, looking much more handsome and sexy than any almost ex-husband should be allowed to look. Really, there should be a law.

"Well," he said as the silence lengthened, a note of amusement creeping into his tone. "Do you have any more questions?"

"You didn't answer the first one." She crossed out her neatly handwritten list with a single pen stroke. "Why are you doing this now?"

"You want the real reason?"

Did she? "Yes," she said, very much afraid she didn't.

"I did it to get one hour where you and I could talk like sensible adults."

Oh, no. She didn't want that at all. It scared her so much she wanted to run. "I'm not here as a sensible adult. I'm here as a reporter."

"You know more about this shelter than I do. I'll give you a couple of good quotes and we're done. Then I want to talk to you."

"I only want to talk about the refuge."

"I got a call from Jeremy. A logger found a peregrine falcon with a broken wing. Hit by a car."

She nodded. The birds sometimes hunted near

highways then got stunned by headlights. The peregrine had been decimated by pesticides and urbanization of its habitat, but through a worldwide breeding program, it was coming back. Still, there were too few. Saving an injured bird was an important service.

"The vet fixed it up, but nobody knows what to do with it. You know as well as I do that it won't have a chance in the wild while it's healing. I decided to fast-track the shelter to give injured animals like that falcon a temporary home. That's all."

He looked a tiny bit pink, as though embarrassed to be thought an animal lover.

Don't ask, she warned herself. *It's not your problem.* But she couldn't stop the words from tumbling out of her mouth.

"Where is it now?"

"What, the falcon?"

"Mmm-hmm."

"At the house."

"The house?"

"I didn't know what to do with it."

"But, Jon, you can't let it become used to humans. It's the worst thing you can do."

He shook his head, looking sad. "This guy's never going to fly again. I thought we'd let him be our first permanent shelter resident."

She wanted to see that falcon, but while she could be strong here at the paper, she didn't think she could stop herself wallowing in misery if she went to the home she and Jonathon had shared.

She could hardly stand thinking of the shelter and how hard they'd worked on it together only to be shut out.

He must know what she was thinking. "Why don't you come by later and see him? He's eating well, but you might have some ideas for improving his surroundings."

No. No. No. She wasn't getting dragged back into her old life. "I have to leave," she said.

She got up quickly, intending to make a fast exit, but dizziness overcame her. She blinked and swayed as the room spun around her.

As she took a staggering step toward the door, Jon was there, his hands warm and strong as they grasped her shoulders.

"Hey, there," he said.

"O-oh." She put a shaky hand to her head, still feeling woozy. "Got up too fast."

It was so familiar, feeling him holding her like this, his eyes focused on hers with warmth and caring.

She swayed into him, inhaling his scent, so familiar and yet already slightly exotic from their weeks apart.

His hands slipped up over her shoulders, one going to rest on her upper back, the other beneath her hair in a gesture that was as natural as it was welcome.

"Are you all right? You look a little pale."

She'd rest here in his arms just for a second until she felt strong enough to walk. Right now her legs would buckle under her if he let her go, which he showed no signs of doing.

His eyes were such a deep, dark blue, and she loved the tiny lines that fanned out from the corners as much as she loved the few silver hairs that threaded through his short black hair. She was a tall woman, but he was a taller man. They'd always fit together so well.

For a long moment they simply stared at each other, each afraid to shatter the moment. She felt herself lean into him even as the sensible part of her tried to resist. But resistance wasn't an option. As his mouth moved toward hers, her eyes drifted shut.

He kissed her softly and she felt herself yearning for more when he pulled back a fraction of an inch.

"I miss you," he said.

"Mmm," she said, her eyes still closed, her lips still uptilted for another kiss.

"Come home with me."

Oh, how she wanted to. "I can't. We're separated."

"We could unseparate."

Her eyes snapped open to find him staring at her with more frustration than passion in his eyes. "I don't—"

"It wasn't about Lori."

"Pardon?" She could not believe he had the poor taste to bring up that woman's name. She took a big step back, leaning against the table for support.

"The reason you ran out on me." He made a frustrated sound. "I've had weeks to think about this. About why you ran so fast and refused to listen to what I had to say."

"Oh, so now you're a psychologist as well as a philanderer?"

"I'm the man who loves you, who always loved you. Probably always will. I never slept with Lori Gerhardt."

"Hmm. And if I'd walked in five minutes later I wonder if that would still be true."

"I wish to hell you *had* walked in five minutes later—you'd have seen Lori on her way out."

Caro curled her nails into her palm, turning her hand into a fist that she dearly wanted to pound him with. "I'm supposed to believe you didn't invite her?"

"I've told you I didn't."

"How did she get in? Climb in the window? Slide under the door without setting off the security system?"

He shook his head, glaring at Caro as though this were somehow her fault. And the worst part was she wanted to believe him. She was that pathetic. "She made up a story for the cleaner, said I'd sent her to get something. That got her in. The cleaner never actually saw her leave, just heard her call goodbye.''

''This sounds like something out of a soap opera.''

''Maybe that's where she got the idea. All I know is she put herself in our bed. What you walked in on was not what it looked like.''

''Lori went to a lot of trouble. She must find you irresistible.''

''Unlike you.''

She sighed. Was it true? Wasn't it true? There was no way she could ever know. ''It's about trust.''

''Yes. It is,'' he said, looking both sad and angry. ''Marriage is about trust. And it's about sticking together in the bad times.'' He stared at her in frustration. ''And when the first excuse offered itself, you took it and ran.''

Caro's jaw dropped and her brows rose. ''Are you saying it's my fault we split up?''

There was a long pause. He shoved his hands into his pockets and rocked back on his heels. ''It was tough on us, trying to get pregnant. I guess we've both always been the lucky ones. Life's been pretty easy and we've always achieved what we set out to do. But this one we couldn't control.''

She glanced down and fiddled with the edge of her manicured nails.

''It took me a while to figure out, but you weren't simply being pigheaded and unreasonable.

You were scared.'' His voice was gentle and he had her blinking rapidly. This was the first reference either of them had made to their failed attempts to conceive a child. Everything in their lives had been perfect. Too perfect, perhaps. Suddenly they had no tools to help each other through it, so they'd backed off, thrown themselves into the animal shelter, both gone to work, but there were tensions they'd both ignored. Troubles they hadn't shared.

''I can't believe how pathetic your excuses are,'' she said in a tone that was meant to be sarcastic but came out sounding wimpy even to her own ears. ''How come you never thought about how hard that year was on me before?''

''Because I was too busy thinking how hard the year was on me!''

''Hard on you?'' She could barely believe she'd heard him correctly. ''You weren't taking your temperature every five minutes and planning your schedule around prime fertility days.''

''Well—'' he grinned slowly ''—I didn't take my temperature, but my schedule definitely got involved in the fertility days. I'm only sorry it stopped being fun.''

''And we stopped talking,'' she admitted, acknowledging their marriage had been threatened and she hadn't even realized it. Not consciously, anyway. ''We probably should have had counseling.''

"We still could."

She glanced up. "I don't know, Jon. I think some time apart is good for us."

"Well, I hate it. I miss you."

She let out a breath.

"Come home with me," he said.

"I can't." She shook her head. "Our troubles won't go away that easily. I don't even know if I want... I have to go."

"What about your quotes?"

"I'll make them up."

"Make them up?" His jaw dropped he was so stunned. "But you're a journalist."

"I work for the *Star*."

He snorted. "Quote this."

Before she could protest, or back away, or run, which she did best of all, he pulled her into his arms and kissed her. He felt her entire body develop an instant case of rigor mortis, so stiff and cold he thought he might contract frostbite from her lips. Then, just as he prepared himself for her to pull back and slap him, all the ice melted.

A warm sigh escaped her lips and she snuggled her body up against him, her arms going around his neck.

It had been so long, she hit his system like lightning, sending heat and electricity zapping through him. He was like a frustrated dieter who'd been denied his favorite foods too long. He devoured her. Nibbling, nipping, licking, tasting, taking them both deeper and deeper into the kiss until he became light-headed and she was swaying in his arms.

He pulled away enough that they could both drag in a breath.

Her eyes were big and glassy, her lips glossy and plump. "I love you," he said.

He knew it had been a mistake to tell her that when she pulled away and grabbed up her notebook and bag. "Tell that to someone who might believe you," she said, and marched out.

6

CARO STORMED OUT of Jon's office, so angry and confused she could barely see straight. She strode along the hallway, knowing her lipstick would be smeared, her hair mussed and her cheeks flaming brighter than her mother-in-law's hair.

She was so angry she marched on autopilot for the nearest washroom. Before she realized it, she was in the newsroom, when she'd have been better to take the other hallway and skirt editorial altogether.

Her brain was as badly disordered as her hair, and her mood was no better. Especially when the first person she all but knocked flying was sports reporter Steve Ackerman, whose eyes widened when he took in her appearance.

"Not one word!" she warned as she stalked past to the washroom.

Fortunately it was empty.

For about thirty seconds.

She'd no sooner dragged her makeup bag out of her leather satchel than the door swung open to reveal two women she really didn't want to see right now.

"Hey, Caro," Tess said with studied casualness. "Everything all right?"

"Peachy," she snapped, pulling out a lipstick with a hand that shook so badly she'd end up looking like one of the Simpsons if she tried to apply the stuff.

"Here, let me do your lips," said Harriet MacPherson, seeing her predicament. "I owe you."

Caro relaxed her grip and let Harriet have the tube. "And look at the monster I created." But she was secretly proud of her protégée. The Harriet who'd been so dowdy and shy when they'd first met had emerged into a beautiful, confident woman. Her taste in clothing still leaned toward fifties Highland fling, but she wore it with attitude. And when she bothered with makeup, as she had to when she was a Pasqualie Braves' cheerleader, she was a stunner.

With competent hands that didn't shake, Harriet repaired Caro's lips.

"Good as new," she proclaimed, handing back the lipstick.

Caro pulled out a brush and fixed her hair, not liking the hopeful expression on Tess's face. Harriet did a better job of looking impassive, but then she hadn't known Caro as long.

"You may think you're being discreet," she said to Tess's reflection, "but Did He Kiss You? is stamped all over your face. In neon."

"And the answer would be?"

She dropped her brush back into her bag. "It was just a kiss. A stupid kiss that shouldn't have happened. I got up too fast and became dizzy and...one thing led to another."

"Right."

Caro glared at her, feeling her cheeks blaze again.

Tess threw up her hands. "Right."

"Well, now that I've made a spectacle of myself in front of the entire newsroom, I'd better get going."

She stalked to the door, turned and said, "I hate this," then slipped out.

Tess met Harriet's gaze in the mirror. "I hate this, too. I've tried to stay out of it—we all have—but they love each other. There must be something we can do."

"I've never believed much in interfering in other people's lives," Harriet said slowly.

Tess couldn't help her own grin. "If Caro and I hadn't interfered in your life you'd still be sitting on the sidelines watching the other cheerleaders," she reminded her friend.

Harriet giggled. "I'll never forget how you and Caro helped me. While you're listing people who interfered in my life, don't forget your mother."

"I think it must be hereditary. It was worth doing the makeover, though, to see Steve's reaction when he saw you at the cheerleading rehearsals."

"Steve doesn't care how I look," Harriet said with the serious tone she'd never entirely shaken.

"I know. It's the best thing about him. His eyes sure did pop out, though, when he first saw you in that skimpy cheerleader outfit."

"I'll never forget that day," Harriet sighed dreamily. "Caro helped make my dream come true, the least I can do is help her get hers back. But are we sure she wants Jonathon?"

"You saw how she looked when we came in here. She was all rumpled and flustered, but her eyes were glowing."

"I thought she was angry."

"She was angry. Also turned on."

"Oh."

Tess paced the tile floor. "We've sat on our hands and watched those two make matters worse. If we don't help them they'll end up divorced and miserable."

"But if Jonathon cheated..." Harriet began, a concerned frown playing connect-the-dots with her freckles.

An unladylike snort, which her mother had never been able to cure her of, came out of Tess. "Lori was a troublemaker. She has a bad habit of stealing other women's husbands. I want to smack Jon for being so dense he didn't figure out she was after him or if he did, for not doing something about it."

"Oh, dear. It's all such a mess."

"But not hopeless," Tess said, already scheming. "If they're necking in the office—something they never did when they were still together—then it's time for us to call an emergency summit meeting of concerned friends."

"But we agreed not to interfere."

"We were idiots. It's obvious they needed a push." Her gaze met Harriet's in the mirror and she started to chuckle. "And I think I have a plan."

"I AM NOT HAPPY about this, Tess," Mike muttered a few hours later when they met Harriet and Steve over a beer at their favorite sports bar. "It sounds like meddling to me."

"Think of it as matchmaking."

"What I'm seeing is match-breaking," Mike argued. "Caro never came back to work after she interviewed Jon. She e-mailed her article and made it sound as if she didn't even know the guy."

"She's angry and hurting. Understandably so. But Caro and Jon love each other. You should have seen her face when she came out of his office. Of course, since I'm the city's top investigative reporter—"

"You mean fiancée of," Mike interrupted.

She winked at him and continued as though he hadn't spoken. "I found a reason to go to Jon's office after she left. I'm telling you, he's got it as bad as she does."

"I wouldn't have had the nerve," Harriet said, her green eyes widening. "What was he doing? Gazing at her picture? Staring into space?"

''Ordering meat from the butcher.''

''Now that's romantic,'' Steve said. ''I hope it was a prime cut.''

''But Caro's a vegetarian,'' Harriet almost wailed.

Tess rolled her gaze. ''The meat's not for Caro. It's for some wounded peregrine falcon. The point is, he must have been thinking about Caro and that made him order food for the falcon. I know he loves her.''

''You're on Jon's side now?'' Mike had his chair tipped back, his pirate's gaze challenging her as it always did.

''No. I'm Caro's friend. But she wouldn't be kissing Jon if she didn't care about him. And he wouldn't be nursing vultures back to health—''

''The peregrine falcon is a raptor, actually,'' Harriet corrected.

''Whatever,'' Tess said. ''If they'd both stop acting so stubborn and—''

''Hey, it was Caro who dumped Jon when everybody knows that Lori is a—'' Mike argued.

''And it was Jon who had Lori in his bed. Believe me, Jon's getting off lightly compared to what I'll do to you if you ever—''

''Think we might be getting off the topic here,'' Mike said, holding up his hands as though to shield himself from Tess's verbal attack.

Harriet tossed her red hair over her shoulder and Steve fingered the bright strands in a habit he was probably unaware of. They were so cute, Tess had a feeling there'd be another wedding in the near future.

"What if Lori and Jon did…*you know…?*" Harriet ended awkwardly.

"If he was doing *you know* with another woman then it's better for Caro to have some closure. They have to talk to each other."

"They'll get around to it when they both cool down," Steve said.

"I found out something that's not going to help them cool down." Tess twisted her engagement band nervously. "Lori's still in touch with a couple of the salespeople at the paper. I hear she's coming to town for a visit—her sister's having a baby. But knowing Lori, that's not all she's coming back for."

"This is not good," Mike agreed.

"No. If we're really their friends, we should try and help them. Caro won't spend any time with Jon, and he's acting like a wounded bear." She glared at Mike, simply for being a man.

"So, we're chipping in for a marriage counselor or what?"

"No." Tess sucked in a deep breath, knowing she needed everybody working together if she was going to pull off her scheme. "I have an idea. Fanny Kushner's birthday party is going to be at the Roadhouse this weekend, right?"

"Right."

"Well." She glanced at Steve and Harriet. "Mike worked there one summer. He's told me stories about how he used to take girls into the wine cellar when he wanted to be...private."

Mike chuckled. "Maybe Fanny will lend me the key and I'll take you on a tour, Tess."

"I do want you to get the key, but not for me. For Jon and Caro."

Mike choked on his beer. "Jon and Caro in the make-out pit? Are you kidding me? Think of all the valuable wine she could destroy if she starts throwing bottles at him."

"Caro never loses her temper. That's part of the problem. I'm suggesting we lure them both down there and lock them in for an hour or so. It will force them to deal with each other."

"What if they have to go to the bathroom or have some sort of emergency?" asked Harriet.

"Have you ever seen Jon without his cell? He'll call one of us and we'll let him out."

"I don't know," Harriet said with a frown. "It's very manipulative."

"I know." Tess sighed. "But I really think it might be the only way to get them talking to each other, before it's too late."

"Lori's got a real reputation for making trouble," Steve said. "If it's Jon she wants, she won't rest until she's got him. I agree we need to move to extreme intervention if we're going to try to save

Jon and Caro's marriage. We're their friends, after all. We only want them to talk.''

Harriet still appeared uncertain, but Steve patted her on the back. ''It's an hour in the wine cellar. What can go wrong?''

THE NIGHT of Fanny's eightieth birthday party was a crisp, clear April evening. Spring had been in the air earlier in the day, but it had cooled off again.

Caro, tired of her own misery and determined to appear happy and carefree, dressed in a chic black cocktail dress, sheer black stockings and heels. The diamond necklace and earrings Jon had given to her would be perfect with the outfit, but she wouldn't give him that satisfaction.

Instead she dug out some costume jewelry with sparkles. It looked fine. Not as perfect as the diamonds, but fine.

Reminding herself the night was about Fanny and not her or Jonathon, she picked up the wrapped present, grabbed her coat and evening bag and ran out the door to wait for Mike and Tess, who were to pick her up on their way. Knowing Mike, he would have opted to take his motorcycle, but Tess knew how to deal with him, Caro thought as she watched for her friend's red BMW.

She'd had to stifle the impulse to offer to arrive early at Fanny's to help; there were paid professionals in charge of this party and showing up early when Jon would be there was too much like old times. Still, even though she'd organized the catering and helped to plan the decorations, it was hard for her to arrive as just another guest.

Mike and Tess appeared and she forced a smile as she got in the car.

"You'll embarrass me," Tess argued as soon as they were moving, and it sounded as though Caro'd dropped into the middle of an argument.

"No, I won't," Mike said. "Let's ask Caro. She'll know."

"I don't want to get in the middle of anything ugly, thanks."

"What did you get Fanny?" Mike asked her.

"I had a jeweler I love make her some chunky gold earrings. Since her hair changes so often, he put stones of every color in them. They'll go with anything."

"Good one," Mike said.

Knowing he was waiting for her to ask, she said. "How about you?"

"I got her boxing gloves," he said in a smug tone.

Caro laughed. She couldn't help it. "Boxing gloves?"

"See what I mean?" Tess said. "He can't give an eighty-year-old woman boxing gloves."

"I had her name stamped on them," he said, glaring at both women. "In gold."

"Well, in that case…" Caro said, having a sneaking feeling Fanny would love them.

"I hope you have your own card. I'm not having

anything to do with boxing gloves. I got her a crystal vase."

"That's a sissy present. She'll hate it."

Since Tess and Mike were arguing perfectly happily without her help, Caro leaned back in her seat and repeated all her favorite phrases from all her self-help books. Especially the one about not looking back.

This would be the first social occasion she and Jon would be at together since the Lori incident. She had to focus on the future, not long for the past.

When they got to Fanny's, the place was noisier than usual and far more crowded. The guest list included Fanny's regulars as well as her enormous number of friends, old and young, and, thanks to Jonathon, the who's who of Pasqualie.

As Caro squeezed through the door she realized that Fanny had a lot of friends.

She and Tess and Mike put their presents on a table that was already stacked to overflowing with brightly wrapped gifts and edged their way through the busy crowd to find Fanny.

They found her looking as regal and courted as a queen bee in the middle of a busy hive. In honor of her birthday she'd dyed her hair silver. At first glance it appeared gray, but there were sparkles shimmering through it. If there was a way to broadcast that she was loving every minute of life as a senior, she'd found it.

Caro kissed her cheek and wished her a happy birthday. The music was rock and roll, the bar decorated with all the funky colors Fanny loved, and the birthday girl bubbled with life.

"It looks great."

"Happy Birthday, Fanny," Mike and Tess said together. Since they were holding hands, Caro assumed the argument over boxing gloves was over.

"Those two look cuter than a wagonful of fuzzy-headed pups," Fanny said. "Kind of reminds me of… Sorry, I must be getting old. I almost got sentimental."

Caro grabbed her hand and squeezed it. She must not be getting enough sleep. For some irritating reason she found her emotions too close to the surface for her liking these days. Finding her way to safer emotional ground, she said, "Did you end up finding a bartender you trust?"

"I handpicked all the bartenders myself," the older woman said, waving her hand in the direction of the bar. "I wanted them to go topless, but it's against the bylaw." She winked. "They're still pretty cute. Go check them out."

Shaking her head, Caro fought her way through the crowd. Knowing Fanny, she'd sidestep the bylaw by putting her bartenders in bow ties and nothing but.

In fact, they were fully dressed. All spectacular specimens of manhood, it was the one in the middle that made her knees weak. She'd been unconsciously searching the room for Jon, never dreaming he'd be working behind the bar. But when she thought about it, she couldn't imagine anything his mother would like more.

Her two older sons were also pouring drinks.

Jon stared right at her, and for a second she simply couldn't move. She wanted to turn and run from his compelling gaze, but she hoped she was made of sterner stuff. She walked toward him slowly.

"Hi," she said, determined to appear calm, even though she hadn't seen him since they'd kissed so unwisely in his office.

He hadn't tried to contact her, so he must realize it was hopeless trying to manipulate her. Although she was a tiny bit sorry he hadn't called simply so she could have the satisfaction of telling him what a worm he was.

Couldn't do it here and now of course. She ought to say hello to his brothers who'd flown in from L.A. and Houston for Fanny's birthday, but they were both busy pouring drinks and catching up with their Pasqualie friends and acquaintances. Only Jon was free; it was as if an invisible force field held every one away from his particular spot.

"Hi yourself. What can I get you? Champagne?"

Her stomach lurched at the thought. Must be the company. "I'll start with sparkling water, thanks."

He got it for her with smooth efficiency, as though he tended bar here every day.

"You look beautiful," he said as he handed her the drink.

"Thanks," she said, feeling suddenly awkward and tongue-tied.

"The diamonds would look great with that dress," he said.

"Diamond mining exploits the poorest African countries and funds wars," she said in her prissiest voice. Getting peeved certainly pushed her past the tongue-tied stage in record time.

"Yours were mined in Canada. I checked before I bought them."

"Oh," she said, her self-righteous bubble bursting.

The way his gaze was roving over her, intimate and warm, reminded her forcibly that she'd lost control in his arms the last time they'd been together. He was obviously thinking the same thing. "I'm free in an hour. Want to go out back and neck?"

He was so outrageous, and she was already feeling off kilter, that he surprised a smile out of her. She recalled Mel's words and he knew the woman was right. Caro had to live in the same town with the man. She might as well get used to being civil. "I bet you say that to all the customers."

"No, ma'am." He shook his head earnestly. "Only the babes."

"I'd better move on. Your brothers are getting overworked."

"Don't run away, will you?"

She shook her head.

"And tell Grundel to get his butt over here. If I have to sling ale, so does he." She nodded once more and turned. "Oh, and Caro?"

She turned and caught his gaze running up and down her back in a way that made her shiver. "You look sexy enough to eat." He winked and turned to serve his next customer.

7

"OKAY, what's the plan?" Steve whispered in a conspiratorial voice. He and Harriet and Mike and Tess were having a quick conference while Caro was busy talking to the mayor and Jon was still tending bar.

"No second thoughts?" Tess asked. She had to be absolutely sure of her team. Her plan required split second timing and nerves of steel.

"No," said Mike. "Jon's my buddy and he's miserable. He at least deserves a shot at winning her back."

Harriet nodded. "I've been watching them. You can see they still love each other."

"Steve?"

"Hey, I haven't locked a couple in a closet since junior high. I'm all over it."

"All right. Since you like that part best, you'll be the one who 'accidentally' closes the door while they're in there. You'll have to hide so they don't see you. As soon as you hear both of them inside the wine cellar, walk past and shut the door. Don't forget to turn the dead bolt."

"Roger, wilco." Steve sent her a mock salute and jogged away.

"Harriet, you go tell Jonathon his mom said he needs to get more champagne out of the wine cellar so she can start chilling it."

"Shouldn't I do that?" Mike argued.

"Honey, if you go, Jon will tell you to get the champagne. But Harriet doesn't even know where the wine cellar is. Besides, she has an honest face. No one would ever believe she could take part in anything underhanded."

"Thanks for that," Harriet said, but obediently headed off to find Jon.

"Are you suggesting I don't have an honest face?" Mike said, his eyes narrowing to slits.

Tess patted his cheek with affection. "You know I fell in love with your bad-boy side."

"Oh, well. For you, I can be bad." He kissed her swiftly and she sighed against him, thinking she could never get enough of him.

"Now what? You tell Caro she needs to haul a case of champagne?"

She shot him a withering glance, glad she could tell him about her stroke of genius. "I enlisted Fanny. When Harriet gives Jon the message, that's Fanny's cue to send Caro on some errand to the wine cellar. Did you remember to set up the table and chairs and put the bottle of wine and two glasses in there?"

"Of course."

"Oh, good. I'm so excited. If we can get Jon and Caro back together, it will be the best birthday present Fanny could have."

"I can think of a few ways we could celebrate, too, as soon as that wine cellar's free."

As she made some laughing comment back to him, she noticed he was looking past her. "Oh, no." An expression of horror crossed his face.

"What is—"

"Emergency. Mayday, Mayday. Trouble's coming through the door."

Tess turned to look and gasped. "I can't believe this!" Lori Gerhardt had just walked in.

"How did she get in?"

"I don't know," Mike said grimly, already striding for the door, "but I know how she's getting out."

"And I'm pulling the plug on the wine cellar gig," she said, seeing how easily her innocently devised plan could be misinterpreted. If Caro found out Lori had been here while she'd been locked in the wine cellar... Tess shuddered.

The first thing she had to do was to stop Jonathon from going down there. She searched for him, and, as though in a nightmare, she watched him work his way through the crowd, obviously on his way to the wine cellar.

Lori Gerhardt, her gaze fixed on Jon's back like a stealth bomber locked on to its target, followed him. Tess raced through the crowd, barging into bodies as she tried to cross the room to cut Lori off, but the other woman was much closer to Jonathon than she. Lori's dyed and teased blond head disappeared through the side door moments after Jonathon, before Tess was halfway across the busy bar.

She shot an anguished glance at Mike, who was only a few feet ahead of her. Doggedly, he kept moving for the door.

Tess decided to leave Lori to Mike. Her best bet now was to stop Caro. She searched for Fanny, and was in time to see her talking to Caro, who had her head bent, listening and nodding. Then Caro headed for the side door, which led to the wine cellar. The one Jon and Lori had just passed through.

Tess started to sweat as she shoved and pushed through. She had to get to Caro.

JON WHISTLED as he entered his mother's wine cellar. In fairness, it was his father's wine cellar, and for a moment the sight of all those bottles his father had lovingly collected during his lifetime brought back poignant memories.

Their house in town hadn't met with Hector Kushner's rigid rules of perfect wine storage, but the huge cellar beneath Fanny's Roadhouse was perfect. She'd complained that he took all the room, not leaving her enough space for a decent beer locker, but her grousing hadn't had any heat behind it, and his dad had gone ahead.

Built into rock, it was consistently cool, but never cold, in winter and summer, and the racks of vintage wine lay in their custom-made bins, quietly aging and mostly undisturbed.

As they gained complexity and flavor, they also gained value. There was a fortune here, Jon thought, shaking his head. He and his brothers occasionally lightened it by a few bottles, but they also added newer vintages to keep the collection going.

Fanny wasn't a big wine drinker and even though she'd threatened a few times to serve the rare bottles as house wine, he had a feeling she took comfort in here remembering her husband, just as he did.

He shook off his memories, along with the sadness that he'd likely never have a son to pass the legacy on to, and bent to fetch another case of the champagne Fanny insisted on having.

It had appeared to him that there was plenty of champagne already upstairs, but this was her business and she had a sense of these things. Besides, she was his mother and he did what he was told.

''Jon, we have to talk.''

He almost dropped the heavy case of champagne when he heard those words.

For an instant, hope leaped in his chest as the woman's voice echoed against the stone walls. But, even distorted, he quickly realized the voice wasn't Caro's.

She didn't want to talk. As far as he could tell, Caro wanted to fry up his liver with onions and bacon.

A bad feeling prickled the back of his neck as he turned slowly, only to have his worst nightmare confirmed.

"I thought you were in Houston," he said to Lori, forcing himself to remember that it wasn't okay to hit girls.

"I came back. Heard you're living all alone now."

Anger at this woman for her contribution to his messed-up marriage consumed him. "This is a private party and you aren't invited," he said as calmly as he could. Any woman who went after married men had to have a couple of screws loose. He tried to remember that.

"A private party is exactly what I had in mind," she said.

He stared at her, wondering how she could possibly think he had the slightest interest in her. Since she wasn't getting the message, he decided to take his champagne upstairs to the safety of the crowd and get somebody else to deal with Lori. If Caro saw them together...

He took a step toward the doorway with the case of champagne heavy in his arms before he noticed the slight movement behind the door.

"Hold the door," he yelled, but he was too late. He heard the heavy door shut before he could stop it, and then he heard the clicking sound as it was locked from the outside.

He felt as if he'd stumbled into a horror movie. He was trapped in the wine cellar with the woman who'd wrecked his marriage. And Caro was out there somewhere.

"Are you behind this?" he all but shouted as he placed the crate on the floor and stomped to the door. As he'd feared, it was locked.

He banged on the door furiously, but there was no reply.

"We were interrupted last time," the woman behind him cooed in what he assumed was supposed to be a seductive whisper but only set his teeth on edge.

He could rant and rail at Lori, but what was the point?

He needed to get out of here and fast. Maybe if he was very, very lucky, he could be behind the bar fast enough that Caro wouldn't know he'd left.

He reached for his cell phone, then realized with a groan that he'd taken off his jacket to tend bar.

Until someone heard him banging on the door, he was stuck here, locked in the wine cellar with Lori.

He didn't think a worse disaster could befall him.

He was wrong.

"Jonathon," Lori said.

He turned around to see her standing there, her dress lying on the floor. All she had on was a see-through black bra and wispy lace thong, thigh-high black stockings and shiny black heels.

8

WHAT WAS SHE doing torturing herself? Caro wondered. She should go home and try to balance her checkbook if she wanted more pain. At least she'd have something useful to show for her time.

"Care for an appetizer?" a waiter said, holding out a tray.

She should stop eating, but the little dainties were so good she was making a pig of herself. She reached automatically for a prawn because she loved seafood, but at the last second her stomach said no and she took a baby asparagus spear instead. Her stomach was acting so strange lately. It was amazing what stress could do to a person.

She wondered how long she'd have to remain at the party feeling miserable, when Fanny interrupted her thoughts. "Thank you for talking Jon out of that stuffed-shirt surprise party. I'm having a ball here in my own place."

"You are the prettiest eighty-year-old I've ever seen," Caro said, kissing Fanny's flushed cheek.

"I'm having more fun than a linebacker at a Friday night buffet."

"I'm glad." And she was. She had to stop thinking about herself and start enjoying Fanny's happiness.

"Look," the older woman said. "Jon's got some kind of fancy cake hiding in the big fridge in the kitchen. I think this is the perfect opportunity to drink some of his dad's frou-frou dessert wine." She handed Caro a slip of paper. "You'll find it in the wine cellar. Bring up two bottles, will you? I wrote the name on there and that's a map of where to find it in the cellar."

"But shouldn't Jon or one of his brothers…?"

Fanny shook her head. "I love those boys, but they fuss more than peacocks in a rainstorm. The stuff's worth a fortune, but their dad would want me to do this."

"All right."

Excusing herself, Caro headed for the cellar stairs.

She'd almost reached them when Tess grabbed her arm. "Caro, thank goodness I found you."

Tess sounded out of breath and one of the shoulder straps on her dress had slipped down her arm. Behind Tess she saw Mike, also breathing heavily, a sheen of sweat on his brow. They must have been on the dance floor.

"We arrived together," she said, wondering what had put the panic on her friend's face. "Where did you think I was?"

Tess laughed a little wildly and glanced at Mike. He started to laugh, too.

Seemed they'd been drinking more than sparkling water. It looked as if she'd be driving them all home. "If you'll excuse me, I have to go get something for Fanny."

"I'll get it!" said Mike. "You stay here and talk to Tess." He bolted through the door, almost slamming it in her face.

Caro's eyes narrowed. "He doesn't know what Fanny asked me to get."

Tess's laugh approached maniacal. "He'll assume it's more beer. Let me know what she asked for and I'll go and tell Mike."

Caro wasn't a suspicious person by nature, but she wasn't a moron, either. Then Harriet appeared, looking pale and nervous. "Caro, I was looking everywhere for you. I need to ask you something." She glanced at Tess as though for inspiration. "In, um…in private. Can we go to the washroom?"

"Okay," Caro said, folding her arms. "What's going on?"

"Nothing," said Tess.

"I'll tell you in the bathroom," said Harriet and, grabbing Caro, began to tug.

Harriet was an amateur athlete who could do back flips and one-handed cartwheels and Lord knew what else, while Caro was willow-slender and excelled in flexibility rather than strength.

It would be no great feat for Harriet to simply drag her to the washroom against her will.

Caro did, however, have a weapon. "Harriet,"

she said sternly, "I'm wearing my Blahniks with the skinny heels. I will step on your foot and bring you to your knees if you don't stop dragging me."

Harriet dropped her arm and blushed. "Sorry," she said, looking sheepish.

"Tess. Move away from that door," Caro said to her best friend, who was leaning against the door.

Tess's shoulders slumped in defeat and she stepped away. "Caro, please don't go down there."

Caro pulled open the door and stepped through.

"Look," said Tess from behind her, "whatever happens, it wasn't Jon's fault. It's mine."

What on earth was going on? She'd never seen her friends act so strange. Not all at once, anyway. As Caro walked down the stairs into the dimness she heard banging—like a fist on a door.

Something very strange was going on and for some reason nobody wanted her to know what.

Her shoes clacked on the cement as she followed Fanny's instructions and made her way down the steps. The banging was louder as she turned left. In fact, the pounding was coming from inside the wine cellar.

Next to the door, Mike and Steve were on their hands and knees, peering at the ground.

"Is that a spectator sport or can anyone play?" Caro asked, feeling amusement curl her stomach.

Mike shot her an anguished glance and rose, as did Steve, who appeared harassed and red-faced.

Mike threw his hands in the air and jerked his head toward the shamefaced Steve. "Guy's got a hundred-and-eighty IQ and he loses the key to the wine cellar. After locking in the wrong woman." His tone had risen with each word and ended on a ferocious shout.

Fanny had a spare key and Caro was about to mention it when she looked more closely at Steve. "Check your shirt pocket," she said. One side was hanging lower, she always noticed details like that.

"What happened? Did the party move down here?" Fanny said, coming around the corner, her own high heels clattering.

With a glare at Steve, Mike grabbed the key out of his hand and yelled, "Okay, Jon. We're getting you out."

"Caro, why don't you—"

"Don't even think about it," she said, overcome by curiosity, angling herself so she'd have a great view when the door opened.

Mike shrugged, shot an anguished glance at Tess, who was all but wringing her hands behind Caro. "I'm sorry. It's all my fault," she said.

Mike unlocked the door. It opened wide and Caro saw her husband's furious face first, and behind him, Lori Gerhardt nonchalantly snapping the front closure of a black bra which left nothing to the imagination.

The woman shot a big-eyed glance at Caro, bit

down on her plump bottom lip and said, "Oops, looks like we got interrupted again, honey."

Jon took a step toward Caro and stopped.

Silence reigned for a good ten seconds.

No one moved.

"Well, butter my butt and call me a biscuit. Look who fell out of the floozy tree and hit every branch on the way down," Fanny said behind Caro.

9

"YOU TOOK my exact measurements," Caro said. "How did this dress end up so tight?" She shifted uncomfortably in her bridesmaid dress, which she and Tess had chosen together. It was a simple and elegant pale green silk with no flounces, ribbons, trains or lace.

But, because of the gown's simplicity, fit was important. The woman had obviously measured wrong since the resulting dress was too tight in the waist and bust.

"You must have put on weight," the fitter said with more honesty than tact.

Caro, who had been wolfing food some days and unaccountably picky on others, supposed it was possible. But she'd spent too many years in modeling to be happy with a less than perfect fit.

"Perhaps you could let it out," she said.

The dressmaker grunted around a mouthful of pins. "I can only do this once."

Did she think Caro was planning to go from a size six to sixteen in a couple of weeks?

Of course, given the way her life had been going lately, she wouldn't be surprised.

She still hadn't recovered from Fanny's birthday bash, but then she wondered if anyone who'd been in the cellar when the door opened would ever recover.

Caro hadn't known whether to laugh, cry or throw herself to the ground and drum her heels on the floor that night. Since her emotions had overwhelmed her, she'd done what she always did when she felt as if she was losing control.

She'd left.

Jon hadn't chased her, as she'd half thought he would. He hadn't called her the next day, either.

Almost a week had gone by and he still hadn't called.

He was the only one who hadn't. She'd received apologies and explanations from Tess, Harriet, Steve, even Mike. Fanny had called to see how she was.

"Fine. I'm fine," she'd said to Fanny as she'd said to them all.

"Jon saw the party through, but I tell you that boy looked like he was rode hard and put away wet."

Fortunately, Tess hadn't been so cryptic. "After you left, Jon tore a strip off Lori Gerhardt and she stomped away so fast she didn't have time to zip her dress." She'd paused. "I know this isn't my business, but I really don't think—"

"You're right. It's not your business." They'd never mentioned it since.

Caro didn't think Lori Gerhardt could have done her a bigger favor. Seeing her once more half-naked in Jon's vicinity, the blinders had fallen from Caro's eyes. If she knew anything about Jon it was that he wouldn't mess with a woman in his mother's wine cellar. And if he wouldn't do that, why would he take that same woman to his wife's bed?

He wouldn't.

Maybe some of those self-help books were getting through to her because she was beginning to accept that part of her despair—and her willingness to run at the first hint of trouble in her marriage—was because of her empty womb.

Had she become so insecure that she believed her husband would cheat on her because she couldn't conceive? It had been easier to run than to face the fact that there were cracks in her once-perfect marriage.

Why couldn't love be enough?

But she was beginning to see that it wasn't enough. It was the foundation on which everything else rested, but they needed ways to work out problems. She had to start facing trouble instead of pretending it didn't exist or running from it, and Jon needed to accept that he couldn't fix everything.

Wouldn't it be wonderful if they could make a new start? Maybe get some counseling, as Jon had suggested. And she must accept that not being perfect was okay. Perhaps they could adopt a child, or take in needy kids.

She sniffed and blew her nose.

When he called, she'd suggest they meet and she'd share with him some of her feelings. It scared her to her bones to think of baring her soul like that, but she knew she had to trust him with her insecurities just as she'd trusted him with her heart.

As soon as he phoned, she'd be ready.

She remembered the image of Lori nearly naked and Jon so mad he looked ready to combust, and she was determined to go easy on him.

He still had to grovel a bit, though. He'd embarrassed and humiliated her all over town, although she had to admit it wasn't entirely his fault. When he called, she'd forgive him.

But every day, her eager anticipation ended in frustration. Her calls were work-related, friend-related, charity-work-related. None was Jon-related.

By Thursday, she wondered whether she should call him.

She was to meet Tess and Harriet at the sports bar after Harriet's cheerleading practice. It would be a great opportunity to figure out how to handle the Jon fiasco.

But when she arrived at Ted's, she discovered it wasn't going to be as easy as she'd thought to have a powwow. Jon was already there, sitting in a cozy corner at a table for two with one of Harriet's teammates, Linda Lou, former runner-up for Miss Georgia Peach.

Caro left before either party saw her, glad she'd been the first to arrive. She waited until she was several blocks away to phone Tess and plead a headache. No way was she going to admit that the husband she'd planned to forgive was unforgivable. She'd decided not to ask Andre, her old modeling buddy, to be her date for the wedding after all, but Jon's latest antics had her punching Andre's number into the phone before the red haze had cleared from before her eyes.

"HE SAYS he'll do it," Caro said to Tess in an excited whisper while she helped Tess pick out lingerie for her honeymoon.

"I can't believe you talked that hunky model into being your date. What about his wife? Doesn't she mind?"

"I introduced them. Besides, Donna's pregnant. She'll be a couple of weeks from her due date when you get married, so she's sending the other two kids with Andre so she can get some rest."

"Are the kids coming on your date, too?" Tess asked sweetly as she tried to decide between a peach bra and panty set and an ice-blue one.

"The blue," Caro said. "And of course the boys aren't coming to the wedding. Andre's bringing the nanny with him. They'll be upstairs in the hotel the whole time. Jon will never know they're there."

Her friend shook her head. "I hope you know what you're doing."

"It was your idea," Caro reminded Tess.

"I'm not sure it was one of my better ones."

"Trust me."

Tess squinted at her over a scarlet thong. "Do you want him back?"

She flinched inside, as though she'd swallowed a sliver of glass, then numbed the pain with anger. "I haven't decided."

"Because there's still time to ditch the hunk and spend the evening with Jon. Well, two evenings. The rehearsal dinner is the night before the wedding."

"Oh, my gosh. That's right. The rehearsal dinner. Can I bring Andre?"

Tess shrugged. "It's your funeral."

The day of the rehearsal, Caro spent longer fussing with her appearance than she had in years. Her hair refused to cooperate. It didn't even feel like her hair. Nothing in her closet fit properly. She couldn't understand how she ate so little and seemed to be gaining weight. Must be the misery she was carrying around.

When Andre arrived to pick her up, which he'd insisted he do, she was trying to jam her feet into her pumps. Even they didn't fit. She stomped to the door with a scowl, one mauve pump on her foot, the other in her hand.

But the minute she saw her date on the other

side of her doorway she began to feel better. He was so stunningly gorgeous he always took her breath away. Andre was also a good friend. She threw herself at him for a hug. "Thanks for doing this."

"Hey, what are friends for?"

He wore a pale gray designer suit and silk shirt. The way he wore it kept the designer in business, she was certain.

"Come on in."

She then spent a couple of minutes hopping on one foot while she tried to shove her stubborn foot into her shoe.

Andre chuckled. "You look like one of the ugly stepsisters trying to get into Cinderella's slipper."

"I feel as though an alien pod person has taken over my body," she complained. "Nothing fits, not even my shoes." She caught a glimpse of herself in the mirror and scowled. "An alien pod person having a bad hair day."

He laughed. "You look beautiful. You always look beautiful. Sit down and give me your foot."

She did and he grunted with effort until he got the shoe on. "Don't you know it's bad for your feet to wear shoes that are too small?"

"They're not doing my temper any good, either," she groaned. "My feet decided to have a growth spurt at thirty. What's that about?"

"Everything about you women is beyond me.

Try living with a pregnant woman through her third. You'll have to put sandals on or something."

"But these shoes match my dress," she complained, hobbling toward her bedroom. "Can I show you my bridesmaid's dress? I picked it up yesterday. They were supposed to alter it, but I think they must have forgotten."

"Sure."

"Fix yourself a drink while I go put it on."

"Okay. Want your usual white wine?"

Her nose wrinkled. "I don't feel much like wine. I'll have a soft drink."

He shot her a peculiar glance, but didn't say anything.

She squeezed into her dress, cursing the dressmaker who'd obviously forgotten to make the alterations and emerged to find Andre sprawled at his ease on the couch, an open copy of the *Star* and a beer and her drink on the table in front of him.

"What do you think?" she asked, feeling self-conscious about the ill-fitting dress.

His eyes widened slightly as he looked her up and down. "Did you get a boob job?"

"Of course not. I've put on a little weight, that's all."

There was an odd expression in his eyes as he studied her more closely. He was probably trying to find a tactful way to tell her the dress was not working. "You look kind of pale. Are you feeling all right?" he asked casually.

She wrinkled her nose. "I've been under the

weather off and on since Jon and I split up. Stress, I guess.''

He rose and stepped toward her, placing a big square hand on her belly. In another man, the gesture would be erotic, but Andre's hand felt more like a doctor's.

He removed it and his eyes twinkled as though he were laughing at her.

''All right, so I've gained a few pounds. Everyone said I was too skinny.''

''For a smart woman you can be awfully clueless.''

''What do you—''

''Honey, I think you're pregnant.''

She sat. That is, her legs trembled so badly they wouldn't hold her and as she dropped, Andre grabbed her and stuffed her into a chair.

''I can't be,'' she said in a blank voice. ''According to modern science I can't be pregnant. The fertility expert we saw said my chances were practically nil.''

''Well, you sure look knocked up to me.''

She'd never even considered the possibility she was pregnant, but what if Andre was right and a semimiracle had happened. That would explain a lot of things.

''Have you been getting your...'' He made a helpless gesture.

When she caught his meaning, she blushed. ''It's never been very regular.'' She shook her head. ''I assumed it was stress.''

If she'd thought about it at all she'd have said

the turmoil with her marital mess had thrown her system off course. Feeling an incredible sense of joy begin to creep through her system, she shook her head. Ever since she left Jon, she hadn't given it much thought.

His eyes were still twinkling with delight.

"Your breasts are bigger. Tender, too, right?"

She nodded.

"Clothes aren't fitting." He pointed to her feet. "Shoes aren't fitting. You're off the booze. Any nausea?"

"No." Well, hardly any. "And I don't crave pickles and ice cream, either."

He laughed. "Donna never gets cravings, but she can't stand cabbage when she's pregnant."

"Fish."

"Pardon?"

"For me it's fish. I usually love seafood, but the past few weeks… Oh, my gosh." Tears filled her eyes as she realized how utterly blind she'd been. After a year of trying and negative test results, it had never crossed her mind that one spontaneous act outside her peak fertility zone could have done the trick. She touched her belly. "How could I be such an idiot. Do you really think it's possible?"

"Want me to run to the pharmacy and get you one of those tests?"

She shook her head. "No." She'd pick up one later. She still wasn't convinced her symptoms weren't stress related.

"Maybe you should stay home tonight and rest."

She shook her head. "I can't. It's the rehearsal dinner."

He sat across from her, a slight frown marring his exquisitely handsome face. "Maybe I should stay home then. Making your husband jealous doesn't sound like such a good idea now he's going to be a daddy."

"We don't know that for sure. Besides, I want you with me."

"Look. Call me old-fashioned, but if you're pregnant, Jon and you need to get back together."

The tears that had filled her eyes when she'd first accepted that Andre's guess was likely correct now spilled over. "I'll take him back for one reason, and one reason only. Because he loves me. Not because I'm pregnant with his child."

"Caro, he has a right to know."

"I know that. But nothing's confirmed yet." She sniffed. "Promise me you won't say a word to anyone until I'm certain."

"I'll tell you what I'll promise," he said, looking as fierce as a Viking warrior.

"What?" she asked with misgiving.

"I promise to bust his chops, that's what." He brandished the splendid muscles that had appeared oiled and bulging in many a woman's magazine. "A man with you for a wife is crazy to look at anyone else."

"Please," she begged him, "don't cause any trouble. This is Tess's wedding."

"Humph. I'm glad I never met him. He sounds like a turkey."

A small, wistful part of her wanted to jump in and defend Jonathon from such accusations. Except that, unfortunately, she agreed.

And with Andre acting so hawkish, she had a bad feeling more than feathers would soon be flying.

"Promise me you won't do anything to embarrass Tess. Or me."

"I won't." He grinned suddenly. "But I am going to put on an Academy Award performance as your new boy-toy."

"Date," she corrected on a laugh.

He stuck out his sculpted lower lip. "Just once in my life I want to be somebody's boy-toy."

"Not going to happen. You've got the looks for it, but not the personality."

"Yeah. I know. Donna never even let me be her boy-toy. Not for a second. Oh, well. Stuff yourself back into that purple number and let's go."

"What about this?" She indicated her too-tight bridesmaid dress.

"Can you wear something else?"

"No. Tess and I chose it specially. It matches the other bridesmaids' outfits."

"Hmm. Oh, I know. I brought Martha, the boys' nanny, with me. She sews her own clothes. I bet she could let it out for you."

She fingered the seam. "There's not much room left. The dressmaker warned me she could only let it out once."

He took it from her and also inspected the seams.

"It'll be tight, but the seam only has to hold one night. Martha will have to do the best she can."

She smiled at him, thankful he was one of the few men in the world who understood fashion in the intimate way she did.

After she changed, they dropped off the dress with Martha, who was happy to have something to do while the boys were sleeping, and then they were off to the church for the rehearsal.

Their stop at the hotel where Andre and the boys were staying, and where tomorrow's reception would be held, had slowed them down, so they were not late exactly, but the last ones to arrive.

Andre pulled open the heavy door of the church and Caro entered to find the bridal party sitting in the first two pews.

All heads turned at their entrance, but her gaze immediately searched for, and found, but one face.

And oh, boy, was it a mad one.

The instant he spotted her, Jon's eyes had lit up just as they had when they were first married. Then, when Andre followed behind her, Jon's gaze narrowed then turned arctic.

She blinked, forcing down the first instinctive impulse to rush forward and explain that her date wasn't really a date. Except that she wanted Jon to get the wrong impression. That was the whole point.

So, instead of following her first instinct, she grabbed her date's arm and together they made their way to the front of the church.

Since Jon was now facing forward, only his rigid

back giving away his emotions, she had attention to spare for the rest of the wedding party. The women—Tess, Tess's mother, Harriet and Cherise—all gaped at the hunk hanging off her arm. But Andre was so accustomed to that reaction from women he barely noticed. Caro couldn't help a tiny thrill of pride that this outrageous hunk was her date, even if he was only a loaner.

Jon rehearsed his role as best man smoothly, giving Mike a pat on the back at the part where he practiced offering the rings. He had a big smile and warm words for Tess, as well. For Caro, Jon couldn't even manage eye contact.

Fine. She told herself. Fine! Let him feel what it was like to imagine your spouse with someone else and swallow a healthy swig of his own medicine.

With a glib explanation he excused himself from the rehearsal dinner and left without a backward glance. Caro knew because she watched him walk all the way out of the church.

10

CARO KNEW SHE'D never forget the day of Tess and Mike's wedding for it was the day she discovered she was going to be a mother. She'd taken the test first thing in the morning and the stick hadn't just turned blue, it had practically sung a lullaby. She danced around, inspecting it under every light, including sunlight, but that magical little stick stayed as blue as her husband's eyes.

Her own eyes filled with tears repeatedly during the ceremony as she watched her best friend commit to her own marriage, and they filled when she caught sight of Jon, her baby's father, and imagined what their child would be like. Jon was formal with her, but she could tell he was affected by the beauty of the ceremony and the words Tess and Mike spoke that were so like their own vows.

Their friends' wedding followed a typical pattern—photos, banquet, speeches and toasts—but it was one of the most wonderful weddings Caro ever remembered attending. Partly because Mike and Tess were two of her favorite people, but also because she was having her own private celebration.

Andre was stuck at the head table beside her and

didn't seem to mind. But then he was accustomed to being on display.

Before she knew it, dinner was cleared and the dancing started and she was able to escape from the table. She couldn't escape Andre's third degree, however, which he'd been giving her since he'd badgered the truth out of her.

"When are you going to tell Jonathon? You should tell him tonight, Caro," he said for about the fiftieth time.

As though he'd heard his name from across the room, Jon glanced over and she automatically sucked in her stomach under the twice-let-out green silk. It irked her that he should see her like this at Tess's wedding. *Less than perfect.* Although she supposed that was still better than his guessing the truth about her changing body before she was ready to tell him.

Of course, as a strategy, concealment was not going to be easy, or permanent, Andre reminded her, watching her antics.

"What are you going to do a few months from now when he asks, 'What happened to you, Caro?'"

He was right, and she knew it, but she felt flippant, partly because Jon had all but ignored her since he'd first seen Andre. They'd performed their part in the marriage ceremony like two strangers and the minute they were free, he'd left her side. If she hadn't seen him cozied up to a cheerleader, she'd feel really bad. But she had. She sniffed and stared at her belly. "I'll say I took a deep breath in the library and sucked in the globe."

Andre's eyes twinkled as he gazed at her. This couldn't be a lot of fun for him since he didn't know anyone, but he was being a dream date to her as he'd promised. "Hmm. The scholarly approach."

"Too sophisticated? Well, I *am* in fashion. I could always say it's the newest trend. A reverse bustle."

"Or go with the food angle." He patted his own rock-hard belly. "Maybe I should have sliced that watermelon before I ate it."

She chuckled. It was a stupid game, but it eased her pain. "Or the pharmaceutical approach. 'You mean a medicine ball's *not* a pill?' No, wait. It's the newest trend in personal boating safety." She tugged on an imaginary string near her rib cage. "Pull cord to inflate."

She was laughing but there was an edge of hysteria in her tone, especially since she felt Jon's gaze all but glued to her. How much more of this could she take?

For all her joking she knew she had to tell him he was about to be a father.

And soon.

From across the room, Jon watched his wife, his bow tie almost strangling him as he saw her giggle and lean against her beefcake date. Since when had she gone for pretty boys with capped teeth and sa-line-implant pecs? And God never gave any man hair that color, with strands of wheat and brown and who knew what fancy shades. Jon stifled the impulse to pop the implants with his fists and knock out the pearly whites currently looking ready to take a bite out of his wife.

Well, it looked as though she'd made her choice. And if that's what she wanted...

Couldn't be. A voice inside him insisted that the woman who married him wouldn't be interested in that sissy boy.

Would she?

He sighed. Unable to bear the thought of standing there glowering at his ex like a chump, he forced a smile to his own lips and went to dance with the bride.

He led Tess to the floor as a waltz began to play.

"Jon," Tess complained, a minute or so later, "I'm getting dizzy."

"Huh?" He'd almost forgotten he was even dancing.

"You're so busy keeping Caro in your sights you're spinning me like a top. With all this fabric, I'm likely to catch an updraft and float away like a frilly white hot-air balloon.

He chuckled with reluctant amusement, forcing his attention back to the woman in his arms. "Sorry. You look beautiful, by the way."

"Oh, like you noticed. My big day and you've

only got eyes for my bridesmaid. I should be jealous," she sighed, "but I want you two to get back together so much it hurts."

"You got any ideas on how I might accomplish that?"

"Look. I can't give away my best friend's secrets, but it's my wedding day so I'm entitled to do a little matchmaking. I can tell you she still loves you. The rest is up to you."

"Who's the beefcake?"

"Beefcake?" She blinked. "You mean Andre? He's hot enough to make me rethink jumping on the back of Mike's motorcycle for our honeymoon. That is one prime specimen of man."

"This is not helping," he said in her ear, but somehow it was. If Caro still loved him, and he had to believe Tess—she wouldn't lie to him—then it didn't take a genius to figure out that Caro had dug up the best-looking man she knew to make him jealous. His wife didn't do things by half measures. Figures she'd find herself an Adonis.

He had to admit it was a damn fine strategy. He was so jealous he was choking on it.

Also, he was being a pig to one of the nicest women he knew, and on her wedding day. He made a conscious effort to slow down, force his gaze away from his wife and concentrate on the bride in his arms.

Tess was already a beautiful woman, but the glow of happiness in her eyes and on her cheeks made him feel extra churlish for his behavior. "I'm an ass. I'm sorry."

She twinkled up at him. Yes, she did. The woman actually twinkled like a Christmas star on top of a tree, she was so happy. "You own the paper I work for. I forgive you."

He chuckled and tried to remember he'd been taught manners, once. But while, on the outside, he was a perfect gentleman, guiding Tess around the floor, his attention focused completely on her, inside, some very ungentlemanlike plotting was taking place.

He'd tried leaving Caro alone to come to her senses and she'd gone and got a job with the *Star.* The *Star!*

He'd tried enticing her by moving ahead on the animal shelter they'd dreamed of together. Well, she'd dreamed of it, and he'd gone along to keep her mind off her unhealthy obsession with pregnancy. And she'd written an article as she'd promised. For his pains, he now had a backyard full of wildlife while the shelter was costing him a fortune in overtime as he tried to get the damn thing built before his neighbors started picketing.

When he'd manipulated Caro into writing the article, his aim had been to get her to move back home with him. But it wasn't his wife who'd moved in. It was a squirrel with a missing ear, a hobbling rabbit, which got the peregrine all het up, and a duck that thought Jon was its mother. At least, he assumed that's why it followed him everywhere.

Caro should be there. She'd make a better mother than he. He felt a small pang of guilt. It wasn't that he didn't want kids, he did. But he loved Caro enough to do whatever needed to be done. More tests, adoption, whatever.

He'd planned to spend some time with her at Fanny's party, but that had blown up in his face and he'd figured she needed some time to calm down before he dare approach her. He'd nearly picked up the phone a dozen times, almost hopped in his car to drive to the house where she was staying more times than he could count. But he didn't. She'd said she wanted some space and he'd decided to give it to her.

But what the hell was she doing dating another man? They'd started out so happy. Where had it all gone wrong?

"It was her obsession with getting pregnant that started all the trouble." He didn't realize he'd spoken out loud until Tess sighed into his shoulder.

"Don't be too hard on her, Jon," Tess said softly. "She's never failed before."

It was a lightbulb moment. One of those slap-yourself-upside-the-head-for-being-a-moron moments that made him secretly believe women were correct when they claimed men were insensitive brutes.

"Of course. You're right. She's *never* failed before,'' he repeated in a stunned way. "That's it. And I've been going about this all wrong.''

He felt a small movement against his shoulder— Tess was nodding agreement.

"Why didn't you tell me?''

She leaned back and stared up at him in surprise. "I thought you'd be smart enough to figure it out.''

He shook his head. "Nope. I'm a moron.'' He hesitated, making another attempt to gather his manners, but like a dry leaf caught in a windstorm, they were gone.

He gave up. "You know nothing happened between me and Lori Gerhardt, don't you?''

She paused, a tiny frown appearing between her brows. "I know Mike believes that, and he's a pretty smart guy.''

"For a guy,'' he finished for her in his driest tone.

She laughed. "I'm giving you the benefit of the doubt here. But if I ever hear one word about Caro not being happy, you're a dead man.''

His heart felt as though it was inflating. A plan so daring and so perfect popped fully formed into his head. "So, you'll help me?''

She bit her lip. "Help you what? Caro's my best friend. I have to be careful.''

"I understand,'' he said. His mind whirled furiously, grabbing and discarding strategies. He had a lot to do and very little time. "I'm not asking you to do anything, I'm just asking you *not* to do anything.''

''Pardon?'' The music changed. The waltz was over and the band was playing rock and roll. Tess and Jon stood motionless while he debated how much to tell her.

He tried to recall all the duties of a matron of honor and best man. The speeches were done, the toasts drunk, there was only the throwing of the bouquet and the changing of clothes before Tess and Mike took off on their honeymoon. ''Look, can you make yourself scarce in about—'' he checked his watch ''—an hour? Then none of this will be your problem.''

Someone bumped him and he realized the two of them must look really strange standing stock-still in the middle of the floor while every one else was dancing. He spun Tess in time to the music. She spun back and narrowed her eyes at him. ''We could go and get changed. Why?''

''I'm not going to tell you what I'm planning, so that you can have a clear conscience when Caro comes after you.''

''But—but…'' He stifled the grin as he watched frustration build on her face. Not knowing what he was up to must be killing her since she was both a woman and one of his most inquisitive reporters.

''Come on.'' She finally cracked, glancing over to where Caro was still flirting with the beefcake in a manner Jon now saw as calculated and determined. "Throw me a bone."

He thought for a second. "I've got an idea. I'm going to let her know I don't need her to be perfect."

She nodded. "And?"

He wanted to kiss Tess for giving him the answer to how to get Caro back. Because it was important to get this just right and any ill-judged blabbing would ruin everything, he said nothing.

One look at his face had her complaining in a hissing whisper, "This is your bone?"

He nodded.

"It's a toe bone."

"Thanks for your help. Really."

"From the baby toe of a mouse," she spluttered in outrage.

"I think you may have saved my marriage." And then he kissed her. A big smacker right on her pretty, pouting lips.

"Hey, you making time with my wife?" Mike said in a booming voice from beside him, heavy emphasis on the word *wife*.

"No." He shook his head, squeezing both of them on a shoulder and pushing them together. "I've got my own wife to make time with."

Mike glanced over at Caro, who was giggling with the beefcake, and sent him a look of pity.

"Well, I don't have her right at the moment, but I will. I've got a couple of calls to make."

He spotted Steve circling Harriet around the dance floor. Perfect. Just the man he needed for a favor or two.

Harriet was wearing a sleeveless turtleneck knit dress in soft turquoise. She seemed to wear a lot of turtlenecks since she'd stared dating Steve. He almost didn't recognize the redheaded beauty without a square inch of tartan among her clothing, though she was wearing a thistle pin in case anyone could doubt her Scottish heritage.

Between her cheerleading duties with the Pasqualie Bravehearts and her new relationship with the *Standard*'s sports editor, Harriet had blossomed. Still, he had to remember she was Caro's friend—she and Tess and Caro stuck together like three peas in a pod as his mother would say. He'd have to get Steve away from her for a few minutes.

Luckily, Steve was a smart guy. Didn't take more than a jerk of the head toward the bar and Jon no sooner had a glass of single malt in his hand than Steve appeared at his elbow. "What's up?"

Jon glanced behind the sports editor. "Where's Harriet?"

"Looked like you wanted to talk to me alone so I dropped her off with the bride. You know women. They won't see each other for two weeks while Tess's on her honeymoon so they've got a lot of chattering to do."

Jon cracked a smile and held out his untouched glass. "Want a Scotch?"

"Isn't that your drink?"

Jon shook his head. "I've got a long drive ahead of me. I need some help. Here's what I want you to do...."

AFTER SPEAKING to Steve, Jon disappeared to make a couple of phone calls, then slipped out for a couple of errands of his own. When he returned, his plan was in place and anticipation in his belly.

He spotted Steve in the crowd and wandered over. "How's it going?"

"Got everything on the list. It's in the trunk of your car. Here are your spare keys."

"Thanks." He held out his hand.

Steve shook it firmly. "Good luck."

Oh, and he needed luck tonight. He checked his watch. Perfect—the hour was nearly up. When Tess and Mike left to change, he'd make his move.

Taking a deep breath, he took a step toward his wife. Step one of Operation Get Caro. He was so focused that he missed the diminutive silver-haired woman stalking him until she poked him in the ribs and said, "I'm going to slap you so hard, when you wake up, your clothes'll be out of style."

His heart sank. He didn't need the lecture he could see burning deep in his mother's eyes. Not now, he didn't. "Mother, please."

But it was hopeless. Once Fanny got started she wasn't easy to stop. "You had that floozy half-naked in my wine cellar—"

"I didn't strip her, she stripped herself!" He felt

stung and was determined to defend himself, though he wondered why he bothered.

"Do not interrupt me, young man." His mother fairly bristled with indignation. The silver beads in her hair and matching silver dress sparkled in the light, causing her to resemble a very wrinkled and angry angel. "What is the matter with you? You haven't even phoned Caro since my party."

"How do you know I haven't?"

"Because I asked her."

He groaned. "Does the phrase 'interfering mother-in-law' mean anything to you?"

"Does the phrase 'stupider than a bowl of mashed turnips' mean anything to you?"

He didn't want to smile, but he couldn't help himself. After knowing Fanny all his life, there weren't many bizarre sayings he hadn't heard. "I'm doing my best to fix things, Mom. All I have to do is get Caro alone."

"How do you aim to do that? She's got company. And he's sticking to her like a bluebottle to flypaper."

"You're my mother. I rely on you to help me get my wife back. Can you distract the beefcake for a few minutes?"

His mother fanned herself with her hand as she studied the bronze god standing far too close to her son's wife. Her annoyance seemed to melt. "My, oh, my. God must have been in a good mood the day he turned out that boy."

Jon had no idea how God felt about Caro's date, but he had a few less than complimentary thoughts of his own. "Mom, will you help me get Caro alone?"

"Why? So you can act like a doofus again?"

He was certain there were men all over the world who had supportive, loving mothers. What on earth had he done to deserve this one? "No. So I can win her back."

She glanced over at Caro and the boy-toy then back at him. "I'll do it this once, and you'd better get it right or I will seriously fix your wagon." She grinned as slyly as an old fox. "I wonder if that boy's interested in a job down at the Roadhouse."

He was momentarily diverted from tonight's plan. "You need another bartender?" His mom usually discussed all her business with him, but he hadn't heard of any openings.

"I've been thinking of adding a male stripper Thursday nights. Call it Ladies' Night. Be good for business." And with a wink she turned and strode toward Caro.

Jon shook his head. Other men his age worried about their mothers, he was sure. But he was certain his problems were unique. *Male strippers.*

Slowly, he followed his mother, waiting until she was already in conversation with Caro and her "date" before he joined the cozy little group. His mother's idea of opening a conversation with a young man she'd never met turned out to be,

"How much can you bench-press with those things?" as she reached up to squeeze the man's biceps.

To his credit, the beefcake merely grinned at the small woman and said, "I could bench-press you with one finger, little lady," which had Fanny chortling with delight.

Then she launched into a story about a wrestler she'd once had in her bar. While Fanny kept the muscle machine occupied, Jon turned to Caro, who was staring at him with an odd expression. "Are you all right?" he asked.

She blinked, looking as stunned as a returning time traveler. "Yes. I'm fine."

There was a pause while he searched her face, sensing something was different but not able to pinpoint what that might be. She squirmed under his gaze and color crept into her cheeks. "It was a beautiful wedding," she said at last, as though they were newly introduced acquaintances instead of husband and wife.

"Yes, it was. I think they're good for each other." But he didn't want to talk about Tess and Mike, he wanted to talk about Caro and him. "Listen, I was wondering—"

The minute his voice dropped, her eyes widened in alarm. "Did you meet Andre?" She tugged Adonis's arm much the way his mother had when she was checking out the man's biceps.

While Caro was doing that, his mother came to

the punch line of her story. "And he lifted me like I didn't weigh any more than a pretzel and twirled me around over his head."

His mother was staring up at Adonis with speculation, and Jon wondered how he was going to prevent her spinning like a roulette wheel over Adonis's head. Fortunately the beefcake helped him out by laughing. "I couldn't do that, ma'am. He must have been some athlete."

"Andre Giardin," Caro said, "meet Jonathon Kushner."

Caro watched the two men shake hands reluctantly and exchange chilly greetings. She had no idea why she found Jon so much more attractive than the gorgeous model who was her escort, but she did. She was tired. Tired of this stupid game she and Jon were playing, tired of pretending. Tomorrow, she was going to phone her husband and suggest they get together. Nothing too rash. Maybe dinner somewhere quiet, where she'd suggest they get some counseling. She wasn't certain she'd tell him about the baby right away. She loved him and wanted her husband back, but she also wanted a strong family in which to bring up their child.

"Do you live around here?" Jon was asking Andre, every inch the possessive stag looking to fight down his competition. She knew it was small and mean of her, but she rather liked being fought over after the way she'd been publicly humiliated.

"I live in Oregon."

"That's not far at all," said Fanny, earning herself a glare from her son. Bless her heart if she wasn't willing to make things as tough for Jon as Caro was. Andre seemed to have caught right on and if he didn't approve, due to her condition, he was more than willing to take a few verbal pokes at Jon.

"Caro and I knew each other in New York," he said, sending her an intimate glance. He'd been taking acting lessons recently and, boy, had they paid off. Even *she* felt as though they'd had a steamy affair, when she knew as well as Andre that they'd never been anything but friends.

She didn't have acting lessons behind her, but she did have a bruised ego that wasn't at all averse to making Jon suffer. "I love New York," she said with a small smile. It was true. She did love the city. If Jon chose to read more into her words, that was his problem.

"New York was a long time ago," Jon said, smooth as silk. "Before Caro met me. I'm surprised she never mentioned your name."

Oh, point to Jon. She was amazed how much she was enjoying being the prize in this absurd verbal tug-of-war.

Fanny made a choking sound and turned to grab a glass of champagne from a passing waiter's tray.

Jon grabbed two more flutes and offered her one.

Andre frowned at him. "She shouldn't be drinking."

Jon blinked and Caro wanted to hit Andre for his tactlessness. Instead she took the flute from Jon and handed it over to her date. "I took a headache pill earlier," she lied. "They don't mix with alcohol."

"Right," said Andre, looking ready to mop his brow. "Listen, why don't we—"

"Dad! Dad!" Two small boys barreled through the crowd, zipping around the dance floor and pelting toward Andre, where they threw themselves against him.

"Hi, boys," he said, putting his champagne down so he could ruffle the heads pressed against him. "These are my—"

"Orphans!" Caro cried, wishing she'd listened to Tess when her friend had tried to warn her about this being a very bad idea.

"Peter and Alex," Andre said, with a quelling glance her way. "My sons. What are you guys doing here?"

"Mr. Giardin, you have to come quickly," the nanny said, puffing slightly as she arrived at the group. "Your wife is in labor."

"Giving birth to another orphan?" Jon asked with a bland glance at Caro, smug humor lighting his eyes.

Later, she'd poke them out. Right now, she had more important things to do. Okay, so her plan had backfired and she'd ended up looking like an idiot. There were worse things that could happen to a person.

She gave Andre a hug. "That's great. Give Donna my best." Her eyes filled with tears of emotion as she watched her old friend flush with pleasure, and hug his two sons, then Fanny.

Soon Caro would be the one in labor, she realized, resisting the urge to touch her own belly. Would anyone be rushing to her bedside?

She sniffed. "Can I drive you to the airport?"

"No. We've got a rental." Andre dug a cell phone out of his pocket. "I'll call Donna and tell her we'll be on the next plane. We'll get there. I haven't missed one yet."

He shot a glance between Jon and Caro and shrugged, gave his charming smile and extended his hand to Jon. "No hard feelings?"

"Not anymore," said Jon, moving closer to her side.

"Oh, how—" she spluttered.

"Take care of her," Andre said, shaking Jon's hand much more warmly than he had earlier.

"Chauvinistic!"

"I will," Jon assured her friend. She couldn't help but notice that Andre may belong in the hunk hall of fame, but it was Jon's nearness that had her pulse fluttering.

Probably because she was still in love with him.

"The father of my child," she mumbled, while she waved goodbye to her temporary date and his children.

"Pardon?"

"I s-said," she stammered, horrified she'd spoken the words out loud and trying to recover, "he'll be the father of another child."

Jon pulled her against him and he touched her cheek. He didn't say a word, simply laid his hand against her face and she felt all the things he wanted to say to her. Their gazes locked and her eyes filled with tears once more. He must be thinking she was sad that Andre was off to attend a birth while she couldn't conceive. She had to tell him the truth. And soon.

"Let's dance," he said huskily.

She nodded, let him take her hand and pull her forward.

"Why, Jonathon and Caroline. It's so good to see you two together again." Cherise swayed toward them. It was obvious she'd been doing quite a bit of celebrating. She seemed to have trouble focusing and her speech was slurred.

"Does this mean you're getting back together?" She stepped closer to give them both a bosomy hug. Caro thought she might get drunk just breathing the same air.

"It means we're going to dance," Jon said in a polite but steely tone. He pulled Caro forward, but Cherise's shoe was firmly planted on the hem of Caro's dress and, as the silk was pulled in two directions, it gave at the weakest point—where the seams had been let out twice.

Caro heard the fabric tear a second before she

felt the breeze on the naked skin of her midriff. She cried out in alarm and hugged her arms around herself, trying to pull the split dress together.

"Jon!" she cried. "Give me your coat."

"Are you nuts? It's hotter than—"

"Your coat. Now."

He stared at her, then blinked as he took in her predicament. Dragging off his jacket, he draped it around her shoulders.

"Take me to the ladies' room and then find somebody with a needle and thread."

He was always quick, she'd give him that. He threw an arm around her so he managed to look casual, yet helped keep everything intact and led her out of the crowded ballroom into the relative quiet of the hallway.

They were almost past the ladies' washroom when she halted.

"Jon, I get off here."

"I've got a better idea," he said, and kept walking. "We're ahead of schedule, but that's all right."

Since he and his jacket were all that stood between her and embarrassment, she stayed with him. When they got to a side entrance leading to the parking lot she said, "Where are we going?"

"My car."

He was a pretty organized man, but unless he'd changed in the last few weeks, he didn't have a sewing kit in his car. "What for?"

"I want to show you something."

It was ridiculous, but she didn't have a lot of better ideas. Besides, it felt so good to be tucked under his jacket, surrounded by his scent, the wool still warm from his body.

The body that had helped conceive a child.

Pregnant. The word shivered through Caro like a wonderful secret. Well, it was a wonderful secret. Her hand settled on her belly where her secret lodged and she gazed at the father of her child.

He helped her into the car and she tried not to let the familiarity of it wash over her. But how could she help it when the smell of the leather interior combined with a hint of his aftershave to taunt her with memories?

She pulled his suit jacket tighter around her as though that could protect her from the past, when the jacket was an even more familiar reminder of his scent.

"You bought a new tuxedo for Mike's wedding? You hate tuxedos."

"Mike wanted to wear biking leathers, but Tess talked him out of it."

While she was picturing what the bridesmaid and best man would have to wear if the groom wore black leather chaps, Jon was snapping her seat belt in place and the next thing she heard was the quiet purr of the Mercedes engine.

"What are you doing?" she asked. "We should get back before we're missed."

He backed out of the parking space without replying and headed out of the lot, the car gathering speed as it hit the main road.

"What are you doing?" she repeated, louder this time.

"You're not going back. Neither am I."

"Oh, yes I am. Turn around."

"You don't seem to have grasped the situation," he said with irritating calm. "I'm kidnapping you."

11

Torn between irritation and a secret thrill at his high-handed tactics, she laughed. "You can't be serious."

"I've never been more serious in my life."

"But…" What on earth could she say to him to make him stop? Did she want him to stop?

She bit her lip and stared out the window as houses and trees flashed by in a blur. She realized her eyes were misty and immediately blamed pregnancy hormones.

"All right, Jon. You've made your point. We need to talk. I'm willing to do that tomorrow, but right now we have to get back to the wedding. We're Mike and Tess's attendants, we can't let them down by leaving before they do."

"Pick out a CD if you'd like," Jon said.

"You're very well-mannered for a kidnapper," she said, her tone brittle.

She could see a dimple develop in his cheek when he grinned. He had a wonderful profile, straight nose, full lips, firm chin. Very firm chin. So firm she'd probably break her fist on it if she punched him, which she was strongly inclined to do.

What she ought to do was call the police. Her ex was clearly a madman. "You must have misread your 'How To Be A Best Man' guide. You're supposed to toast the bridesmaid, not kidnap her."

"Actually, it's the groom who toasts the bridesmaids. I'm running away with one. I was improvising. Do you think it's a custom that will catch on?" He turned to her and the light from a passing streetlight touched his cheekbones and left his eyes in shadow, giving him a sinister aspect.

"I think you're insane. Where are you taking me?"

"Somewhere outside of town."

"Outside town?" She'd assumed he'd take her to their house, or to the riverfront park where they could talk. But out of town? The man must be losing it.

"Hand me your cell phone. I have to call Tess so she doesn't worry."

"All arranged."

The statement hit her like a slap. "You mean Tess knows you're kidnapping me?"

"No. Of course not. I simply let her know we'd be leaving early."

"Oh, I am so glad we are getting a divorce. That's just the sort of arrogant—"

"Are you?"

His interruption stopped her cold.

He turned to glance at her. "Are you glad we're getting a divorce?

As glad as she'd be if somebody pulled her hair out strand by strand. But she wouldn't admit that. Not yet. Instead of answering him, she said, "I still need to let Tess know. I'll apologize to her. Let me have your cell." She held out her hand for it.

"I didn't bring it."

Didn't bring it? He always had his phone with him. "I don't believe you. What if a hot news story breaks?"

"It will break without me."

"What if...what if Fanny needs you?"

"Fanny's fine. Steve will take her home."

"Steve?" She was flabbergasted. "Steve's in on this, too?"

He laughed softly. "Give it up, Caro. They're all in on it. Our friends want us back together."

She made a disgusted huffing sound. "None of them has ever tried living with you. You're impossible. At least pull over and let me use a pay phone."

"I'm being as flexible as a kidnapper can be, but I have my image to uphold. Sorry."

She couldn't help the smile that stole over her face in spite of her annoyance. "Your image as a kidnapper. Well, one thing for sure, your image as a staid newspaper publisher will be shot to pieces when you turn up on the front page as a kidnapper."

"Staid? Is that how you see me?"

He glanced over at her and she took a moment to answer, listening to the quiet purr of the powerful engine, watching his hands in perfect control on the wheel. It was one of those spring nights in the Pacific Northwest when the last rays of daylight seem to hover like a friend standing at the doorway still chatting, reluctant to leave.

It seemed to be similar to the way Jon felt about their marriage. She'd shown him the door, but he seemed reluctant to walk through it.

"Yes. You can be staid. But you can also be surprising." She shot him a laughing glance. "Kidnapping me, for instance, is a surprise."

"Was that the problem?" he asked softly. "Was I too conventional?"

Instinctively her muscles tightened. Every darned one of them from her scalp to the soles of her feet. Her knee-jerk reaction was to throw his infidelity in his face, but maybe it was time to look deeper than that, at the problems that had hovered below the surface of their seemingly perfect marriage like jellyfish, floating lazy and almost invisible but ready to sting. "It's not…" she began, not certain at all what she wanted to say.

"I'm sorry," he said. "I promised myself I wouldn't get into this until we reached our destination. Let's talk about something else."

Only too happy to concur, she looked out the window. "Where are we going?"

He shook his head. "Now, I know this is your first kidnapping, so I'm going to go easy on you. But it's questions like that that get a kidnappee into trouble."

She hadn't thought she'd ever laugh again in Jon's company, but the giggle coming out of her mouth surprised her.

He turned to her, his expression just readable in the near dark. "I missed hearing you laugh."

"I haven't been doing much of it lately," she admitted.

"You look tired. Why don't you close your eyes? I'll wake you when we get there."

Amazingly, she found she could relax. He was right. She *was* tired. She felt as if she could sleep around the clock and still wake up wanting a nap. Between the pregnancy, and the stress of the past few days, she was as tired as she'd ever been.

"What's the ransom?" she mumbled, her eyes closed.

"The ransom?"

"The kidnapping ransom. I hope I'm expensive." A woman had a sense of her own value, after all.

"Oh, you are," he said. "And worth every penny."

She might have replied, but her eyes were so heavy, and she was so tired....

IT WAS FULL DARK when Caro woke. She blinked muzzily, responding instinctively to Jon softly calling her name. *Oh, good,* she thought in that moment between sleep and waking, *Jon's here.* But then she woke completely and reality slapped her. Their separation was more than a bad dream, and she wasn't waking in her own home in her own bed, but in the car, and where it was parked she had absolutely no idea.

He had her door open and was offering his hand to help her out. She was so tired she took it.

As she rose to her feet, she felt the chill in the air and inhaled the moist sharp scent of evergreens. She glanced up and saw a million stars bright in the black sky and knew they were miles from the city. "Where are we?"

"A friend's cabin. Come on, I opened it up already."

She took a step back, toward the car. "This is where you brought me? A remote cabin in the middle of nowhere? Who else is here?" Panic beat at her like tiny fists.

He shoved his hands on his hips, frustration in every line. "There's no one else here. That was the whole point of kidnapping you. It's the only way I can get five minutes of your time for you to listen to me."

She stared at him, and even though she couldn't see more than his outline, she heard the anger simmering in his tone.

It sparked her own temper. "Don't you start with me. I didn't ask to be brought here without so much as a toothbrush." She glanced at the squat outline that had *rustic cabin* written all over it. Oh, man, she really hoped it had indoor plumbing. She had nothing but the clothes on her back. One torn bridesmaid's dress, matching silk pumps in eau-de-nil-green, one pair of cream silk panties, a matching silk bra and a clutch purse containing tissues, a lipstick, a comb and her house keys.

"Relax, you won't get a cavity before tomorrow. Anyway, I—"

"Tomorrow?" she screeched. "I'm not spending the night with you."

"Yes. You are."

"Give me those car keys!" She stuck out her hand, palm flat and shaking with anger.

She heard the jingle of keys and in the back of her mind thought how poor-spirited of him to give them up so easily, even as she envisioned driving off in a spurt of dirt, leaving him to enjoy his rustic outdoors weekend alone.

He held them up and she saw a flash of silver. "You want the car keys?"

"Yes."

"Then go get 'em." And he pulled his arm back as if he were a baseball pitcher.

"No! Don't you dare…" But there was no point finishing the sentence. The keys flashed through the air like a shooting star and she heard a distant rustle of bush when they landed somewhere out in the blackness.

"STILL MAD AT ME?" he asked her. She sat in front of a fire, an old hand-crocheted afghan wrapped around her and an earthenware mug of tea in her hand. In the hour they'd been here, she'd calmed down. The cabin was quiet and soothing after the excitement of the wedding. It was so quiet she could almost hear the forest outside settling for the night. Inside, she was comfortably warm in front of the fire Jon had lit in the woodstove. The furniture was old, overstuffed and comfy, perfect against the cedar-paneled walls.

The tea was hot and soothing. Her companion was also hot, but the opposite of soothing. He made her think about things she didn't want to face. He made her vulnerable.

"Mad doesn't begin to cover it." Secretly she was a bit impressed at his ungentlemanly methods. He'd always been so mannered, it was intriguing to see this rough-and-ready side of him. She thought of the speck of life growing inside her body. It wouldn't be a pushover, then.

She had to think of their communal gene pool, hers and Jonathon's, in ways she never had before. Beneath the concealment of the afghan she laid a hand across her tummy. It didn't stick out yet, but there was a hardness there that had nothing to do with sit-ups.

She'd relaxed a bit on discovering the cabin boasted two bedrooms and that Jon had brought some of her clothes from their house, along with a brand-new toothbrush and toiletries. He knew her so well, he had most of the brands right.

"Are you tired?" he asked, settling down into an old leather recliner across from the couch where she sat.

"No." Her sleep in the car had revived her. "You went to a lot of trouble to get me here for a talk. So talk."

She'd decided that the sooner she listened to what he had to say, the sooner she could get out of here. She had no doubt Jon had a spare key to his car hidden somewhere, along with a cell phone. She'd never known him to cut himself off from the world. Never.

He seemed to hesitate and she glimpsed a hint of vulnerability before it disappeared.

"I don't want children," he said.

12

An inarticulate sound came out of her throat. Part moan, part plea, part cry. Then nothing.

The fire crackled loudly in the emotion-filled silence and tears slowly filled Caro's eyes. "You don't want children."

"No." His voice was quiet and steady and she couldn't have a clue how much effort it took him to keep it that way.

"Why...why not?"

"Because I've been an idiot." He stared into the fire, unable to look at her while he lied.

"But—"

"Caro, I want you to listen to me. Please, just hear me out.

She blinked back tears, seemed to hug herself beneath the multicolored throw, and nodded. Her face appeared pale and he realized she was probably tired from all the wedding preparations.

"Would you rather talk about this in the morning?"

"No. Let's get through it now. I think it's best. So, you don't want children."

"No."

"Why didn't you say something months ago? Before we drove ourselves half-crazy with basal temperatures and charts?"

He had to get this right so she'd believe him. Even though it hurt like hell to put his dream of a family away, he knew he had to do it for Caro's sake. For the sake of their marriage. He'd been such a fool not to recognize that she'd latched on to the first excuse to run, not only from her own failure, but, if he knew his wife, she'd wanted to give him an out. If they split up he could find another woman to have a family with. She had that kind of generosity.

"I went along with the child thing because you wanted it so badly. What do I want with kids? It's all dirty diapers and two o'clock feedings and a house with no peace."

Jon continued to talk, but she only heard the same words echoing around in her head. "I don't want children."

The words swirled in the air like gremlins, laughing and mocking her.

It was a joke. This had to be a joke. She forced a grin, but it frayed at the edges. "Did Andre put you up to this?"

"Andre? What's this got to do with him?" He was so obviously appalled at the idea of discussing their attempts to have a baby with Andre that she had to believe him.

She stared at him. Had he been pretending all

that time? She could have sworn he'd been as anxious as she to have a child. At least in the beginning.

"You're not just saying this to make me feel better about not being able to conceive, are you?"

"No. Of course not." He colored and turned away to look out the window.

She bit her lip. She'd smile if this weren't the cruelest irony of her life. Jon was no more used to failing at anything he set his mind to than she was.

It must have choked him to utter those words.

Well, he might be sincere that he really didn't want children and he might be saying it to make her feel better. Either way, they'd made a child their last night together and they were responsible for that baby's welfare whether together or apart.

He'd never been any good as a liar, and the sweetness of his gesture warmed her. Still, they were stuck here for the weekend and she wanted to get to know him again. She wasn't nearly ready to tell him about the baby.

They had a long road back, but it was time to take the first step.

"You hurt me," she said softly.

For her pains she ended up at the receiving end of a groan. "I can't keep telling you over and over there was nothing between me and Lori. It's up to you to trust or not trust."

She shook her head. "I do believe you. I knew the minute the door opened in that wine cellar, and there you were looking ready to murder her while she stood there half-nude.'' She snickered at the memory. She couldn't help it.

''I don't find the memory one bit funny. It was publicly humiliating.''

''Kind of like me finding her in our bed, and then the whole town somehow learning all the details.''

He stared at her as though she were crazy. ''You don't think I told anyone, do you?''

''No.'' She shook her head. At first she'd been ready to believe anything she'd been so mad, but later she realized it was probably Lori who'd spread the story, or the cleaning lady. Or both.

''I've had some time to think. I never knew Lori very well, but I don't think she was subtle around the men she wanted. She must have been coming on to you before that day.''

He rose and grabbed another log, shoving it on the already blazing fire. ''Yes,'' he said, watching the wood snap and crackle. ''You're right, she did. I thought I could handle it, but I guess she wasn't getting the hint that I wasn't interested.''

''Why didn't you tell me?''

''I don't know. Things were kind of strained between us. I didn't want to make a big deal about something that didn't matter.''

''But don't you see? If you'd told me, I wouldn't have believed you were having an affair when I saw her in our bed. I was so angry, and so hurt...''

"I was hurt, too. And angry that you didn't trust me. That you would think for one minute I would do that to you. And in our bed."

She chuckled softly, amazed she could see the humor in what had been, hands down, the worst moment in her life.

"I was so angry, I didn't look beyond the obvious. Besides, you were staring at her with this bemused expression on your face."

"I was stunned. I'd come home, run up to the bedroom to change and there was a nearly naked woman in my bed. It would have been great if she was you. But she wasn't."

"She looked pretty good in a G-string."

"I'm not going to insult your intelligence and pretend I didn't notice that, but believe me, it did nothing for me." He took the step that separated them and ran a fingertip down her cheek. "I'm in love with my wife."

She recognized the rush of emotion she felt as joy. Pure, unalleviated joy.

"I've been an ass."

She nodded in full agreement

"But so have you."

It was tougher to accept that she'd been as much of a fool as he. She furrowed her brow and glared, ready to argue her case.

He merely raised his eyebrows, challenging her to face the truth. It wasn't easy, and when she considered how she'd felt that day when she'd walked in on Jon and Lori, she was certain any woman would have felt the same.

"You have to admit, Jon, it looked bad."

"Of course it looked bad. But you jumped to the most obvious conclusion—the one that did the least credit to either of us, and then never budged from that position. Why?"

This was the part where he had a point. "Okay. Maybe I *was* a bit of an ass. I should have agreed to hear you out."

He blew out a breath in a big, "Whew," then grinned at her. "That wasn't so hard was it."

"Yes. It was. It's not easy for me to admit I was wrong."

"No. That's not the problem." He took her hand in his and sat beside her on the old couch. She almost wept to feel that strong, loving connection she thought they'd lost. "This was the part that took me a while to figure out." He leaned back, keeping her hand tight in his. "We've always been the lucky ones. Leading charmed lives, successful at our careers, finding each other and falling into a great marriage. We didn't know it wasn't perfect because it had never been tested. Then we decided to have a child and discovered we weren't perfect."

Reluctantly she nodded.

"All that time we were trying to create this new life, our marriage was slowly dying. Loving became work and we forgot what brought us together in the first place.

"I've had a lot of time to think about this while we've been apart, and I realized I don't want to lose what we have. That's why I don't want kids."

The fire popped and crackled, sending warmth and the fragrance of burning cedar into the room. Beneath the granny-square afghan, Caro felt cuddled and comforted.

If she'd needed proof that Jon loved her, could it have come any clearer? Did he think she didn't remember their conversations when they first started trying for a child? How he'd felt so alone growing up with almost a generation between him and his older siblings, with parents who were old enough to be grandparents physically, although, of course, his mother had never entirely grown up.

Jon was giving her an out and she loved him for it, but she had to be honest about her shortcomings if they were going to be able to weather the next storm. And there'd be a next storm. She was coming to realize that in a marriage the squalls had to be battled together. It would make the smooth sailing all that much sweeter.

"I didn't trust you to love me if I wasn't perfect. If our marriage wasn't perfect. Running away, refusing to hear your version of the Lori story was an easy way for me to leave." She heard the huskiness in her voice as she fought tears. "I'm sorry."

He pulled her against him and touched her lips softly with his. She wanted to cling to him, to deepen the kiss and to take their reunion to the next stage, but it had been so long since they'd talked and held each other that she didn't want to give that up.

Besides, once he had her naked, Jon would almost certainly notice the changes taking place in her body, and she wasn't ready yet to tell him her news. They needed to heal as a couple first. She pulled away slowly and laid her head on his shoulder. He put his arm around her and snuggled her close.

"Mmm. This is nice. I missed it," she admitted. "I missed you."

"I thought, after the wine cellar, that it was all over."

"You should have seen your face when the door opened. I don't know if you were madder at Lori for trying to seduce you, Mike and Steve for locking you in, or me for seeing the spectacle."

"I was angry with myself for getting caught a second time with a half-naked Lori." He groaned. "I had such big plans for that night. I was going to woo you with my charm. It was my idea to work behind the bar so I could show you I wasn't a snob. And, correct me if this is male ego talking here, but I was getting some pretty good vibes from you that my plan had a shot."

She smiled sleepily against his shoulder. "Not

to cater too much to your male ego, but I was yours for the taking.''

He sighed grumpily. ''Then Lori pulled Home-wrecker II and I saw history repeating itself.''

''I'd already decided to hear you out. Maybe suggest some counseling. Then I saw her in the wine cellar and I knew there was nothing between you two.''

He grabbed her chin and turned her to face him. ''How did you know?''

''When you looked at her, it wasn't a bit the way you used to look at me.''

He tilted her face up so they were staring at each other. ''The way I still look at you,'' he said, and she could see that was true. His gaze sent shivers down her spine.

''The way I'll always look at you,'' he insisted, and she believed him.

''Could we…''

''Yes!'' he said.

She laughed, tamping down her own desire because she simply wasn't ready yet.

She'd punish him for pretending he didn't want a child, but, because she loved him and because she knew he'd made the gesture out of love, she wouldn't make him pay too dearly. There'd been enough of that.

''No. Not that. You know what you said before, about planning to woo me the night of Fanny's birthday party?''

"Sure."

"I was completely wooable."

"How was I supposed to know that? You stomped away so fast you were sprinting."

"I was being discreet. It was embarrassing for Lori—not that she didn't deserve it—awkward for Fanny and our friends, and pretty unpleasant for you. It seemed that if I got out of the way quickly it would be the easiest."

"You did that all right."

She glared at him. "Then you never came near me the rest of the night."

"How was I supposed to know you still wanted to be wooed?"

She rolled her eyes. She could see she still had a lot of work ahead of her. "I stayed, didn't I?"

"I thought that was for Fanny!"

"Well, you were wrong. I love Fanny, but I wanted to be with you."

He groaned. "I really blew it, didn't I?"

"Not as much as you blew it by bringing Miss Georgia Peach to the sports bar on Thursday."

"What? I never saw you there."

"That's because I saw you first."

"I bumped into her there and we had a drink."

"I hope you don't end up hurting her," Caro said, concern pulling her eyebrows together.

"I probably shouldn't tell you this, but if it's to save my marriage, I know she'd understand. She was using me to make a certain quarterback jealous."

Her jaw dropped. "Rock Richards? The one who dated Harriet for a while?"

"The very same. I guess making men jealous is something all you women delight in."

In spite of her own tangled love relationship— or maybe because she was back on the road to bliss and wanted everyone to find their own path to happiness—she was delighted to think of Rock and his cheerleader finding each other. "Did it work?"

Jon rubbed his jaw, his eyes dancing with mischief. "Let's just say, I feared for my life when he saw us together at the sports bar. Not wanting to be flattened by those steamroller muscles of his, I gracefully made way for him."

She wasn't fooled for a minute. "You were playing matchmaker," she said, delighted with him.

He shifted, the picture of manly embarrassment. "No way. I was lucky to get away with my life."

Okay, so he wouldn't admit it. She kissed him anyway. "Those two are perfect for each other. Do you think it will work out?"

"They were certainly wrapped up in each other when they left the bar together."

She clapped. "Now the only one we have to worry about is Lori."

"Houston can worry about Lori. What we have to worry about, my love, is us."

He laid a palm against her cheek and kissed her, a long, slow kiss that made her toes curl.

"About us," she said, pulling away slowly. "We need to keep working on this marriage and never let it get stale."

"I have a few ideas right now that would freshen things up."

She chuckled. "I was thinking of counseling. Maybe it would be a good idea for us to get used to talking things through."

He groaned. "I don't want to spend three hours a week whining to some shrink."

"If it was important to me would you do it?"

He screwed up his face as though in pain. "Any shrink will take one look at my mother and figure I'm a hopeless case."

She laughed. "Maybe your mother should be our counselor. Can't you imagine the advice she'd give?"

"I know one thing she did teach me is 'never go to bed mad.'" He made a big production of yawning. "I'm ready for bed. And I'm not mad." His eyes were half humorous, half serious. He was leaving the decision to her, she knew. She bit her lip, torn between wanting him so much it hurt and wanting to continue the sharing and touching. The wooing.

She thought about her baby and how important a strong marriage would be to the child they'd created and decided her hormones would have to wait.

She kissed Jon lightly. "Much as I'd love to crawl into bed with you right now, if we did, we wouldn't crawl out again until Monday."

"I think you're exaggerating," he said with enormous dignity.

"Remember Paris?"

He grinned. "One of the best weekends we ever spent."

"We didn't see a single sight," she said, warming with the memories.

"I remember the Eiffel Tower distinctly."

"Only because it was the view from our bedroom window."

He chuckled. "Okay, you're right. If we go to bed now, we'll stay there all weekend. And that's not a good idea because…?"

She sighed and snuggled against him. "Let's not fall into our old routines. We need to do some communicating."

"Well, here's a communication for you. That fellow you brought to the wedding can thank his new baby that he didn't end up eating his capped teeth."

She happened to know that nature had endowed Andre with perfect teeth along with his good looks and magnificent physique, but she decided now probably wasn't the time to explain that to Jon.

"I still want the wooing. I want us to talk and go for walks and get to know each other again."

"All right," he said. "But I'm giving you fair

warning. In my opinion, sex is a big part of wooing.''

''I know, and I appreciate you letting me have
my way in this.''

She got ready for bed, feeling happier than she
had in weeks. They loved each other and they had
a future, but they'd also learned their marriage
wasn't perfect, and neither were they. This recon-
ciliation was an important step for both of them.
She was determined to get it right.

She readied herself for the night in the cabin's
single bathroom, thankful both for the indoor
plumbing and for how well Jon had remembered
her favorite products.

When she emerged, he was stoking the woodstove in the kitchen.

His eyes kindled brighter than the burning logs
when he saw her. ''Do I get a good-night kiss?''

She nodded, feeling absurdly shy. They'd been
married for five years for goodness' sake, but this
felt like a new relationship. Of course, she realized
that in many ways it was.

She licked her lips as he halted inches away from
her. She smelled the wood smoke and fresh air
smells of him and the underlying scent of his skin.

''Good night, Caro,'' he said, and lifting her
chin, kissed her softly. She'd been prepared for a
deep, hungry kiss, and the gentle brush of his lips
was so unexpected, and so surprisingly sexy, that
she leaned into him and sighed. She didn't know

if it was the hormones at work, but she'd never felt so female, so…womanly. All he had to do was take her hand and lead her to his bed.

"See you in the morning," he said, and it took her a minute to realize he'd left her standing there, needy and restless.

As she moved back inside her room, she was tempted to lock the door. Not to keep Jonathon out, but to lock herself inside.

As she snuggled under the blankets, she rubbed her hand over her belly. "You're a good chaperon," she whispered, grinning to herself. "And one day, believe me, I'll be returning the favor."

13

THEY DROVE BACK to town the next morning. As she'd suspected, he'd brought a spare set of keys along, although he'd really come without a cell phone. Since she'd more than once complained that he wouldn't go anywhere without one, she had to assume he'd spent a weekend phoneless to please her.

And it did please her. She yawned as they drove down the windy mountain road she hadn't seen on the trip up. She wasn't nearly as rested as she would have liked to be. He'd wanted her to come to him last night. She understood that, even as she understood that they still had some hurdles to cross.

By unspoken agreement, they stayed on safe conversational topics until they reached town. Then all her chitchat seemed to dry up. In fact, her tongue seemed to dry up until it felt like a piece of beef jerky in her parched mouth.

What if she was wrong and he really didn't want children?

The car slowed as they passed through a school-crossing zone. She gazed at the sign with stick figure renditions of a boy and girl crossing the street and her eyes misted.

She had to get a grip.

They were turning into the street where she was staying. She clasped her damp palms together. She had to tell him.

Jonathon pulled the car to the curb and cut the engine. In the sudden silence they stared at each other. He lifted a hand and touched her hair. "Well, the weekend didn't exactly go the way I planned it, but—"

"I had a wonderful time," she interrupted. "It was like old times."

He grinned at her, that devastatingly charming grin that got to her every time. "When are you moving back home?"

"I'm, um…" Oh, what was the matter with her? She ought to have seen this one coming. She took a deep breath. "I'd like you to come for dinner one night this week. What about Wednesday?"

The grin faded, and he was as serious as she'd ever seen him. "I don't want to play any more games. Let's make it tomorrow. And if I come for dinner, I'm going to want to stay for breakfast."

Her breath caught on a combination sigh and sob. Without answering, she opened the car door, digging the borrowed house keys out of the cream clutch from the wedding. She had to go by feel since she could barely see.

She made it to the door and managed to get it

open before he appeared with the case of her things he'd brought along.

"All right," she said shakily. "Tomorrow."

"Why don't we have dinner tonight?"

She took a deep breath, making sure she was on the other side of the open door. "I'm pregnant. See you tomorrow."

"I NEED A CHISEL," Jon announced.

Bert of Bert's Hardware, stared at him. They knew each other through the chamber of commerce, not because Jon was a frequent visitor to the store. In fact, as far as Jon could recall, he'd never crossed the threshold before.

Places like this made Jon nervous. It was all tools he had no idea how to use, and nuts and bolts and pipes. Jon's tools of choice were a calculator to estimate costs and a phone to call in the experts. Any job requiring more macho tools could be hired out to a macho guy who knew how to use them. He didn't know a chisel from a planer. Which was a problem, because he needed both.

He'd blown it and blown it good. He'd been amazingly successful in convincing Caro he didn't want children. Now he had to make her believe the truth. That he wanted children as much as she did.

He must have stood like a fool staring at the door Caro had shut in his face for a good ten minutes. At first he'd been numb with shock at her announcement that she was pregnant, then delighted. He'd been about to bang down the door to be with her, kidnap her a second time in as many days if necessary, but then he realized that if he'd drawn up a plan to destroy his future happiness he couldn't have come up with a better weapon than to tell her he didn't want kids. Getting her to believe the opposite would take some doing.

Words wouldn't cut it a second time. He had to convince her through an impossible feat of manly daring.

He picked up the pages he'd photocopied from the book he'd bought earlier: *How to Build Your Own Nursery.*

His airways had felt restricted as he'd leafed through the book looking for a way to show Caro with his hands how much he wanted a baby with her.

He'd balked at the crib. He wouldn't entrust anything so precious as a baby to any crib he would build. But the cradle was a two-hammer job, signifying minimum difficulty on the book's handyman scale according to the authors. Minimal tools, minimum skills and he'd liked the time frame. According to the instructions, he'd have a cradle built in just over eight hours.

Perfect.

Jon had always been a quick study. He'd managed a four-year business degree in three; he was certain he could shave a couple of hours off the estimated cradle-building time. He figured he'd have his home-built cradle ready for occupation in under six hours.

All he needed was the correct tools.

"You need a chisel?" Bert repeated, looking at him as though he'd lost his mind.

"Yes. And a coping saw."

Bert nodded, then paused to scratch his ear. "You want to show me what you've got there, Jon? Maybe I could help."

Oh, yeah. He'd help, all right. He'd help spread the story that Jonathon Kushner was building a cradle. Wouldn't the good people of Pasqualie love to hear about that? He could already hear the whispers and speculation.

He slapped the photocopied pages against his chest. "No. It's, uh...I want to do this myself."

"Okay, keep your shirt on," Bert muttered. "Shout out what you need and I'll get it for you."

"Great. Excellent." If Jon had been thinking straight he would have prepared a list and faxed it, then picked all the stuff up. But he was like a traveler in a foreign land in the do-it-yourself department. His normal rules of behavior didn't seem to apply.

So he called out his list of tools and materials, and Bert loaded them on a trolley. When Jon had double-checked that he had everything, including what looked like most of a butternut tree, the trolley was packed high with tools, three grades of sandpaper and something called filler-stain. He had everything right down to the nontoxic varnish.

Bert rang up the total. "Comes to $783.08."

Jon pulled out his credit card, thinking he probably could have ordered a cradle from Tiffany's that wouldn't have cost as much. But it wouldn't have meant as much to Caro, either. She knew he'd never built anything in his life and this was the gesture that would tell her his real feelings.

He was counting on it for the sake of his marriage and his family. He couldn't quite keep the grin off his face as he and Bert manhandled the dolly of stuff out to the parking lot.

"You want me to deliver this for you?" Bert said, eyeing the Mercedes.

"No. I want to get started right away."

Between them they managed to wedge everything in, lashing the butternut to the car's roof. He drove away slowly, feeling more like the Beverly Hillbillies moving all their worldly goods than a prospective father with nothing more than the makings of a baby cradle.

He got home and parked outside the garage, having already decided that would be the command center for Operation Cradle.

He set up his new portable workbench, put an alarming number of tools out and hauled in the piece of wood that, within six hours or so, was going to be transformed into a cradle.

He glanced at his watch—11:00 a.m. Good. By

five he'd have the cradle done, sooner if he really focused, in plenty of time for dinner, and then he could get back to wooing his wife. He figured he had all the time in the world.

Taking a deep breath, he rolled his shoulders, and pulled out the instructions.

He read them thoroughly. Baffled, he frowned. Maybe the light in here wasn't that good; he couldn't seem to make any sense of the directions.

He took the instructions into the house and brewed himself a pot of coffee in the bright kitchen. While he was waiting for his coffee he read the directions again, with a highlighter pen in hand so he could highlight each step in the process.

Butternut was an open-grained hardwood, he learned, so it must be filled before staining. Right, filler-stain. He had that.

Round all corners. Well, duh. It was a cradle. Aha, that's where the coping saw came in. He scratched his head, trying to remember which one was the coping saw.

Even as a drop of cold sweat rolled down his back he reminded himself that he could do this. He was an intelligent, educated man with two ad-vanced degrees. This was a two-hammer level pro-ject for the beginning handyman. How hard could it be?

Back into the garage. By one o'clock he was ready to take those two handyman hammers and bash the *How to Build Your Own Nursery* authors senseless.

In two hours he'd managed to gouge a small well in the aptly-named hardwood. He'd also managed to injure his thumb badly enough that he was pretty sure he was going to lose the nail, to break the handle off his new chisel when he accidentally threw it against the side of the house, and to give himself a black eye when he lost control of the block of wood that was no closer to being a cradle than it had been two hours earlier.

He pulled out his cell phone, wincing at the pain in his thumb, and considered offering Bert a thousand bucks to come over and build the damn cradle.

With a soft curse he shoved the phone back into his pocket knowing he had to do this himself.

14

CARO WATERED the plants Tuesday morning, which she'd intended to do on the weekend. "You must be female," she said to the healthy-looking ficus. "You retain water."

She was up much too early to go to work and much too upset to do anything that involved concentration.

Jonathon had stood her up last night, after she'd cooked his favorite dinner. His six o'clock phone call had been harried and bizarre. He'd sounded so strange she had a feeling he'd been drinking.

"I hope your father's not turning into an alcoholic," she said to her tummy. "Is that hereditary? If it is, I apologize right now. I never knew. Honest. Seems funny to feel guilty over your father's faulty genes, but I guess I might as well get used to guilt. It's a mother's burden. I'm guilty you won't have a normal home life with a mother and father, guilty I'm not a better cook, and I should probably tell you I'm hopeless with nursery rhymes. It's like jokes. I get so far then don't remember the punch line."

She sighed at her shortcomings as a mother,

thinking of her little girl growing up not knowing what happened after Rapunzel let down her golden hair.

Was that the same story where the little guy spun straw into gold?

And what were the names of Snow White's seven dwarfs?

"Sleepy, Dumpy..." No, that couldn't be right. Humpy, maybe. Depression washed over her as she contemplated her inadequacies as a mother, and the heretofore unknown discrepancies in the Kushner gene pool. She brightened up a little, however, when she thought ahead to the fashion-doll stage.

"If there's one thing I know, baby, it's fashion. Barbie will never look so good."

Cyclops seemed to have picked up on her anxiety and was pacing and meowing until she picked her up and cuddled her.

With the cat purring against her neck, she heard a car pull into the driveway. It wasn't even seven yet, who could possibly be visiting at this time of the morning? She opened the front door only to feel her jaw drop.

There was Jon. At least, she thought it was Jon. That was certainly his car. But this guy looked as though he'd gone twelve rounds with Tyson in a very bad mood.

"Jon?"

He turned to her and she gasped. "What happened to your eye?"

"Had a little accident."

He limped toward her and in spite of her anger, her heart twisted. "What about your leg?"

"I dropped a— I forget what it's called. A big metal thing on it."

He was bleary-eyed, his hair was a mess and her usually scrupulously neat husband didn't smell all that good.

Annoyance and pity warred within her. "Where have you been?"

"I have a surprise. Go inside. I'll bring it in."

She didn't move. "Jon, have you been drinking?"

"A few pots of coffee. Give me a break, will you? I've been up all night. Just go inside."

He'd been up all night, he appeared to have slept in his clothes, he smelled sweaty and unwashed and if he hadn't been brawling, she'd eat her new maternity dress. She wasn't anywhere near ready for maternity clothes, but she hadn't been able to resist.

Well, she wouldn't eat her dress, of course, because she didn't suppose designer clothes were the optimum diet for an expectant mother.

She muttered as much to the cat, settling them both at the kitchen table. Cyclops leaped away, still restless, pacing and mewing.

She heard Jon bash something against the front door and call her name. He sounded out of breath.

"I'm in the kitchen."

He limped in, carrying something about the size

of an armchair wrapped in a yellow sheet with an inexpertly tied bow around it.

"What on earth?"

He grunted as he placed it to the floor. "Open it."

She glanced up, but it was hard to read his expression through the black eye and unshaven stubble.

For some reason her fingers trembled slightly as she undid the bow and removed it. She took a deep breath and wiped her suddenly damp palms on her slacks before flipping the sheet away.

She had no idea what she was looking at. A piece of modern art? An incredibly strange salad bowl on a wobbly stand?

She stared at Jon, speechless, and he dropped to his knees beside her, wincing as he hit the tile. "Do you like it?" he said, sounding so hesitant she barely recognized the self-assured man she was used to.

"Yes," she said politely, wondering what on earth this thing was and what she was supposed to do with it.

Maybe it was a bird bath?

For pterodactyls.

"You don't have to use it," he said, still in that soft, diffident tone.

Okay. A clue. It was something you used. "Oh, of course I'll use it." For what she had no idea. A planter? But surely the plants would topple out.

"I'll have to fix it so the baby doesn't fall out," he said.

"Baby?" What this lumpy, strangely yellow hunk of wood with a crater gouged in it and a baby had in common, she couldn't work out.

"Yes. It's a baby cradle. I made it myself."

It was too much of a shock. Those two statements together. He'd made her a cradle. For their baby. With his own hands. She turned to him, so choked with emotion she couldn't form a single word.

"I know it's not very good. It was a lot harder than the directions indicated. And I've never made anything before. I planned to have it finished in time for dinner last night, but I wasn't nearly done, that's why I had to cancel. I worked all night. I just finished. I didn't want to miss you before you went to work, so I didn't stop to shower or shave." He stopped talking long enough to sniff and grimace. "I was so scared I'd miss you. Please say you understand."

The tears were coming and she couldn't stop them.

"You made it?" She touched a finger to the odd-shaped lump and it wobbled alarmingly.

"Yeah." He lunged for it, settling it back in place, holding on until he was certain it wouldn't topple.

"Well?" he said. "What do you think?"

She bit her bottom lip. "I think that that is the

worst cradle I've ever seen." She blinked rapidly, though nothing would stop the flow of tears. "And the sweetest thing you've ever done."

Even through Jon's blurry, sleep-deprived eyes, he could see she had a point. He'd never let any child of his spend five minutes in that pathetic excuse for a cradle. "What I was trying to say is..." He glanced at her, hoping she'd finish the sentence for him, jump in and help him out, but she merely gazed at him, her eyes like rain-drenched violets.

"I'm trying to send a message here."

"And that is?"

"I love you. I told you I didn't want kids because I love you. With children or without them, I want you. I..." It hurt to tell her this, but it was time for full and complete honesty. "I need you."

Another pair of tears tracked down her cheeks and he saw the hope, and her own need. He stepped forward and pulled her into his arms. "We'll make mistakes, and we'll fumble. We won't be perfect parents, but I promise you here and now that I'll be the best husband and father I know how to be. I love you." He kissed her lips then dropped to his knees and kissed her belly, which would soon bloom with his child. "I love both of you."

She sniffed and wiped her streaming eyes. "I love you, too. I'm sorry I didn't trust you. Sorry I was such a fool."

"There's nothing like almost losing something precious to make you appreciate it."

He rose and kissed her, a long deep kiss that promised more than words ever could. She was light-headed and short of breath when he pulled away.

"Speaking of something precious, what are we going to do with your cradle?"

He shrugged. "Kindling."

"No!" she cried. "You made it and that makes it beautiful. Although, of course, I couldn't put our baby in there." She sniffed. "Why don't you take off the legs before somebody gets hurt?"

While he did that and put the cradle on the floor in the corner of the kitchen, she said, "You look like you could use some breakfast."

"Thanks. I could. Are you sure it's okay? Should you be standing? Do you feel all right?"

She laughed. "I have never felt better."

"You've never looked better, either." He pictured her growing round and couldn't suppress the smug pride. They'd done it.

They were so busy talking at once, making plans, eating breakfast and sometimes falling silent simply to stare at each other, that neither noticed Cyclops until a strange noise came from the corner, almost spookily like a crying baby, and had them both jumping to their feet.

"Oh," Caro cried, dropping to her knees. "Look!"

Jon glanced over at the litter of tiny kittens snuggled in his homemade cradle against the proudest-looking cat he'd ever seen. He thought of the hours he'd worked and the injuries he'd sustained on behalf of a one-eyed tabby. Then he turned and saw Caro laughing as she helped a blind and mewling newborn kitten find a teat. And he knew he couldn't have spent his time better.

When she rose, he snuggled up behind her and wrapped his arms around her, resting both hands possessively on her belly. With a wry grimace he glanced at his wobbly cat cradle. "If I donated another thousand bucks to the animal shelter, would you let me burn that thing?"

She leaned back against him in a gesture so familiar it brought an ache to his throat. "No. I want that always, to remind me that something can be imperfect and still wonderful."

He groaned. "Five thousand." She turned into his arms and nuzzled his neck.

"Ten thousand."

She rose on tiptoe and ran kisses along his jaw.

"Fifty thousand."

She shook her head. "Nothing in the world could tell me you love me the way that cradle does."

"Fifty thousand to the animal shelter and I Love Caro tattooed across my chest."

She laughed. "Well, in that case…"

We've been making you laugh for years!

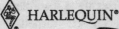 **HARLEQUIN®**

Duets™

**Join the fun in May 2003
and celebrate Duets #100!
This smile-inducing series,
featuring gifted writers and
stories ranging from amusing to zany,
is a hundred volumes old.**

This special anniversary volume offers two terrific
tales by a duo of Duets' acclaimed authors.
You won't want to miss...

Jennifer Drew's You'll Be Mine in 99

and

The 100-Year Itch by Holly Jacobs

With two volumes offering two special stories every
month, Duets always delivers a sharp slice of the lighter
side of life and *especially* romance. Look for us today!

Happy Birthday, Duets!

Visit us at www.eHarlequin.com

HD100TH

HARLEQUIN®
Duets™

TWO ROMANTIC COMEDIES IN ONE FUN VOLUME!

Don't miss double the laughs in

Once Smitten
and
Twice Shy

From acclaimed Duets author
Darlene Gardner

Once Smitten—that's Zoe O'Neill and Jack Carter, all right! It's a case of "the one who got away" and Zoe's out to make amends!

In *Twice Shy,* Zoe's two best friends, Amy Donatelli and Matt Burke, are alone together for the first time and each realizes they're "the one who never left!"

Any way you slice it, these two tales serve up a big dish of romance, with lots of humor on the side!

Volume #101
Coming in June 2003

Available at your favorite retail outlet.

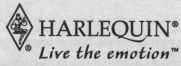

HARLEQUIN®
Live the emotion™

Visit us at www.eHarlequin.com

HDDD99DG

If you enjoyed what you just read,
then we've got an offer you can't resist!

Take 2 bestselling
love stories FREE!

Plus get a FREE surprise gift!

Clip this page and mail it to Harlequin Reader Service®

IN U.S.A.	IN CANADA
3010 Walden Ave.	P.O. Box 609
P.O. Box 1867	Fort Erie, Ontario
Buffalo, N.Y. 14240-1867	L2A 5X3

YES! Please send me 2 free Harlequin Duets™ novels and my free surprise gift. After receiving them, if I don't wish to receive anymore, I can return the shipping statement marked cancel. If I don't cancel, I will receive 2 brand-new novels every month, before they're available in stores! In the U.S.A., bill me at the bargain price of $5.14 plus 50¢ shipping & handling per book and applicable sales tax, if any*. In Canada, bill me at the bargain price of $6.14 plus 50¢ shipping & handling per book and applicable taxes**. That's the complete price—what a great deal! I understand that accepting the 2 free books and gift places me under no obligation ever to buy any books. I can always return a shipment and cancel at any time. Even if I never buy another book from Harlequin, the 2 free books and gift are mine to keep forever.

111 HDN DNUF
311 HDN DNUG

Name	(PLEASE PRINT)	
Address	Apt.#	
City	State/Prov.	Zip/Postal Code

* Terms and prices subject to change without notice. Sales tax applicable in N.Y.
** Canadian residents will be charged applicable provincial taxes and GST.
All orders subject to approval. Offer limited to one per household and not valid to current Harlequin Duets™ subscribers.
® and ™ are registered trademarks of Harlequin Enterprises Limited.

DUETS02

eHARLEQUIN.com

**Sit back, relax and enhance your romance
with our great magazine reading!**

- **Sex and Romance!** Like your romance
  hot? Then you'll *love* the sensual reading
  in this area.

- **Quizzes!** Curious about your lovestyle?
  His commitment to you? Get the
  answers here!

- **Romantic Guides and Features!**
  Unravel the mysteries of love with
  informative articles and advice!

- **Fun Games!** Play to your heart's content....

**Plus...romantic recipes,
top ten lists,
Lovescopes...and more!**

**Enjoy our online magazine today—
visit www.eHarlequin.com!**

INTMAG

A "Mother of the Year" contest brings
overwhelming response as thousands of women
vie for the luxurious grand prize....

Kate Hoffmann

Jacqueline Diamond

Jill Shalvis

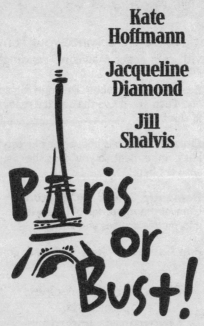

Paris or Bust!

A hilarious and romantic trio of new stories!

With a trip to Paris at stake, these women are
determined to win! But the laughs are many as three of
them discover that being finalists isn't the most
excitement they'll ever have.... Falling in love is!

Available in April 2003.

HARLEQUIN®
Makes any time special®

Visit us at www.eHarlequin.com

PHPOB